# The Realm B
# Two Brothers

PHOENIX GREY

ISBN: 9781793874092

# CONTENTS

# PROLOGUE

## EARTH - September 8th, 2057

It was a horrible sound. The sound that no parent ever wants to hear when they're sitting at the hospital clutching their unconscious son's hand.

Flatline.

One long beep that means it's all over. That the hours spent hoping and praying were fruitless. That whatever Radical Interactive had done to their son had failed.

Panic set in. Both parents stared at Will in complete shock. Mrs. Galvan had already begun chanting the word 'no.' Will's father's gaze jumped between his son's body and the machine that was signaling his death. This could not be real.

The room filled with sorrow like a noxious gas, choking the devastated couple out. Mr. Galvan was a man of few emotions, but this was just too much. While there had been no sign of Will waking up in the nineteen days since he'd been in the hospital, there had also been no decline in his health. This just didn't make any sense. It was too sudden.

A nurse walked in, the sight before her making her stop in her tracks, her hand moving up to her chest in sympathy. Her lips opened to speak, but then she decided against it and walked out of the room. Minutes later, she returned with both the doctor and Michael Coleman at her side. The doctor immediately went to offer his condolences and then check the machines before pronouncing a time of death.

Mr. Coleman, Radical Interactive's Medical Director of The Realm Project, couldn't force such sympathies. He wasn't well-versed in dealing with grieving families, even though he'd been through this dozens of times before. The Realm was far from perfect. More often than not, the participants didn't survive. Though, it was against company policy to tell the parents and spouses that. It was bad enough that they knew this was an experiment.

*Another failure,* he thought, though he couldn't place if it was disappointment or remorse that he was feeling. No doubt, Will would have died long ago if they hadn't put him in The Realm. The implant that carried the game was stimulating parts of his brain that otherwise would have laid dormant in his unconsciousness.

But Radical Interactive wasn't just trying to achieve a medical miracle. After suffering such harsh criticism for their initial failed launch of The Realm, they wanted to strike back with a game that was leagues ahead in technological advancement. A level of psychological immersion so intense that the player could no longer tell if the world was real or not. That required tapping into parts of the brain that no gaming company had dared to venture into before because of the high risk of damage. No one would dare test this stuff on a healthy human being...even if they volunteered for it. But one that was as good as dead—well, that cut through a lot of red tape. If the player survived, it was a miracle and a success. But if they died, what did it matter? They were already expendable. Maybe that's why it was so hard for Michael to look at these people as people anymore. They would likely be dead otherwise. Now, they were just test subjects.

"What happened to him? He's been doing just fine all this time," Mr. Galvan asked, clearly distraught.

"I don't know. This just happens sometimes," Mr. Coleman lied.

How could he possibly tell the man that his son had been murdered by a demon? It would spark outrage and more questions than Mr. Coleman felt like dealing with. To be honest, the initial cause of Will's coma, slamming his temple against the edge of a kitchen counter, would have been a much better way to go. If you don't see death coming, you can't really be afraid of it.

No one wants to hear that their child felt sheer terror before they met their demise. And while not the scariest thing that Radical Interactive had conjured up for The Realm, demons were pretty high on the list.

As soon as the nurse had come to report that Will had flatlined, Mr. Coleman put in a call to his visual team back at Radical Interactive—the people who monitored the live-feed being projected from the implant. The information on William Galvan's death would then be relayed back to multiple departments in Radical Interactive. The developmental department would start tweaking the game slightly to increase survivability, while the medical team would analyze the spikes in Will's brain activity to try to isolate the actual cause of death. Every deceased player had a purpose in modifying the game.

The doctor held up his wrist comp and tapped it to access William's file. "Time of death is exactly 9 o'clock in the morning."

Mrs. Galvan bellowed from the announcement.

The nurse walked over to shut off the machines, her eyes staring at the lifeless body to avoid having to look at the grieving parents. Death was an uncomfortable thing for everyone involved.

Just as her finger touched the button to kill the insufferable beeping, William Galvan inhaled a breath with such force that his chest puffed up and his body jerked. The entire room seemed to jump from the unexpectedness of seeing a dead body suddenly come back to life. Then Will began to cough. Violently. The machines beeped, his heartbeat racing critically fast. It was the most activity they'd seen from him since he had been brought in.

The doctor rushed to Will's side, taking his stethoscope from around his neck to give Will's chest a listen. "It's like he's choking on water," he said.

All that they could do was watch and wait for Will to either stabilize or fall back into death.

"Will, baby. I'm here," Mrs. Galvan told her son as she clutched his hand, standing by the side of the bed and brushing his hair away from his face. "We're here." She looked back at her husband, her pale blue eyes alight with hope.

Mr. Coleman's wrist comp buzzed. He stepped to the corner of the room to take the call. On the other end of the line was Will's Visual Supervisor. They exchanged a few words, and then Mr. Coleman ended the call, a grin spreading across his face.

By the time he turned and looked back over at the hospital bed, Mr. Galvan was walking towards him. For someone who had just gotten his son back, he didn't look happy. If Mr. Coleman was a smaller man, he might be intimidated, but he was well-trained to handle hostile family members. It was just a part of the job.

"What's happening to him? What did you do?" Mr. Galvan's voice was almost accusing.

Mr. Coleman patted him on the shoulder, gazing past him at Will. "I didn't do anything. It appears that William's story isn't over just yet."

## CHAPTER ONE
THE REALM – Day 28

"This has been bothering me for a while." It was an awkward conversation. A conversation that would most likely start an argument, which is why it was essential to wait until Lonnell was asleep.

They had just changed guarding duty. Azure had engineered it so that it would be his turn after Lonnell's. That way, Lonnell would still be asleep when it was time for him to confront Uden.

Part of him wondered if it was even worth bringing up when they were all stressed out from the idea of having to face such a fearsome foe as the demon. But nothing would be dumber than wandering into a dark cave with someone who was secretly your enemy. It was difficult for Azure to believe that was the case, though. While the half-imp might not give two shits if Azure died, he cared about his brother.

"What's up?" Uden asked as he stretched. No doubt, the half-imp was more refreshed than Azure. While he and his brother had gotten to sleep for six hours straight, Azure's sleep had been chopped in the middle thanks to taking the center shift. It was the shift that no one ever wanted. Something they often rotated for the sake of fairness.

"When the goblins had me captive and I was walking through their settlement, I noticed something." There was no tactful way to approach this topic without sounding accusing. "Do you remember the cook from the goblin camp? The one with the bite on its collarbone. It ran away when we attacked, and you were supposed to have gone after it and killed it."

"Yeah?" Uden dragged the word out, shifting his weight. "What about it?"

"It was at the settlement," Azure told him with as much certainty as he could muster. "Which means you didn't kill it. Which means you lied," he said pointedly.

The half-imp huffed and rolled his eyes. "Do you really think I'd be so stupid as to let it live? I told you I hunted it down, and I did. Whatever goblin you saw at the settlement was not the same one." He waved Azure's assertion away.

Azure cocked an eyebrow, not willing to drop the subject. "I'm about 99% sure it was the same goblin. I haven't seen any other goblins with bite marks on their neck."

"Then you haven't been looking," Uden insisted. "I've seen plenty."

"That were also cooks?" He prodded.

The half-imp's entire body sulked with annoyance. "You are just determined not to trust me. Why would I let it go if I knew it was just going to go tell the others? That would put me in danger as well, and I don't like being in danger."

That was a laughable statement considering how much danger Uden had put them all in by mounting a surprise attack on the goblin camp when they were clearly outnumbered. The half-imp was nothing if not a thrill seeker, it seemed.

"You tell me." Azure crossed his arms.

Uden snorted. "Are you trying to say that I'm somehow in cahoots with the goblins?"

"That's not what I'm saying. I don't know what's going on. I just know that the same goblin that was at the camp was also at the settlement and that you lied and said you had killed it. If you would stop lying and explain shit to me, then maybe I would understand."

"There's nothing to explain." The half-imp threw his arms up in frustration. "I said I killed the goblin. I killed the goblin. I'm sorry your eyes deceived you. I don't know what else you want me to say, but this conversation is starting to piss me off." Uden seated himself heavily by the fire, his jaw set with stress.

Azure sighed. He had known they would argue about this, but he hadn't expected to get nowhere. For the briefest of moments, Azure wondered if Uden was telling the truth—if he had just been imagining things. But then he brushed the thought away. It was the same goblin. He knew it was. There had to be some reason why Uden was lying? Maybe he was embarrassed by his failure and hadn't wanted Lonnell to know.

Still. Killing the goblin had been important. Not just for them but for Cragbell's safety and the safety of Uden's parents. It was hard to believe that he wouldn't have gone above and beyond to find and kill the goblin unless there was some ulterior motive.

"Go to sleep," the half-imp told him, giving Azure a look that would suggest he might want to sleep with one eye open tonight. "We still have a full day's journey before we reach the cave. You'll be no good to us if you're not rested."

Azure half-expected to see a notification that his Relationship level with Uden had dropped. They definitely weren't on good terms right now, and he felt uneasy in the half-imp's presence. Maybe the points only went one way. If Uden wasn't an NPC, he definitely would have gotten the notification on his end.

*I have to trust him*, Azure told himself as he bedded down.

*When we're in that cave with The Dark One, my safety will be partially in his hands.* As he closed his eyes for sleep, he wondered if he was being naive.

Not surprisingly, sleep didn't come easily. For most of what was left of the night, Azure tossed and turned, replaying the events of when he and the half-imp had been searching for The Dark One alone. The way Uden had insisted that they hadn't been walking in circles when they obviously were. How he had suggested that they split up when they had found the three goblins. But most of all, trying to match up the cook from the camp to the cook from the settlement.

Admittedly, Azure wasn't the most observant person. He couldn't count the number of times that Sheila had changed her hair and he hadn't even noticed. But Azure sure remembered the earful he received after every occurrence. You'd think that would have made him more observant, but he seemed to be selective when it came to, what he considered to be, small details.

Maybe he was wrong. Perhaps it had been a different goblin. But what were the odds?

The morning came way too soon. It was like Azure had just closed his eyes and then he was being shaken awake again. His body felt extra heavy from the lack of sleep, but that had never stopped them from pressing on before.

Now that they were all partied up again, Uden wasn't being his usual lazy self. He barely looked at Azure as they ate breakfast before setting off into the forest, clearly still sore about last night's accusations.

After having traveled together for so long, the silence between the men had become a normal, natural thing. Today it was filled with tension, though. At least, on Azure's end. He still wanted to talk about the goblin, but what was there left to be said? Uden would just continue to deny it. Lonnell would likely take his brother's side. Then they'd all be upset. Besides, having an argument when they had already entered into goblin territory definitely wasn't a good idea. It was best to just drop the subject and pray that the half-imp hadn't been lying.

By the time they reached the river that led up to the demon's cave, Azure had leveled up his Archery and Stealth skills to 3 just from all of the hunting he had done on their journey. While leveling his Archery skill didn't provide a bonus, he gained a 3% damage bonus while Stealthed. It was now clear to him that the bonus went up by one point for every level increase. At least, that's how it seemed to work.

His fear of the demon had mostly subsided, though Azure certainly wasn't looking forward to seeing it again. Having his friends beside him helped to abate most of his dread. There was strength in numbers, and he knew he wouldn't be the creature's sole focus once they finally encountered it.

They met the river where Azure had washed ashore and made the arduous climb upstream. He was surprised to find that it was only about a quarter mile to the waterfall he had tumbled down after he had escaped from The Dark One. Azure hadn't drifted far. In fact, he was so close that it wouldn't have taken much for the demon to have come after him. That meant the creature hadn't even bothered.

Perhaps this was like other games he'd play where if you ran out of a boss' range, it stopped giving chase. While he was certainly grateful, that seemed like an archaic concept to him. The Dark One had traveled much farther to reach the goblin settlement and retrieve him. It would have taken less effort to follow the river. But perhaps it had just assumed that he'd washed farther downstream, or maybe that he had died from the fall and was no longer worth pursuing. It needed a live sacrifice, after all.

They diverted from the waterfall to find a less steep climb up to where the demon's cave resided, joining back with the river once they had ascended. It wasn't long before the companions came upon the small bend that revealed the entrance to the cave. Lonnell stopped and immediately backed up, causing Uden to bump into him.

"What is it?" the half-imp whispered.

"Goblins," Lonnell told them.

It had become a familiar word that spiked both excitement and anxiety in Azure. "How many?"

"Two at the mouth of the cave, guarding it. Both warriors."

"Did they see you?" Uden's hand was already reaching for his dagger.

"I'm not sure, but I don't think so." Lonnell stepped back a few more feet before stopping and grabbing his staff.

"Did you have time to Analyze them?"

"I didn't." He shook his head. "But they are big."

They stood there in near silence for several moments, listening for approaching footsteps the best they could with the sound of the rushing river in the background. Azure's heart drummed in his chest, adrenaline pumping through him as he carefully drew his sword. It was disconcerting not knowing the strength of their foes. The urge to peer around the bend was great, but Azure knew well enough from his first journey here with the demon that there wasn't much cover. It would be dumb luck if the goblins hadn't seen them.

Minutes felt like hours as they waited for the fight to come to them, but it never did. Not turning from the direction of the cave, Lonnell motioned for them to continue retreating. They stayed vigilant as they backtracked a few yards downstream before clustering together to discuss a plan of action.

"They will probably be strong," Uden commented. "The demon suspected we were coming."

"That is fairly obvious," Azure shot back in annoyance.

"If they didn't see us, we'll have a chance to Analyze them

before we engage them," Lonnell said.

"But only before we immediately engage them," the half-imp pointed out.

"Whatever the case, we're three against two, and we have ranged weapons. From what I could see, they do not. We should be fine," Lonnell assured them.

"I'll go first with my bow since it has the longest range. As they get closer, Uden can attack with his throwing knives. Lonnell, you can jump in when they get within close range. If we haven't killed one by then, they should at least be weakened," Azure suggested.

"That sounds like a solid plan." Lonnell nodded before glancing over at his brother.

"You will hear no complaints from me." Uden held up his hands in surrender. It was as if he thought they had expected him to argue. To some degree, Azure had. The half-imp had been full of nothing but stupid decisions and a need to take control these past few weeks. Hopefully, he would stick to the plan this time.

“Are you guys ready to do this?" Lonnell inhaled a deep breath.

"I was born ready." Uden spun his throwing knives in his hands, a blood-thirsty grin spreading his lips.

"You enjoy this way too much." Azure raised an eyebrow at him.

"Go on. We're waiting on you." Uden gestured impatiently for him to ready his bow.

"How many yards away are they, would you estimate?" Azure asked as he nocked an arrow.

"A little over one hundred yards," Lonnell informed him.

"I'll have to get closer to make any type of impactful blow," he said more to himself than anyone else. That means the goblins would have a chance to come at him, clearing some distance.

"We've got this, brother." Lonnell clapped him on the shoulder.

"Stop dawdling. We don't have all day." Uden tapped his foot impatiently.

Azure cast a disdainful side-eye at the half-imp before heading towards the cave. His steps were hurried with the urgency to get the deed done, but he knew he couldn't let adrenaline rule him. He had to think strategically because he had a finite amount of arrows and didn't know how many levels deep the dungeon went down.

It was something they had discussed in length during their journey. Lonnell had told him that dungeons could be up to ten levels deep. Strong bosses always had ten levels. Weak bosses could have less, but it also wasn't uncommon for them to have ten as well, just with less powerful monsters along the way. Really, it was a crapshoot. There was no way to tell until you descended.

Azure had burned through all of the extra bronze arrows that Lonnell had brought with them when he was hunting. Now, only the fifteen Bronze Arrows of Minor Light Magic remained. If he divided them by level, he could afford to use only one or two per level. Inside the cave, close-range would likely be the most effective way to fight. He wanted to save at least five arrows for The Dark One. For this particular task of vanquishing the goblin guards, he needed to use his bow. It pained him to waste the magic arrows on foes that he wouldn't gain a bonus on, but there was no other choice. In hindsight, he probably should have let Uden do some of the hunting instead of being so obsessed with trying to level up. He had felt the anxiety when he started running low on regular arrows. But he also hadn't imagined that there would be goblins waiting outside of the cave entrance for them.

Azure rounded the bend, quickening his pace as he raised

his bow. The goblins spotted him instantly, one drawing a longsword while the other straightened himself and gripped the halberd he had been supporting his weight on.

Lonnell had been right. The goblins were big. Both Analyzed as yellow—challenging opponents. They readied their weapons, but to Azure's surprise, they didn't leave the mouth of the cave.

He continued to approach, waiting until he was in range before letting his first arrow sail at the goblin with the longsword. The arrow would have hit its mark in the center of the goblin's chest had he not held his sword in front of him like a makeshift shield and deflected it.

"Watch out!" Lonnell called to him, but Azure had no idea what he was watching out for until he heard the whoosh of an arrow whizzing by his head and felt the sting of an arrowhead grazing his shoulder.

A quick upward glance revealed a goblin archer at the top of the cliff.

*Clever goblinses*, Azure thought before realizing what a shitty situation he was in. The archer on the cliff had the advantage. He was too high up for Azure to reach with much accuracy. Noticing his distraction, the goblin warriors finally moved forward to attack. Azure thought to draw them further out, but he doubted he could get them to go outside of the archer's range. His mind swam with indecision, wondering what he should do.

"Cover us!" Uden passed Azure on the right, practically a blur in his peripheral vision.

Lonnell was right behind him, staff raised.

*Well, there goes Uden acting on his own again. I guess it can't be helped this time, though.*

Azure turned his attention back up to the archer. It loosed another arrow at him that he was easily able to dodge, possibly because it seemed distracted by the new attackers. The next time it nocked, it aimed for Lonnell. Clearly, it no longer saw Azure as a threat.

While he was unsure of his ability to hit the archer, he nocked an arrow and aimed at it anyway. It had been understood by Uden's words that this was now his job, protecting them from downward fire, which was much easier said than done. There was still that dread from the idea of wasting the magical arrows, but what other choice did he have?

Aiming the best he could, he loosed an arrow at the archer. It hit the side of the cliff about two feet short of the top and splintered into pieces. The archer merely scowled at him before returning its attention to the foes engaged in close-combat. What was even more infuriating was that the goblin Analyzed as blue, so if they were face-to-face, Azure would definitely win.

The word *coward* flashed across his mind, but it was quickly replaced by *strategic planning*. The Dark One was protecting his dungeon well. The low-level archer was practically untouchable, guarding from above while the warriors took care of any threats that may try to slip past on ground level. If he was being honest, he was more upset that they hadn't come up with the idea to double back, scale up the side of the cliff, and simply snipe both of the goblin guards. Though there was no guarantee that would have worked either. The goblins always could have just retreated into the safety of the cave.

"Shit," he muttered as he watched the archer nock another arrow and take aim for Uden.

The two brothers seemed to barely be holding their own. Lonnell was mostly defending against the goblin with the longsword while Uden kept the halberdier distracted and dashed in to take a cheap shot at the swordsman's backside whenever he could. He had positioned himself between the two goblins, which was a dangerous place to be. Thankfully, the one that was busy fighting Lonnell was too stupid to think of the same backhanded tactics that the half-imp was resorting to to try to turn the odds in their favor.

Still, it wasn't working well enough. And it didn't take long for Azure to realize that the brothers were outmatched. He was only one level below them now, which meant there was a decent chance that the goblins had Analyzed as yellow to them. He needed to think fast, or they were going to lose.

There was no time to distract the archer. If it weren't for Uden stepping to the side to avoid a blow from the halberd, the arrow would have hit its mark, penetrating the half-imp's head and putting an end to him. He sliced Azure with his gaze, shouting out, "Fuck's sake, man."

Giving up on fending off the archer, Azure moved out of its range, backing away towards the river. With his speed, Uden seemed to be doing better against the goblin he was facing, so Azure turned his attention to the swordsman. He nocked an arrow and concentrated his aim. It was a dangerous shot to take. If the goblin moved at just the right moment, there was a fair chance he would hit Lonnell. But Azure felt more confident in his abilities with the bow at a safe distance from the archer than he would with the distraction of the possibility of being sniped down from above.

He held his breath before letting the arrow sail. By a stroke of luck, it hit the back of the goblin's neck, the arrowhead piercing all the way through to the front of its throat. A spray of blood and light gushed forth from the wound, and the swordsman gurgled in shock. The distraction was all that was needed for Lonnell to finish the goblin off with his staff.

*Defeated Level 7* ***Goblin Warrior****. 56XP rewarded.*

With the swordsman out of the way, Lonnell went to help

his brother. Azure thought to try shooting the halberdier as well, but with both brothers on it, it was too risky. Instead, he drew his sword and rushed in to join the melee, effectively surrounding the last remaining goblin warrior.

It glanced up at the archer as if asking for help, then swung its halberd in a wide arch to keep its attackers at bay. Just as the three adventurers were about to set in on the goblin for the kill, a pained cry rose up from the fray.

Panic took over Uden's expression as he saw the arrow sticking out of Lonnell's back, and sickness roiled in Azure's stomach as he realized he had failed at the only job they had given him. More importantly, his friend had been injured, his health bar cut by a good twenty percent. If the archer had been a higher level, it might have been a kill shot.

Distracted by Lonnell's injury, Azure barely saw the halberdier plunge his halberd forward. He dodged, but not quick enough to avoid a glancing blow to his side. A hiss of pain escaped his lips as he felt the weapon slice into him, his own health bar falling to about equal what Lonnell had lost. Just as the archer had done less damage from being a lower level even though that normally would have been a critical shot, the warrior did more damage from its glancing blow for being a higher level.

*You are **bleeding**. You will lose 5 health every second for the next five seconds.*

"Oh shit," Uden cursed, barely avoiding getting shot by another incoming arrow.

"Fuck!" Azure mirrored his frustration. Never before had he felt like their lives were more in danger.

The fight at the goblin camp had been different. In the end, Azure had been the only one seriously injured. To see Lonnell wounded and staggering was unsettling. They needed to end this as quickly as possible.

Azure rushed forward with his sword, but the goblin parried with his halberd before pushing Azure back, nearly knocking him off balance. As his muscles clenched to keep him standing, he felt the wound. There was a cool spot on his armor where blood was leaking through and soaking into the leaves. He was definitely bleeding. It felt as if someone had shoved a spigot into his side and turned it on. Every second made blood pump from the wound, bringing with it a feeling of weakness and disorientation.

"You've got this," Uden called to him in encouragement.

Azure could barely see him around the behemoth of a goblin, but the two brothers were now together. Lonnell's arm was around the half-imp's neck. The look that Uden was giving Azure was pointed as if speaking to him silently. It might have made sense if the two of them were actually in sync. But they weren't.

With the goblin's attention almost wholly focused on Azure, Uden began half-helping, half-dragging his brother to the cave, leaving Azure to handle the foe—one that would most definitely kill him if it managed to land another blow—on his own. For a split second, Azure thought about running for the cave as well, but what would that accomplish? The goblin only had one small visible injury, a slash on its side that Uden had undoubtedly landed at some point. It wasn't critical, and it wasn't slowing the goblin down one bit. If he ran, it would give purchase. Making it to the cave would ensure that the archer no longer had a shot at him, but it would also put Lonnell in danger again. A quick glance at the cave showed Uden examining the wound. Azure wasn't sure if he had been left to die or if there was a bigger plan, but for now, he had to consider himself as on his own.

He felt like easy prey, favoring his wounded side and using all of his remaining strength to stand and defend with his sword. The only advantage he had was that he was now facing the cliff so he could see whenever the archer was ready to loose an arrow at him. As the halberdier came forward, Azure continued to back up towards the river. He tried to concentrate on finding an opening—one small drop of the goblin's guard that would allow him to dash in and make a critical hit—but the goblin's defense was solid. His halberd had far better reach that Azure's sword, and he knew how to use it well. It would be a battle between speed and strength. Right now, strength was winning, Azure realized as the goblin continued to push him back towards the river.

A flash of deja vu played through Azure's mind as he quickly glanced over his shoulder at the rushing water, thinking that jumping into it might be the only way to save himself. But that would be cowardly. Briefly, Azure wondered which was worse, being branded a coward or surviving. At least surviving meant a second chance.

He was only about three yards away from the river now. He dug his heels into the ground, determined to make a stand. If the goblin was able to strike him again and he didn't die from it immediately, he would take his chance with the river. At least he had his arms this time. He might not have to plummet over the waterfall.

The goblin swung his halberd down. It struck the metal of Azure's sword, the weight behind the blow making Azure's muscles ache from fighting against it. His back foot slipped a little, creating a rut in the dirt behind him. Who knew a goblin could be so strong?

*This is it*, Azure thought. *I jump into the river and live a coward or I stand my ground and die a hero.* There was no way he had enough stamina left to parry another blow. His arms were trembling. It was taking every ounce of adrenaline left in him to keep from buckling, and it was quickly becoming not enough.

There was a wicked smile across the goblin's face as it continued to press down on the halberd. Azure was crumbling back, the blade inching closer to his head with each passing second. If his muscles atrophied, it would be all over. He had hoped the goblin would let up to swing at him again, allowing him the chance to roll towards the river, but it didn't look like that was going to happen. The warrior was not stupid. He had Azure right where he wanted him. With a dull emptiness, Azure realized there would be no escape. Within a few seconds, what was left of his stamina would be depleted, and he would meet his gruesome demise on this riverbank. Whether he wanted to or not, he was going to die a hero.

Azure blew out a breath, trying to prepare himself for death. Hopefully, he had at least bought Uden and Lonnell enough time to escape into the depths of the cave. It was strange to think about how he'd gotten caught up in all of this. The curse on Crescent Island wasn't even his problem, and yet he was going to die for it, nonetheless.

Azure watched in his peripheral vision as the remaining color in his stamina bar drained down to nothing. He wished it was more like seconds on a clock so each one could seem precious. But oddly, nothing seemed remarkable about what was happening.

The goblin jerked the halberd, and Azure fell back. His arms gave up their defensive hold on the sword, letting it fall to the side. The blade of the halberd crashed down, the top of it hitting Azure's hip, piercing through flesh and bone and causing excruciating pain to course through him and his health bar to drop to just under twenty percent.

"Die, you son of a bitch!" a familiar voice hissed with unbridled hatred.

Through a blur of pulsing agony, Azure looked up to see Uden practically riding the goblin. His legs were wrapped around its waist, his arms poised with a dagger in each hand, the blades driven deep into the goblin's neck on either side. Its eyes were wide. It reached back to throw off its attacker, but Uden twisted the blades, causing the creature to scream—a strange high-pitched grunt that made Azure shudder.

He was too worn out to do anything but watch. The goblin staggered, still trying to reach back and grab at Uden, though his aim seemed to be horribly off.

Uden was unyielding. “I said fucking die,” he raged as he pulled his daggers out and drove them into the goblin's neck over and over again. Blood sprayed from the wounds, making Azure's side injury look like a mere trickle.

The goblin cast its gaze up to the Heavens, its mouth agape, its black beady eyes somewhere distant. Then it finally fell, landing face down in the dirt a few feet away from Azure. Uden still clung to its back, digging his blades in even deeper as if he feared the goblin might rise again. After a few seconds of heavy breathing, he looked over at Azure. “Are you all right?”

As it had happened at the goblin camp, Azure found himself deliriously happy just to still be alive. He honestly hadn't thought that Uden would come back for him.

"I didn't get any points for that kill," he commented, feeling that it was slightly unfair for all of the work that he'd put in. Usually, if he and one of his companions teamed up to kill a monster, he'd earn his share of experience points. That did not seem to be the case this time. But to be fair, he hadn't even been able to land a single blow on the goblin.

Uden snorted at him. “That's some gratitude.”

"It took you long enough to get here." Azure looked past him to the goblin archer. He hadn't even realized that he had somehow managed to coax the warrior out of its range. The archer sat on the edge of the cliff, looking unhappy, waiting for them.

"I had to tend to my brother," Uden replied without remorse. "Plus, I needed to wait for the most opportune time to strike."

"Like when I was on the verge of death?" Azure said with a scowl.

"Like when you had the warrior outside of the archer's

range." There was no humor in the half-imp's voice. It was strange to see him so serious. As soon as he pulled his blades from the goblin's neck, he turned his gaze to the archer. "We are going to have to make a run for it."

"Or you could take my bow and try to shoot it," Azure suggested.

"I am not an archer." Uden cast a side-glance in Azure's direction as if to say he should know that by now. "Besides, the range and angle are bad. That bow is shit. I likely wouldn't get enough power to reach it.

"Yet you sent me out to do just that." He narrowed his eyes at the half-imp.

"If any of us would have been able to hit it, it would have been you."

The compliment caught Azure off-guard. Was he really a better archer than even Lonnell? He wasn't so sure, but he wasn't going to argue.

"My stamina is depleted," Azure said as if Uden couldn't see it. "My hip is pretty close to crushed. I'm not going to make it to the cave."

"Oh, don't be so dramatic." Uden rolled his eyes, pulling a red vial from his bag and uncorking it before coming to Azure's side, kneeling beside him, and bringing it up to his lips. "And don't fight me on this. I know it's embarrassing for both of us."

Being embarrassed was the last thing on Azure's mind as he drank down the liquid. He'd let Uden bottle-feed him in front of his entire family if it made the pain go away.

"Another," he demanded as soon as the contents of the vial were drained.

Uden didn't hesitate to oblige, feeding him four vials of the red potion in a row. While it rapidly healed Azure's wounds, it did nothing to recover his stamina. He wasn't in as much pain, but he still felt as weak as a kitten.

"You wouldn't happen to have a Potion of Minor Stamina on you, would you?" Azure asked. "Otherwise, it's still going to be a while before I can move."

"I can spare one," Uden replied, pulling a vial of yellow liquid from his bag, though he hesitated to open it. "We don't have anywhere near as many of these. I'm not sure we should waste it."

"Waste it?" His head jutted back. "If you haven't noticed, I'm pretty much a quadriplegic right now. I seriously don't know how I'm even able to stay sitting up."

Uden glanced back at the archer and then sighed. "He won't leave his post as long as we're here. We probably have time for you to regain your stamina naturally."

"Do you know that for sure? I'm assuming they're working in shifts. Who knows when they'll change again."

The half-imp thought for a moment then nodded and uncorked the vial. "You are right. The best thing we can do is get into the cave as quickly as possible. If we give them a chance to change shifts, we'll be in trouble."

Azure gulped down the contents of the vial, trying not to make a face. It was like egg whites and plastic had a baby. While it wasn't the worst thing he'd ever tasted, it was still strange in an unpleasant way. The potion restored 25 points of stamina. It didn't seem like enough. Though he could move, he felt as unsteady as a newborn calf, his arms and legs shaking just from the effort of getting them to work.

"Are you sure you can't spare another?" Azure gave Uden a hopeful look.

"Can you stand?" The half-imp straightened himself, offering his hand down to Azure.

Azure clasped Uden's wrist and tried pulling himself to his feet. It was like he was drunk; his muscles were jello. Somehow, though with so much stumbling that he almost pulled the half-imp down, Azure was able to make it to his feet. How he had managed to fend the goblin warrior off when his stamina had been so low was a mystery. Perhaps his adrenaline had been working better than he had thought. While Azure had been at almost zero, for some reason he still had strength. Now, he was just pathetic.

"This isn't going to work," he said as he clung to Uden's side. Now *this* was embarrassing.

"At times like this, I wish I was stronger." The half-imp sighed. "You and Lonnell both weigh a ton."

"Yeah. No offense, but I wouldn't expect you to be able to carry me." He glanced down at Uden's lithe frame. The half-imp was strong for his size, no doubt, but some tasks were definitely beyond him. "I know you don't want to waste it, but I'm going to need another Potion of Minor Stamina if you expect us to make it to the cave with any kind of speed. We will be easy targets if we don't move quickly. We need to zigzag towards the cave...separately so that the archer doesn't have a wide target and will have to choose between us."

"He is going to aim at you," Uden told him matter-of-factly. "I would."

"So would I," Azure admitted with an exhale. It looked like he wasn't out of danger yet. "Regardless, we'll both have a better chance of making it if we move independently."

The half-imp stared out into space for several moments, seemingly lost in thought. Then he nodded, though he didn't look pleased about his decision, and extracted another yellow vial from his bag. "Two is all you get," the half-imp said with a hint of resentment. "To think that we haven't even made it inside the cave yet."

It was a harrowing thought.

"Do the goblins make up any part of the first floor?" Azure asked.

The look of sarcasm on Uden's face was all the answer that he needed. “Are we inside the cave yet?”

"Yeah..." Azure drew the word out. "I suppose that was a stupid question." He drank the contents of the vial and immediately felt more steady on his feet. Running still seemed like an arduous task, but Azure was pretty sure he could at least make it to the cave entrance.

"There's no such thing as a stupid question. Just stupid people." Uden smirked at him.

"Oh please." Azure rolled his eyes.

"Just saying." The half-imp shrugged nonchalantly, taking a few steps away before stuffing the empty vial back in his pouch and turning to Azure. "So are we ready to do this?"

"Shouldn't we loot the body first?" Azure glanced over at the dead goblin.

"Do you want the halberd? It would be a cumbersome thing to carry." Uden knelt to scour the body for any valuable items but came up empty-handed.

"Let me at least check it out first." He walked over and picked up the halberd. The stats of the weapon appeared in front of him.

*You have received the following item:*

| **Iron Halberd** | **Attack:** +9-12<br>**Type:** Two-Handed Weapon<br>**Durability:** 12/20<br>**Item Class:** Common<br>**Quality:** Average<br>**Weight:** 3.0 kg |
|---|---|

"Hmm," Azure mused. The halberd did deal more damage than his crude goblin sword, and it still had pretty good durability. It might be worth taking. But Azure didn't have the Two-Handed Weapons skill yet, and he was concerned that a dungeon might not be the best place to start leveling it up. "I suppose I could take it now and then drop it later if I decide not to use it." He gripped it with both hands. It definitely felt weighty in comparison to his sword. Unnatural. As of now, he barely had the stamina needed to wield it.

"You know that's going to slow you down when you run, right?" Uden raised an eyebrow at him, clearly implying that taking the halberd wasn't a great idea.

"Well, it won't fit in my bag, and I don't want to leave it." Azure sighed, staring up at the archer. It smirked at him as if spotting his idiocy from a mile away.

"It's your choice." Uden gestured to him as he walked past. "Just don't make me regret using those Stamina potions on you."

"Like I said, I can always drop it if it slows me down too much." Azure wondered if he had the skill to use the halberd to block incoming arrows, but he doubted it.

"So, are we ready to go?" Uden asked.

"No, but what other choice do we have?"

"None." The half-imp smiled. "I'd say that I'll race you, but we both know I would win."

"Yeah. Because I'm going to be busy dodging arrows." Azure fought the urge to roll his eyes again.

"Maybe I won't even bother zigzagging."

Honestly, that wasn't a bad idea. “Maybe you shouldn't. That would take the attention off of me. I can only assume that that goblin is going to go for whichever one of us is the easier target.”

"Even if I zigzagged, you'd still be the easier target. You're bigger than me, slower, and more clumsy." That smile just wasn't going to go away as Uden continued to jab at Azure with his remarks.

"Whatever," he said with a sigh. "Let's just do this. Should we count before running?"

"Nope." And with that, Uden took off at a jog back towards the cave.

"Oh you asshole," Azure muttered under his breath as he gave chase.

To his surprise, Uden didn't zigzag. In fact, he was moving pretty slowly. It wasn't until they got within the archer's range that the half-imp dug his heels into the dirt and left Azure in a cloud of dust. Good God, he was fast.

The archer raised his bow and took aim. Uden still wasn't zigzagging. He ducked as an arrow came sailing at his head but didn't stop running.

Azure was a snail by comparison, sloppily weaving left and right. There was nothing to dodge, though. The goblin was focusing entirely on Uden. Realizing that he was wasting time and the advantage of the situation, Azure followed suit, giving up the zigzagging routine to make a beeline for the cave while the half-imp was affording him the time to do so. It was no surprise that Uden reached the cave first, holding the goblin's attention until he was near the entrance. Once it became aware that pursuing the half-imp as a target was useless, it switched back to Azure, at which point Azure switched back to zigzagging. His heartbeat sped up, but he wasn't sure if it was because he was overexerting himself or from the adrenaline of seeing the goblin lining up his next shot.

An arrow came sailing in his direction, barely missing. The second one was aimed in front of him, causing Azure to stop and divert. The goblin got in two more missed shots before Azure finally made it to the mouth of the cave. He slowed down to a trudging crawl, panting and leaning on his new halberd. He was finally safe—for now—he thought with much relief.

Lonnell was a bit further in, sitting down as he waited for his two companions to return. Upon seeing them, he didn't bother getting up. Like Azure, despite all of the health potions he'd drank, he still wasn't fully recovered. They were a sad bunch, if truth be told.

"We made it!" Azure breathed out, throwing an arm up in jubilant rejoicing.

"That we did." Lonnell smiled at him.

"We're not out of the woods yet." Uden stared out of the cave as if he expected a swarm of goblins to come around the bend at any moment. "We need to proceed inside as quickly as possible. You both have about fifteen minutes to rest, then we move on." He turned away from the cave entrance and leaned against the wall opposite from Azure.

Wincing, Lonnell pulled himself to his feet. He hobbled over to his friend and brother to join them, resting next to Azure. “Do you think the goblin will stay and wait for us to come out, or do you think he'll go back to tell the others?”

"He knows we're not coming back out," Uden told him. "He knows what we're here for. More than likely, he'll go back to camp to tell the others."

"Then more will come, and they'll follow us into the cave," Azure commented with dread. They had barely escaped with their lives as it was. The thought of being trapped in the dark cave with a hoard of goblins, most of them probably warriors as strong as the two they had just faced, didn't give him much hope that they were going to survive this ordeal.

Uden shook his head. "They won't come into the cave. Their job here is done."

"What makes you say that?" Azure knitted his brow.

"They are every bit as afraid of the demon as we are. Trust me when I say they will not venture in here."

Azure wasn't sure he believed Uden, but he quickly decided that he wanted to. "Well, that's a relief."

"There will be more dangers up ahead." The half-imp gazed into the darkness of the cave. "Your bow will be of little use. We need to stick close together and remain vigilant."

It was strange getting a lecture on safety from Uden. This was usually Lonnell's department. Right now, though, Lonnell was busy pulling torches from his Bag of Holding. The inside of the cave was so dark that one could barely see a few feet inside. Unnaturally dark, Azure thought. The light from outside should have been able to reach much farther.

He also noticed that the inner walls weren't the gray of stone, but instead pitch black, the surface having a smooth quality, like obsidian.

"What is up with this cave?" he asked finally. "It's not like anything I've ever seen before."

Uden turned to run his hand over the stone. "This is not a cave, Azure. It's a dungeon. It is not a naturally made structure. The demon created it.

"Unlike caves that are formed by the dissolution of

limestone, dungeons have a supernatural quality to them. They can form anywhere that a powerful monster deems necessary. They can look like anything. This is simply the surface. There's no telling what awaits us further inside."

"Too bad we don't have a pickaxe," he mused. "This stuff looks valuable."

"It does, but it's just an illusion. Remember that when we're further in. Everything you see besides the beasts we face is just an illusion."

"Interesting," Azure responded as he watched Lonnell lay the torches out on the ground before crouching over them, clenching one fist, and waving his other hand over his fist while whispering an incantation in a language that Azure didn't understand. When he opened his clenched fist, there was a small flame. He picked up one of the torches and lit the oil-soaked cloth with the flame, then reached out to hand the torch off to Uden before he did the same with the other two, giving one to Azure and keeping one for himself before closing his palm to extinguish the flame. It was a useful little spell, one that Azure definitely wanted to learn if he ever reached a place where he could acquire magic. Everything in The Realm seemed to take forever, but perhaps it was the path he had chosen. He could have always opted to go straight to the mainland instead of helping the brothers, but that would have just been a dick move. Besides, he had a score to settle with this asshole demon.

"Are you guys ready for this?" Lonnell asked with a sigh, clearly not looking forward to venturing deeper into the dungeon.

"Well, there's certainly no going back now." Azure mirrored his exhaustion.

Since Uden was the only one who had escaped the melee with the goblins uninjured, he took point. With his torch in one hand and his dagger in the other, he proceeded with caution. Every step seemed surprisingly careful, his eyes dancing around to cover every bit of the dungeon that was revealed by the light.

The cave was small and cramped, approximately fifteen feet wide and only nine feet to the ceiling. It made Azure feel claustrophobic. He had never liked caves. The fact that this one seemed to be made from one solid piece of stone was probably the only thing keeping him from freaking out. It wasn't so much that he had a fear of confined spaces as it was the fear of a cave in and being trapped. Suffocating sounded like a horrible way to die.

The three men kept close, almost awkwardly so. The type of closeness that people keep when they venture into a haunted house. At any other time, that would be considered invading someone's personal space. But when you're afraid, it's somehow okay and natural.

They hadn't ventured very far inside before the mouth of the cave was no longer visible. Enveloped in darkness, Azure wondered if they went back if they'd even be able to find the entrance again. There had been no twists or turns, but he had a sinking feeling that they were trapped now. Though there was an urge to ask Uden, he didn't really want to know the answer.

Light bounced off of the walls of the cave, but the smooth stone reflected nothing else. For a while, it was eerily silent. So quiet that it was almost unsettling listening to nothing but the sounds of their nervous breathing. What was worse was the fluttering of wings that could suddenly be heard up ahead.

Uden stopped dead in his tracks, and the other two followed suit. He dug his heels into the dirt, preparing for the attack.

"What is it?" Azure whispered, clutching onto his halberd with a white-knuckle grip.

"I don't know," came the disconcerting response.

"Let's form a wall," Lonnell suggested, moving to stand beside his brother.

"If they surround us, back into a circle," Uden added.

Much like they had done when they had first seen the goblin warriors after they had rounded the bend, they simply stood there and listened, preparing to be ambushed. The wings did not get closer. Azure tried his best to discern how many pairs he heard, but the sounds overlapped each other, and none were distinct from the others. It was definitely more than one creature but probably less than a dozen, he surmised, though he knew he could be grossly off.

Lonnell motioned for them to proceed forward. They took one hesitant step at a time, their weapons brandished. The goal seemed to be to approach the creatures without disturbing them, but none of them were stupid enough to think it would end well. The monsters inside the dungeon had been generated to protect it. They would attack at the first sign of intruders.

A few more steps forward and the fluttering suddenly grew louder. The few wing flaps that Azure had heard turned into hundreds. Yes, he had grossly miscalculated. Chirps and screeches came from deep within the cave, and they were quickly approaching.

"Brace yourselves!" Lonnell called, obviously no longer worried about remaining quiet.

Azure expected some hideous monster to emerge from the dungeon, but what he saw instead was a cloud of bats. Regular everyday bats. Nothing special.

He barely had time to Analyze a few of them before they were swarmed. The bats struck like razor blades raining from the sky, darting down to scratch the men with their tiny claws and bite them with their sharp teeth. It felt like Azure spent more time prying the small creatures off of him than he did swatting at the air with his halberd. The weapon was horribly cumbersome to wield, and he felt slow with it.

*Congratulations! New skill learned:* ***Two-Handed Weapons*** *Level 1. From spears to claymores, two-handed weapons deal great* *damage if you have the strength to wield them. Used as both a weapon and a shield, fight strategically to smite down your enemies!*

Azure didn't have time to be excited about acquiring the skill. In all honesty, he wished he was using his sword instead, but he didn't have time to switch weapons. Each bite and scratch chipped away at his health and stamina one point at a time. The bats would have just been an annoyance if not for the fact that there were so many of them.

*Level 1* ***Bat*** *delivers 1 damage and drains 1 point from your stamina.*

The notifications in his vision popped up so frequently that he was almost blinded by them. A quick thought of his irritation made the text turn so light that he could see through it, making it less of a distraction.

*Defeated Level 1* ***Bat****. 8XP rewarded.*

*Defeated Level 1* ***Bat****. 8XP rewarded.*

*Defeated Level 1* ***Bat****. 8XP rewarded.*

*Congratulations! You are now* ***Level 5****! Your base stats have been boosted. You have earned 3 points to assign to your characteristics. Please note that adding points to some* *characteristics(Vitality, Intelligence, and Strength) will further boost your base stats. You may also advance any 1 skill of your choosing by 1 level.*

*Defeated Level 1* ***Bat****. 8XP rewarded.*

*Defeated Level 1* ***Bat****. 8XP rewarded.*

*Defeated Level 1* ***Bat****. 8XP rewarded.*

*For fucks sake, when will this end?* Azure thought in exasperation.

*Defeated Level 1* ***Bat****. 8XP rewarded.*

*Defeated Level 1* ***Bat****. 8XP rewarded.*

*Defeated Level 1* ***Bat****. 8XP rewarded.*

*Defeated Level 1* ***Bat****. 8XP rewarded.*

*Congratulations! The skill:* ***Two-Handed Weapons*** *has reached Level 2. This skill enables you to use all manner of two-handed weapons to defeat enemies. Increasing your Strength will make them easier to wield.*

Azure took notice of the fact that it was the first time that a skill offered him a clue on how to use it the most efficiently. But he barely had time to think about it with the relentless barrage of bats assailing him.

*Defeated Level 1* ***Bat****. 8XP rewarded.*

*Defeated Level 1* ***Bat****. 8XP rewarded.*

*Defeated Level 1* ***Bat****. 8XP rewarded.*

The bats were doing far more damage to his stamina than his health. A foe that wasn't designed to kill them but to weaken them until they couldn't fight anymore.

Sixteen more bats later and the fight was finally over. As Azure took a deep breath, prying the last bat from his bloodied arm and squashing it under his heel, he could feel the trembling in his body once more from the loss of stamina.

Turning to his companions, he could see that they were all a bloody mess, the appearance of the damage much worse than the health points actually lost.

"I bet we all leveled up from that one," Lonnell commented with a chuckle.

"I didn't level up." Uden scowled.

"Well, I guess now we're the same level." Azure jabbed the half-imp in the side with his elbow to add insult to injury.

"I don't know how," Uden huffed. "I'm pretty sure I killed more than you."

"Shall we tally it up?" Azure suggested, already scanning back through his list of kills to take count. He liked that he could bring up these details just by thinking about them.

"Thirty-six." Uden gave him a pointed look.

Now it was Azure who was scowling. Would the half-imp be able to tell if he was lying? “You win,” he grumbled.

"Nope. You don't get out of it that easy. Tell us how many you killed."

"I killed thirty-four, so I wasn't far behind you, brother," Lonnell chimed in.

"I killed less than both of you," Azure replied stubbornly.

"Clearly," the half-imp said.

"But at least I leveled up." Azure smirked.

Uden's expression twisted in annoyance. “Oh, fuck you.”

"Stop it," Lonnell chastised them. "This isn't a competition. And we all got pretty messed up in the stamina department on that one."

"We did," the half-imp agreed. For having the most kills, he had also lost the most stamina, though he wasn't anywhere near at a critical level like Azure was.

"I think I'm going to need another stamina potion," Azure confessed.

The two brothers looked at each other as if carrying on a silent conversation. Then Lonnell put words to his thoughts. “Should we go forward or move back a bit? I think we've all had enough adventure for one day. We should camp for the night. I could see in your stats, Azure, that your stamina increased twice by 25 points. That means you used two stamina potions. You're pretty bad off right now, and I don't want to use another potion since we're only on the first floor of the dungeon and who knows how much further down it goes."

Uden let out a long sigh. "I really don't like the idea of camping in a dungeon."

"It can't be helped," Lonnell told him with an air of sympathy.

The half-imp looked toward the direction they were headed in, then looked back at where they had come from. "We don't know what lies ahead, but I really hate the idea of losing any of the ground we gained today."

"Why would we go back?" Azure furrowed his brow.

"Because it's safer," Lonnell replied plainly. "Moving forward without your stamina restored could put us in great peril. And we can't stay here because the bats will respawn after some time."

"So what you're saying is that if we go back and make camp in an area that is safe, we will still have to face the bats again tomorrow." Azure didn't really like that idea.

"That is exactly what I'm saying."

"What are the odds that another foe waits not far up ahead?" he asked.

"There's no way to tell without venturing forth," Uden said. "Even attempting to proceed forward a little bit holds its own dangers. We don't know how far the bats' reach extends. If we don't go far enough, they could respawn right on top of us. If we go too far, we could encounter an even greater threat.

"If you hadn't noticed, all of those bats were level one. The foes will only get stronger the further in that we go."

To be honest, Azure had used the goblins outside as a starting mark. He was relieved to know that inside the cave, things were easier to some degree. If they had all been at max health and stamina when they had entered the dungeon, there would be no question about pressing on.

"If we retreat back a bit, is our safety guaranteed?" he inquired.

Lonnell shook his head. “No. But the odds of an attack are much less, and even if we are attacked, it shouldn't be as great as the swarm. Maybe one or two straggler bats who happen to find their way to our location. It shouldn't be anything stronger than that.”

"Shouldn't be?" Azure snorted. He wasn't very confident in that, especially given their luck with the goblins.

"Or you could just feed him another stamina potion, and we could get on with it," Uden suggested, impatiently tapping his foot.

"No. We all need rest," Lonnell insisted. "It's better if we face whatever comes tomorrow fully healed. Besides, since Azure and I both leveled up, we'll be in a better position tomorrow. And I'm fairly certain that if we go through the bats again, you'll level up, too. Maybe we all will."

*A loophole,* Azure thought. The first opportunity he'd seen in the game to truly level grind. He had killed twenty-nine level one bats and earned 232 experience points for it. It was an immense amount of experience compared to everything else he'd done in the game. Definitely an exploit.

"I say we go back," he spoke up. "Go back, then go forward again. Kill as many bats as we can. Gain as much experience as we can. Then go back, wait for them to respawn, and do it all over again."

"Why would we want to do that?" Uden raised an eyebrow.

"I got 232 experience points from the fight with the bats. That is an insane amount of experience. We could probably all use a few extra levels for when we face The Dark One," he explained.

Lonnell looked tired. “I'd rather get this over as quickly as possible. We don't want to linger in the dungeon and give The Dark One a chance to emerge.”

"What do you think?" Azure asked Uden, hoping to appeal to his greedy nature. Even though he didn't trust the half-imp, they were often on the same page when it came to looting and gaining experience.

Uden thought for a moment. “It's not a bad idea. Who knows how strong the foes ahead will be. It would take a bit of time, but I'd rather gather strength while we can.”

Yes. At least the half-imp could be counted on for something.

"Fine," Lonnell blew out a breath, obviously not agreeing with the plan but willing to go along with it nonetheless. "Let's head back until we know it's safe and make camp. We'll go through the bats as many times as we can tomorrow. But we are only wasting one day on this," he insisted, his voice telling that there was no room to argue.

"That seems fair," Uden agreed, turning to Azure for his reaction to the decision.

"That does seem fair." He nodded, quickly calculating how many times they'd be able to go through the bats again without having to waste potions on stamina. The number was three, by his estimation. That should be enough to level them each up once or twice. Whether they liked it or not, they'd have to use healing potions, but of those they had plenty.

"But first let's gather our loot." Uden knelt and placed his torch on the ground. Then he picked up one of the bats and cut off its wings, layering them together before moving on to the next.

Azure followed suit, assuming that the wings could be sold

at the market for coin later.

*You have received the following item:*

| **Bat Wing** | **Quantity:** 1/1<br>**Item Class:** Common<br>**Quality:** Average<br>**Weight:** 0 kg<br>**Uses:** Loot. Sell for coin. |
|---|---|

They don't sell for much because they're so common," Lonnell informed him. "Only a copper a wing, if I remember correctly."

"Any money is better than none. With this many wings, it equals a lot," Uden said, justifying his desire to pluck the wings from every single bat.

None of them could argue.

Once they were done looting the bodies, they walked back about thirty yards before finding a spot to bed down for the night. Much of the cave looked the same, and Azure couldn't tell if it was night or day anymore given the pitch blackness inside. All he knew was that he was exhausted from all of the fighting.

"Don't forget to allocate your characteristic points and level up your skills," Lonnell told him.

"Yeah," he replied nonchalantly before setting to the task.

**Name:** Azure

**Race:** Human

**Level:** 5, 36% of the way to next level

**Health:** 98 / 180

**Mana:** 150 / 150

**Stamina:** 17 / 160

**Vitality:** 13

**Intelligence:** 10

**Strength:** 11

**Agility:** 12

**Dexterity:** 11

**Charisma:** 10

**Luck:** 12

**Skills:** Archery Lvl 3; 36% of the way to next level

Stealth Lvl 3; 36% of the way to the next level

Analyze Lvl 4; 90% of the way to next level

Cooking Lvl 5; 40% of the way to next level

Alchemy Lvl 3; 0% of the way to next level

Foraging Lvl 5; 94% of the way to next level

One-Handed Weapons Lvl 4; 18% of the way to next level

Tracking Lvl 1; 70% of the way to next level

Two-Handed Weapons Level 2; 95% of the way to next level

**Languages:** Common Tongue, Sprite, Goblin-Tongue

This was the easiest allocation of points he had to make so far. If this quest had taught him anything, it was that he needed more Stamina and Health. Without a second thought, he put two points into Strength and one into Vitality.

Picking which skill to level up wasn't much more challenging. Normally, he would have leveled up Alchemy, since it was the furthest away from leveling. But he wasn't really in a situation where he needed it right now. The next skill furthest away from leveling was his One-Handed Weapons skill. Just from the fight with the bats, Azure had come to realize that the halberd wouldn't be his weapon of choice. The only thing keeping him from passing it off to Lonnell to hold for him was the fact that it did more damage than his crude goblin sword. As soon as he found a better sword, though, it would undoubtedly be getting sold.

*Congratulations! The skill:* ***One-Handed Weapons*** *has reached Level 5. This skill enables you to use all manner of one-handed weapons to defeat enemies. What you do with your other hand is up to you.* ***One-Handed Weapons now do 20% more damage.***

Sweet! A perk. Twenty percent more damage was a pretty good increase.

Closing his stats, Azure settled against the cave wall, staring at the darkness across from them. It amazed him how little the torches illuminated. It made him feel vulnerable, and it almost made him want to stay up and keep watch with Uden. But he needed rest more than any of them. The only reason they had even stopped was because his stamina was so depleted.

"Thanks for saving me, by the way," he mentioned, wanting to smooth over any lingering tension between him and the half-imp.

"Don't worry about it." Uden waved his appreciation away. "You would have done the same for me."

"I would have." It wasn't a lie, Azure realized. The half-imp had left him behind once but had saved him twice as many times. Whether Azure fully trusted him or not, they were in this together now.

All for one, and one for all.

## CHAPTER TWO
THE REALM – Day 30

There was a faint unease throughout the night. The strangest feeling. It was as if Azure's subconscious mind was trying to force a nightmare. The images that flashed through his head were always on the cusp, but not quite there.

When what he perceived to be morning finally came, Azure found that neither Uden nor Lonnell had gotten much sleep. That had impeded the recovery of their stamina, but not so much that they weren't both nearly fully charged.

"Sleeping in this place was definitely a bad idea," Uden said between yawning and stretching.

"I don't feel rested at all," Lonnell groaned.

Azure could only surmise that his Armor of Light had protected him from the bad dreams that had plagued the others. He was grateful that he had it.

"Did you guys run into any trouble last night?" he asked, thinking about how his watch had been silent. Eerily so.

"No," they both responded.

"And thank the Gods for that. We all needed every bit of rest we could get since sleep only came with unpleasantness," Lonnell added.

"Ah yes. The lovely nightmares," Uden remarked sarcastically.

"I think the armor kept me from having them," Azure confessed.

"It would." Lonnell nodded. "You're lucky you have it."

"You'll be lucky if I don't steal it from you tonight if we don't make it out of this forsaken place," Uden grumbled.

"I'd like to see you try and take it." Azure snorted in jest.

"Do not put it past me to undress you." The half-imp glared at him.

"If we follow your plan and don't proceed forward after fighting the bat swarm again, we will be stuck in here another night," Lonnell reminded them. "Is it really worth it?"

"I think so," Azure quickly replied.

"You would since you have the armor." Uden brushed Azure's shoulder, flicking up a few of the leaves.

"Our stamina did recover, but I'm not feeling it." Lonnell shook his head, looking exhausted. The dark circles under his eyes could be seen in the flickering light of the torches. Uden sported them as well.

"Let us get through the swarm one more time and then see how we feel," the half-imp suggested. "While I'm all for leveling up, I'd rather do what's necessary to make it out of here alive."

A soft huff passed through Azure's lips. Perhaps he hadn't

found a loophole after all. There were definitely consequences for staying in the dungeon too long.

They shared a light breakfast of dried meat before heading back towards the bats. Already knowing what was coming, they were ready when they heard the flapping of wings headed in their direction.

"Here they come!" Azure shouted, fully energized and ready to earn some sweet experience points.

Again, the barrage of bats descended on them, and they all swung their weapons and pried the bats off of them that managed to get through. Again there was a rapid fire of notifications in Azure's vision.

*Defeated Level 1 **Bat**. 8XP rewarded.*

*Congratulations! The skill: **Two-Handed Weapons** has reached Level 3. This skill enables you to use all manner of two-handed weapons to defeat enemies. Increasing your Strength will make them easier to wield.*

*Defeated Level 1 **Bat**. 8XP rewarded.*

*Defeated Level 1 **Bat**. 8XP rewarded.*

*Defeated Level 1 **Bat**. 8XP rewarded.*

This time, it was more like a game to him. He desperately

wanted to beat Uden's kill count for bragging rights. Both brothers seemed slower, somehow, but at the end of the swarm, Azure still only managed to garner twenty-nine kills, the same as the day before.

"Did you guys level up?" Azure asked as he knelt to start cutting the wings off of the downed bats.

"I did," Uden replied, though he didn't seem particularly excited about it.

"I did not," Lonnell told them.

"I didn't either, but my Two-Handed Weapons skill did. Maybe next round."

The battle had depleted nearly a quarter of his Stamina and Health. Uden was the worst off, having lost a third of his Stamina and Health equally. That meant they would only be good for one more round with the bats before they'd need to either heal with potions or rest up. Azure had miscalculated the day before by only factoring in his own Stamina and Health.

Glancing at Uden's stats in the bottom of his field of vision, he began to wonder if he might actually be stronger than the half-imp despite Uden's higher level. He doubted that Uden took the brunt of the attack. They had all been standing side by side.

"Thirty-four this time," the half-imp commented, obviously wanting to keep the game going.

"I beat you, brother," Lonnell said with a smile.

They both looked over at Azure.

"I don't want to talk about it," he muttered, which garnered a chuckle from Uden and thankfully no further prodding.

When they were done cleaning up the field, Lonnell distributed a healing potion to each of them.

"Don't you think we should disperse these in case we get separated from one another?" Azure suggested after downing his potion.

"You would probably waste them," Uden said, not bothering to hold back the harshness in his tone.

Azure gritted his teeth. “Or I could just die.”

"We have to be careful with our supply," Lonnell told him. "We haven't even cleared the first level, and we've already used up eleven healing potions."

Had they really gone through that many already? Now that he was counting, the math made sense. While he could understand the need to conserve and ration, he didn't get why Lonnell wouldn't entrust him with his own supply. Perhaps it was a mechanic of the game where he was only given things on rare occasions—a way to force him to purchase and craft potions on his own. Still, this seemed like one of the times for the game to not be stingy.

"Fine." He sighed.

"Having said all that," Uden began, "should we go through the bats again? That took a pretty big chunk out of my Health and Stamina. I'm good for maybe one more round. I wouldn't risk a third. If we go again, though, we're all going to come out the other end weak. We won't make any more progress for the day, and we'll have to double back again to heal. Honestly, my opinion on this has changed. I think we should press on."

"I am in agreement." Lonnell nodded. "It's not worth the drain on our supplies to fight the bats again. Whatever is up ahead we will still gain experience from."

While Azure was disappointed, he could see their logic. They still potentially had a lot of floors left to go, and their supplies were quickly dwindling. They hadn't planned to run into an experience fountain like this. “I suppose we can always come back once we defeat The Dark One.”

"It doesn't work that way," the half-imp told him. "Once we defeat the demon, the dungeon will disappear. A path should open up and port us to the surface. There will be no going back."

"Well, that kind of sucks." Azure frowned. He really loved the easy experience from fighting the bats.

"Let us move forward." Lonnell pressed on ahead, taking point and forcing the two to follow him.

They walked for about fifteen minutes before coming to a set of stairs.

"We made it," Lonnell said with relief. "One level down. Who knows how many more to go."

"Progress is progress." Uden jogged down the stairs past them.

As they proceeded further into the dungeon, the scenery began to change. The closed-in path they had been walking on doubled in size as did the distance to the ceiling. The obsidian walls were replaced by rock. It was beginning to actually look like a cave. And smell like one, Azure thought as he shied away from the strong smell of ammonia.

"Is it safe to breathe the air?" he asked as the odor grew more intense.

While Uden seemed unaffected by the stench, Lonnell kept drawing his hand up to his face, clearly bothered by it as well.

"It's just bat droppings," the half-imp informed him. "I'm surprised the smell wasn't stronger on the level above."

Oddly, Azure hadn't noticed the smell at all on the higher level. If anything, the air had just seemed stale, trapped and unmoving within the confines of the dungeon.

"It should not be poisonous," Uden assured him.

He was proven wrong a few minutes later when Azure received the notification.

*You have been infected with **sickness**. You will now move 5% slower and will lose one health point per second for the next 10 seconds.*

"Oh you've got to be kidding me," Azure grumbled as a wave of nausea overtook him. It was like the ammonia scent was clinging to every hair inside of his nose and crawling down his throat. When he retched, it was all he could taste.

"What happened?" Uden paused, looking at him with concern.

"It's sickness. I just got it, too." Lonnell's face turned a pale shade of green, and he pinched his brow, undoubtedly trying to push back the headache that Azure was now feeling as well. A green icon in the shape of a face throwing up blinked next to Lonnell's name at the bottom of Azure's vision to confirm his assertion.

"That's strange. I feel fine."

"You may be genetically immune to it, but who knows," Lonnell suggested.

"Should we tear our clothes to cover our noses. I still have my old tunic," Azure offered.

"I doubt that will stop you from getting sick. The smell is everywhere." Uden's eyes roved the cave to point out the scope of the problem.

"I'm willing to try anything at this point." Lonnell gestured for Azure to pull the shirt from his bag.

They took a few moments to tear pieces of the shirt and create makeshift masks for themselves. Uden took one too, even though he seemed immune to the smell. By the time they had finished, both men's sickness had passed.

"I didn't expect these kinds of defenses," Lonnell confessed, his voice slightly muffled now that his mouth was covered.

"I honestly didn't know what to expect," Uden muttered. "Just that it would probably be bad."

"Everything in this place seems designed to weaken us," Azure commented.

"That's so it will be easier to kill us when we do finally reach The Dark One," the half-imp pointed out.

"I wish I would have invested in some cures, but sickness was the last thing I thought we would encounter in here," Lonnell told them.

"It's too late to worry about it now. All we can do is keep pressing forward. The stench has to subside eventually. Like most other things in this dungeon, it's probably unique to this floor," Uden said before taking the lead.

About fifteen more yards into the dungeon and they were greeted by the fluttering of wings again. This time, the sound was louder, and it was accompanied by a guttural screech, more ear-piercing than that of the bats—a stronger noise indicating a bigger creature.

"What's that?" Azure whispered, staying close.

"Considering what we just encountered," Uden kept his voice low, "I would guess they are large bats."

"I'm getting the obvious difference between the two," Azure said so that the half-imp wouldn't have the chance to mock him, "but how large are we talking about?"

"They're about the size of a sheep," Lonnell told him.

*Odd comparison*, Azure thought. But Lonnell was a farmer, after all.

Despite their efforts to be quiet, the creatures still heard them. There was a whooshing sound from the beating of oversized wings, and the cave shook slightly as the monsters approached.

When the large bats finally made it into the light, it was like seeing something from a horror movie. Dark brown with black beady eyes and upturned noses, they were blown-up versions of the smaller bats they'd faced before. Two crawled along the cavern walls on either side. Two more made faster purchase dragging themselves along the floor, and four flapped their powerful wings as they used flight as their method of attack. It reminded Azure of seeing ants erupting from a disturbed ant hill. They covered whatever space they could to reach the adventurers. As soon as they were close, the ones that had been crawling on the walls took to the floor. Thankfully, they were slower than the large bats in the air. Azure had time to Analyze two of the bats before they reached them. Both Analyzed as purple, an even match. That would have been all well and good if there weren't so many of them. This wasn't going to be an easy battle.

That became even more apparent when one of the bats easily swooped past Lonnell's defenses, gripping him by the shoulders and nearly biting his head off. He popped the bat in the chin with the butt of his staff just before its fangs had a chance to reach him. Large droplets of slather fell on Lonnell's face, blinding him and causing him to fall back.

Within seconds, the scene was pure chaos. Uden's speed once again gave him an advantage. He was quick with his dagger, slashing and stabbing any bat brave enough to approach, though he didn't seem to be focusing on a single one with so many upon them.

Thankful for being armed with the halberd for the first time, Azure was mostly relying on defense to keep the bats at bay.

The weapon's reach helped to put a reasonable distance between him and his attackers. Occasionally, he would slash forward with it, and the bats would recede before he could land a hit. The bravest of the three that was on him was the one in the air. It dove to attack every now and then, and the distraction it caused allowed the two that were crawling to move in.

Uden seemed to be having the most luck of the three adventurers. Not afraid to engage in close combat, he ran and dove, skidding on his knees until he was beneath one of the bats before driving his blades up into its throat and putting a quick end to it.

*I have to man up and get in there. I won't make any leeway if I wait for them to come to me,* Azure realized.

He watched in his peripheral vision as Lonnell smashed one of the bats against the cave wall with his staff. A sharp crack to the back of its head, and it was dead.

Throwing caution to the wind, Azure let out a battle cry and attacked one of the bats on the floor. It tried to move out of his range, but it didn't go far enough. He practically cleaved its head in half. It was a much easier triumph than Azure had expected, but not one that came without consequences. As he was attacking, the other floor bat moved in to swipe at his leg with its thumb, effectively slashing through his armor to his flesh.

*Defeated Level 5* ***Large Bat****. 35XP rewarded.*

*Level 5* ***Large Bat*** *delivers 35 damage.*

Azure's adrenaline was pumping so fiercely that he barely even felt the cut. Seeing his attention diverted, the remaining floor bat backed away, leaving the next attack to its flighted friend. Azure slashed at one of its wings but missed. When it dove for him a second time, it gripped the pole of his halberd with its foot, engaging Azure in an unsteady battle of tug-o-war. The floor bat saw the advantage, quickly crawling in to strike again. Azure saw this attack coming, though. He kicked the bat in the nose, causing it to screech and cower back. It afforded him enough time to reclaim his weapon, and with it to cut off one of the flighted bat's feet with a lucky stroke. This seemed to only piss it off, and it charged at him, baring down for the kill.

Wrong move. Azure plunged the axe of his halberd into its gut, causing its entrails to spill out. The smell of iron and ammonia assaulted his nostrils.

*Congratulations! The skill:* ***Two-Handed Weapons*** *has reached Level 4. This skill enables you to use all manner of two-handed weapons to defeat enemies. Increasing your Strength will make them easier to wield.*

*You have been infected with* ***sickness****. You will now move 5% slower and will lose one health point per second for the next 10 seconds.*

The bat fell heavily with the weight of its death, causing Azure to lose his balance and tumble to the ground with it.

*Critical hit! Defeated Level 5* ***Large Bat****. 35XP rewarded.*

In an instant, the ground bat was upon him, gnashing its teeth at Azure's face. He barely had time to block with his arms, which proved to be a mistake. Seeing his fleshy defense, the bat buried its fangs into Azure's forearm, making him cry out in pain.

*Level 4* ***Large Bat*** *delivers 20 damage.*

To add insult to injury, it then stepped on his leg, seeming to accidentally cut through his armor with its sharp claws.

*Level 4* ***Large Bat*** *delivers 20 damage.*

For a few seconds, Azure felt trapped and panicked. His halberd was stuck in the body of the other bat. Due to the length of it, it was useless against a foe at this close range. But then Azure snapped to the fact that he had another weapon. Too bad it was tucked into his boot.

Sacrificing the arm that was still in the bat's mouth, Azure wiggled to reach his dagger with his other hand. Between his headache from the sickness and the searing agony from his arm being mauled, moving was excruciating. But pain was better than death.

Realizing that it wasn't getting any closer to killing Azure, the bat let go of his arm to strike again. The removal of the pressure allowed Azure to move more freely. He reached his dagger just as the bat was lurching forward to attack again, plunging it into the creature's eye when its face was only a mere foot from his. Despite the stab that penetrated its eye socket and stopped somewhere in its brain, the bat still pushed forward with its last remaining life. Azure grunted as he held it back, his hand trembling from the effort. Luckily, the bat's life force expired before his strength did. Its body went limp, and then its head followed, dragging Azure's hand down with it.

*Defeated Level 4* ***Large Bat****. 28XP rewarded.*

*Congratulations! You are now **Level 6**! Your base stats have been boosted. You have earned 3 points to assign to your characteristics. Please note that adding points to some characteristics(Vitality, Intelligence, and Strength) will further boost your base stats. You may also advance any 1 skill of your choosing by 1 level.*

Azure just wanted to lie there until the rest of the battle was over. His health was down by nearly forty percent, and he was feeling it. But the fight wasn't over yet.

He used his remaining strength to push the dead bat off of him, deciding to leave his halberd for now since he couldn't use it with just one arm anyway. Azure forced himself to his feet and drew his sword. Thankfully, the large bat had bitten into his left forearm, so he could still wield the sword with his dominant hand. His effort seemed unneeded, though. Uden and Lonnell had teamed up to finish off the last bat. While Lonnell distracted it from the front, Uden jumped on it from behind like a maniac, thrusting his blades into its back and dragging them down with his weight. The bat arched its spine, screaming in pain before falling to the floor.

Azure wondered how Uden always made killing things look so bad-ass. Maybe it was because he enjoyed killing so much that he was able to do it with such style. Whatever the case, Azure admired him for it.

"Well, that wasn't as bad as I thought it would be," Lonnell said, panting for breath. He leaned over and placed his hands on his knees. A familiar green tint took over his face, and he retched.

"Speak for yourself," Azure muttered, sheathing his sword and then clutching his injured arm.

"I see you went and got yourself all fucked up again." Uden smirked at him mockingly.

"I don't understand how you never get seriously hurt."

The brothers' wounds were about on par with what they'd received from the swarm, though their stamina wasn't quite so drained.

Azure stared at Lonnell, waiting for him to dish out another healing potion. He was officially the healer of their group.

"I'm just that good." Uden cockily blew on the back of his knuckles.

"Yeah, yeah. Whatever." Azure brushed his bravado away. "Explain something to me," he said as he watched Lonnell start digging into his Bag of Holding for healing potions. "I don't really understand the battle mechanics of this."

"What do you mean?" Uden gave him a queer look.

"This has been bothering me for some time. The large bats Analyzed as purple for me. I killed all three of them in one hit, yet they weren't able to do as much damage when they struck me.

"I've noticed variations in the fighting abilities of other creatures of different levels as well. No matter the strength of the monster, I feel like it's possible to kill even the strongest foe with one hit."

The half-imp thought for a moment. "Monster level has little to do with its abilities. Everything has its own attack power. And no matter what level you are, a critical hit is a critical hit. Though highly unlikely, someone who is a level one could kill a level ten monster if they hit it just right. Everything has weak spots. It shouldn't be that hard to believe."

Azure sighed. "I am clearly grateful, especially given our current predicament. It just seems a bit unbalanced, I guess."

"Think of it this way." Uden walked over and leaned against the cave wall next to him. Though he wasn't panting like his brother, Azure assumed that he must be tired as well. Out of all of them, he exerted the most energy during his attacks. "How a monster Analyzes for you is directly proportionate to its level in relation to yours. Nothing more. You can encounter docile beasts that are a much higher level than you. Just because they're capable of inflicting more damage doesn't mean that they will. Part of what makes up a monster's attack power is its level of aggression. The more aggressive a monster is the more damage its likely to do. As far as humanoid species go, the weapon or weapons they're carrying also plays into the amount of damage they can do."

"By that logic, the lecture you gave me when we first met was bullshit," Azure commented dryly.

"It was not." The half-imp crossed his arms over his chest. "More often than not, you won't be able to kill anything orange and beyond on your own. You have to be partied."

"If you say so." Azure waved the explanation away, deciding to leave the mysteries of the color system alone. He had more important things to think about right now anyway, like allocating his characteristic points.

A mere thought brought up his character sheet.

**Name:** Azure

**Race:** Human

**Level:** 6, 2% of the way to next level

**Health:** 156 / 200

**Mana:** 160 / 160

**Stamina:** 131 / 190

**Vitality:** 14

**Intelligence:** 10

**Strength:** 13

**Agility:** 12

**Dexterity:** 11

**Charisma:** 10

**Luck:** 12

**Skills:** Archery Lvl 3; 36% of the way to next level

Stealth Lvl 3; 36% of the way to the next level

Analyze Lvl 4; 95% of the way to next level

Cooking Lvl 5; 40% of the way to next level

Alchemy Lvl 3; 0% of the way to next level

Foraging Lvl 5; 94% of the way to next level

One-Handed Weapons Lvl 5; 2% of the way to next level

Tracking Lvl 1; 70% of the way to next level

Two-Handed Weapons Level 4; 3% of the way to next level

**Languages:** Common Tongue, Sprite, Goblin-Tongue

Feeling pretty good about his Health, Azure decided to place a point in Agility and one in Dexterity. Because this particular dungeon seemed to be pretty big on draining their Stamina, he put his final characteristic point into Strength, just to be sure he had enough for whatever they were to face next.

Choosing which skill to level up was a bit more difficult since his One-Handed Weapons skill and his Two-Handed Weapons skill still had a ways to go before the next level. Remembering the increase in damage from leveling his One-Handed Weapons skill to 5, Azure wondered if he'd get the same perk from leveling his Two-Handed Weapons skill to the same level. That would add +2.4 max damage to his halberd. For curiosity's sake, and because he'd most likely be using the halberd for the remainder of this dungeon, Azure decided to go with leveling up his Two-Handed Weapons skill.

*Congratulations! The skill:* ***Two-Handed Weapons*** *has reached Level 2. This skill enables you to use all manner of two-handed weapons to defeat enemies. Increasing your Strength will make them easier to wield.* ***One-Handed Weapons now do 20% more damage.***

Sweet! It was just as he had suspected. The more damage he could do, the better.

"I think that's enough for one day." Lonnell stepped forward to hand him a healing potion.

"Have you recovered, brother?" Uden asked in concern.

He nodded. “The sickness has passed.”

"We haven't made much progress," Azure noted before drinking the potion.

"Better to be safe than sorry. And better to not waste stamina potions when we might need them later." Lonnell extracted another vial from his Bag of Holding and handed it to Uden.

"I'm not sure it's so safe to drag this out." The half-imp turned his gaze to the unexplored depths of the cave as if he expected something to creep out of the darkness. "Yes, if we rest we'll recover stamina naturally, but if we continue to lose sleep, we may become infected with insanity."

“Insanity?” Azure asked, instantly thinking of Call of Cthulu.

"Yeah. I'm honestly surprised you didn't get it after the demon scratched you and you didn't sleep for several days. Insanity typically kicks in after three days of not sleeping. It leads to hallucinations that often cause you to attack your own comrades. It's one of the most dangerous things that can happen in a party."

Azure thought back to when he had wandered through the woods aimlessly after escaping from The Dark One. Every time he had closed his eyes, he had seen the demon's face, and the fear of it had roused him back awake. Sheer exhaustion was the only thing that had afforded him an hour of sleep here and there, but it definitely wasn't restful. Five nights he had spent tossing and turning. According to Uden, that would have been enough to cause insanity.

"Maybe I'm immune." Azure shrugged.

The half-imp gave him a sarcastic side-eye. “No one is immune.”

"Well, I didn't get it." He huffed.

"Maybe you got enough sleep to avoid it," Lonnell suggested. "Insanity is a strange thing, and people are more prone to get it in certain situations. As odd as it sounds, being in a party increases your chances of getting it."

"And this is also the perfect environment for such an illness," Uden pointed out. "A perfect environment for many of the ailments. I think we should press on." He kicked at a rock.

"We are only two floors in. There could be eight more to go. We only have eight stamina potions left," Lonnell argued. "Out of all of us, you are the most at risk of running out of stamina."

"Then give me a stamina potion and let's move on. I want to get out of this bloody dungeon as quickly as possible. You guys are probably both good for one more encounter. We can't keep stopping at every floor to sleep. If we continue this pattern and there are ten floors, both of us will definitely end up with insanity and will probably kill each other. Do you really want that?"

"I think he's right," Azure chimed in. "Besides, if we keep backtracking to rest, we're just going to deplete our supplies that much faster. It's better to take the chance of moving forward."

"Fine," Lonnell relented with a sigh. "I don't like this, though." He dug into his Bag of Holding for a stamina potion and handed it to Uden who promptly uncorked it and downed the contents.

"Now, let's loot these things and get out of here before those large bats respawn." The half-imp returned the empty vial to his brother and then knelt to lift the head of one of the dead bats. He wedged his blade into its mouth and began cutting out one of its fangs. It seemed like a laborious task.

"Are we taking the wings, too?" Azure asked as he walked over to one of the large bats that he had slain.

"Pick and choose what you want to take. Some of us have limited inventory space." Uden glanced at Lonnell's Bag of Holding.

The elder brother seemed to be slower to want to dissect the creatures for their parts. "You have five minutes to loot before we need to move on. We've already wasted too much time here." His tone was stern.

Prying the large bat's tooth from its mouth proved to be challenging. The root was well-seated. Azure could only assume that the fang would be more valuable than the wings, though it seemed that he could have collected much more of them in the same amount of time. It took him a bit over five minutes to extract the tooth, and once he did, it was a bloody mess. He made a face as he stuck it in his bag, thinking about how he'd probably have to wash it later. What was worse was the smell, like an old dog's mouth with rotting gums. Azure certainly hoped it would be worth the effort.

*You have received the following item:*

| **Large Bat Fang** | **Quantity:** 1/1<br>**Item Class:** Common<br>**Quality:** Average<br>**Weight:** 0 kg<br>**Uses:** Weapon Forging, Jewelry Crafting |
|---|---|

Checking out the uses for the large bat fang, it definitely seemed more valuable than the wings had been.

Finally, the three adventurers pressed on. It seemed like they had walked a good hundred yards before coming upon another set of stairs.

"Thank the Gods," Lonnell said with relief.

"It seems that there's only one set of foes per level," Azure pointed out.

"That could always change," Uden told him. "I've heard of dungeons of super strong bosses spanning for miles and having an almost endless supply of monsters."

"Those are probably just stories," Lonnell said, making it sound like the tales of children.

"There's truth in most stories," the half-imp mused.

"You're obviously not very well read." Azure snorted then immediately wondered if he was being ignorant. Without encountering a sizable library, there was no way for him to tell if the books contained within The Realm were mostly fact or fiction. Hell, he wasn't even sure which side the scale fell on in his own world"a world that was seeming more like fiction with each passing day. Whether this was a game or not, it was his reality now. He had accepted that much as the truth.

As they descended the stairs, Azure noticed that they gradually became weathered the further down they went. The stone was cracked and crumbling in some places. One misplaced step and he nearly fell, though luckily he was able to regain his footing before his ass met the ground.

"Careful," Lonnell warned. Completely unnecessary, as the error had already been made. Azure had known to be careful when he was walking down the stairs. That hadn't stopped him from stepping on a weak spot.

At the bottom of the stairs, the cave opened into a large circular chamber. It was a gigantic space, and oddly well lit with torches adorning the walls every five feet. The ceiling must be a good fifty feet tall, with sandy-colored stalactites hanging from it. Water dripped softly from their tips, making the floor moist and slick. The walls appeared to be made of the same weathered stone bricks that comprised the stairs. Some were missing in spots, making it seem as if the walls could cave in at any moment. A few large stalagmites dotted the outer ring of the room, but the inner portion of it was bare aside from a giant egg-looking stone. It seemed strategically placed, perfectly set in the center of the floor, signifying some importance that Azure wasn't catching onto.

*You have been infected with **sickness**. You will now move 5% slower and will lose one health point per second for the next 10 seconds.*

Azure exhaled in annoyance. “Are you kidding me right now?” Almost the second the words left his mouth, nausea hit him.

"Shut the fuck up and get back up the stairs." Uden threw his arm out, practically pushing Azure back towards the stairs.

Lonnell was staring wide-eyed at the egg, a mix of shock and panic on his face. “Seriously?”

"Go, go, go, go!" Uden urged them on as the egg made a strange noise, like that of a humpback whale followed by a rattling purr, and began to move.

Seeing Uden literally running for the stairs told Azure just how afraid of the creature he should be. Quickly Analyzing it, he saw why. It showed up as orange. Now that they were all the same level, Azure knew it Analyzed as a hard kill for his companions as well. Even with the three of them together, this would likely not be a creature that would be easy to defeat, especially given its scale.

At a distance, Azure could tell that it was about twenty feet tall in its egg form. Glancing back, the last thing he saw before he made it up the stairs to the point that he couldn't see it anymore was it...unfolding, for lack of a better word. Its skin looked hard and armored like that of an armadillo, but it shared the gray and brown patterning of a snake. To be honest, Azure wasn't sure what he had just seen. The egg seemed to open up, and there was only darkness inside.

"What is that?" he asked, following Uden who was taking the stairs two at a time. Sediment flew back as their shoes tore up the dilapidated staircase. Due to his sickness, Azure was at the rear, which made running feel like a desperate act.

"It's a dawnflayer. Now keep running," Uden responded.

"A what?"

"Don't worry about it, just run."

Once they were about halfway up the staircase, Lonnell began to slow. “I don't think it saw us.”

Uden stopped finally, hunching over a few steps above them to catch his breath. He took in air in gulps, pausing to listen between them. There was thankfully no sign of further movement at the bottom of the stairs.

Azure refused to tear his eyes away from the steps below as he slowly ascended them until he was on the same level with Lonnell. Bile raced up his throat from a mixture of his sickness and exertion, and he had to steady himself against the wall as he retched and emptied his stomach acid onto it.

The half-imp let out a long sigh and straightened himself. “I think we're safe for now.”

"I certainly hope so. Running for your life while sick is miserable." Azure rested his head against the wall, trying to get the room to stop spinning. A few seconds later, the sickness passed, leaving him feeling fine again.

"We're going to have to plan this attack strategically." Lonnell rubbed his chin, obviously already working on a plan inside of his head.

"What are we up against, exactly?" Azure raised an eyebrow.

"It's a dawnflayer," Uden said again. "Basically an unholy mix between a dragon and a bat. They have almost impenetrable defenses and can inflict deafness with one good screech, making it difficult to coordinate attacks," he explained.

"So how do we kill it?" Azure asked the obvious question.

"Most of their bodies are covered in a protective skin so

thick that it's impregnable by arrows and blades. Only their stomachs and eyes are vulnerable to attack."

"That sounds easy enough. So I snipe it in the eye from a distance, and we're done with it." He shrugged as if it were no big deal.

"Did you even get a look at its face?"

Azure shook his head.

"Their eyes are set back in their heads, so tiny that you almost can't see them. The way they're sunk in provides a type of protective shield with the skin around them. Even the slightest movement of their head would be able to deflect an arrow. To easily shoot one in the eye, you would have to be an expert marksman.

"Like bats, they mostly use echolocation. Once we rouse it, it will screech loudly and often. Without charms to protect us, we will all succumb to deafness. There is no way to avoid it."

"Then we go for the stomach..." Azure said hesitantly, knowing that the half-imp would have a counter for that as well.

He crossed his arms over his chest. “As I mentioned before, most of the skin is an armor. Their heads are oversized and hang low, guarding against what would otherwise be an easy shot. They also have massive wings that they use as shields. Pretty much the only way to get a good shot is at point blank range, and that puts you right in line with their massive jaws.

"Being in range of their breath will immediately cause sickness, further weakening you and making it harder to focus. They kill in two ways, with their teeth and by crushing victims with their massive claws. Thankfully, they can't fly far, but they will make the distance to put you under them. And if it lands on you, you are dead."

"Can you make this sound anymore bleak?" Azure gave

him a sarcastic look. "Give me the silver lining." He gestured.

Lonnell inhaled deeply. “Unfortunately, there isn't one.”

"But it is still possible to kill it from afar. I would just need the right angle." Azure began working up his own plan.

"It's unlikely that you'll be able to kill it with your bow, considering the level difference," Uden told him.

"But my arrows are imbued and do +4 damage against dark magic. That has to count for something." Azure glanced between the brothers.

The half-imp nodded slowly. “Yes. It will help. But you have to get the shot in, first. The way their eyes are set, you'd have to shoot at the perfect angle to penetrate all the way to the brain. I'm not sure if the bonus would be enough to do the trick.

"And honestly, even if the creature does move in just the right way for you to go for a body shot, the odds of hitting a vital organ are few and far between. I hate to put so much pressure on you, but your sword will be the best weapon we have against the beast. My small blades might be able to slit open its stomach if I'm lucky, but they're not long enough to hit a vital organ like a lung or the heart. For this battle, my role is best as a distraction while you go in for the kill."

Azure was both honored and mortified that the half-imp was willing to hand off this important task to him. While he had been longing to feel like a hero, the weight of this responsibility was crushing.

"My staff won't be much use against it either," Lonnell said with a frown. "I think my brother has the right idea. He can distract from one side with his throwing knives while I attack with the bow and arrow. Hopefully, we can keep the dawnflayer occupied while you make the close-range attack."

"I think you guys are missing a big advantage that we

have." Azure gazed back down the stairs.

"And what would that be?" Uden hummed.

"The stairwell is narrow. If we lure it here, it won't be able to come inside. It would just snap at us from the outside. We could shoot at it with the bow until we hit it in the eyes, then lunge in to make the kill when it's blind. Easy peasy."

The half-imp chuckled and shook his head. “There is still much you don't understand.”

"Dungeons have certain rules," Lonnell began to explain. "Most creatures cannot move from floor to floor. We headed for the stairs to escape, not just because it was the obvious choice, but because the dawnflayer can't come up here. Its range of attack is to the bottom of the stairwell. Similarly, we cannot attack beyond the stairwell if we are standing on it, meaning that the monster is protected from unfair attacks as well."

"In many dungeons," Uden continued, "once you reach the next floor, the way back will close, trapping you in with the monster. We were actually very lucky that didn't happen." There was clear relief in his voice.

Azure was still a little confused. “If the dawnflayer can't come up here, then why did we run so far to get away from it?” A Flock of Seagulls song played in his head for half a second.

"Because we don't want it waiting at the bottom of the stairs for us when we go back down, and because it also still holds an advantage. While it can't physically pass the barrier between floors, its screeches and putrid breath would still affect us.

"It's bad enough that it began to stir. It knows we are near. It will be alert now." Uden lowered himself so that he was sitting on the stairs.

Azure tried to think of some other advantage to having the dawnflayer follow them to the edge of the stairs, but he came up empty-handed. The plan that Lonnell had laid out seemed the best. There would be no easy way to finish this.

"Now I think we should rest," Lonnell announced. "Facing the dawnflayer tomorrow will take everything we have. We need to approach the battle clearheaded and focused if we hope to succeed."

"It's hard to be clearheaded and focused when you're sleep-deprived," Uden commented beneath his breath but then relented. "Yes, it is best if we rest tonight. I don't believe we have much farther to go. In most circumstances, a dawnflayer would be considered a mini-boss. And the mini-boss almost always comes right before the main boss. We are very near to the demon now. I can feel it." He gazed down the stairs, looking distant.

Azure hesitated. “You can...feel it?”

"Yes." The half-imp dropped his head.

Lonnell walked over to where Azure was standing, keeping his voice low. “In many ways, they are made up of the same kind of dark energy. I'm not surprised he can feel it nearby.”

"If Uden is made up of dark energy, then how can he use light magic? Don't the two contradict?"

"He can use light magic because of his human half, and because his heart is good. If he were evil, he would not be capable of wielding light magic."

"You guys know I'm right here, right? I can hear you." Uden raised an eyebrow at them.

Lonnell chuckled. “Sorry, brother.”

“Oh, don't be so sensitive,” Azure teased him.

"If you think I'm grumpy now, you should see me tomorrow after another night of no sleep." The half-imp closed his eyes and rested his head against the cold stone wall.

"Well, we should eat before we sleep." Lonnell rummaged through his Bag of Holding for enough dried meat to feed the three of them.

"I'm too tired to eat," Uden groaned.

"I've never known you to be so whiny." Azure smirked, taking a strip of meat from Lonnell.

The half-imp opened his eyes, but he still looked tired. “I don't think you understand how much energy it takes being me.”

"I don't want to know." Azure shook his head and laughed.

They spent the rest of their time eating in silence. The stairs did not provide a comfortable place for them to rest, and Azure was eventually able to convince them to ascend the rest of the way so that they'd at least have flat ground to lie on. But sleep would not come to his companions no matter where they were...because the demon was always watching.

## CHAPTER THREE
THE REALM – Day 31

Since he was the most well-rested, Azure offered to take the loathed split shift. While he didn't encounter anything while he was on watch, Uden said that a large bat had appeared when he was guarding. Lonnell had immediately risen to help defeat it, having not really been asleep, just lying there.

The evidence of the melee lay in a stinking heap about four yards away from where Azure had been sleeping. It was merely just the toothless carcass since Uden had taken the time to loot everything else. Thankfully, both brothers were uninjured, and since they had teamed up to fight the creature, hadn't had to use much stamina to defeat it.

"We should probably solidify the plan before we go back down there," Azure suggested as they ate breakfast together. It was strange how he'd almost gotten used to eating the same thing for every meal. Back in his world, eating had been something he'd often done for pleasure. Here, it was just what he did to stay alive. With little flavor in most of the foods they ate, consuming was more of a chore than anything else"something he wanted to be over quickly so that they could get on with whatever task they happened to be attending to.

"The first thing we need to do is Stealth ourselves before we reach the bottom of the stairs. We barreled in like a stampede last time without even thinking. We're lucky that didn't cost us our lives," Uden said. "I think that Lonnell and I should skirt around the room, taking cover behind the stalagmites. We'll both attack from the side, drawing the dawnflayer's attention away. Then Azure can come in from the other side, hopefully make it past the dawnflayer's defenses, and land the killing blow."

He made it sound so easy. But most of their plans sounded easy until they actually put them into action.

Nervousness swirled in the pit of Azure's stomach. One wrong move and he could end up dead. Considering the level of the dawnflayer, it had the potential to kill him in a single hit. He felt like he only had one chance to do this, and he had to get it right.

"Give me your halberd, and I'll stick it in my bag," Lonnell offered, gesturing for the weapon. "Also, I'll need your bow."

Worry flooded Azure as he handed over the quiver of imbued arrows. “Use them sparingly. We should save some to face the demon.”

"I will only use what I need to keep the dawnflayer off of you and Uden. I plan to aim only for its eyes."

"I wouldn't go for the eyes," Uden told him.

"We need to get its attention, brother. With the rest of its body well-armored, the only thing worth going for is its eyes."

The half-imp exhaled slowly, seeming concerned. “If that's your plan, then you'll need to be careful. Even its face is armored. A deflected arrow could hit Azure.”

Azure drew his hand up to his chest in mock surprise. “Aw, are you actually worried about me?”

"Shove it," Uden bit back, his expression all seriousness.

"This isn't a game. Your life will be on the line. More than ours. If you fail, I doubt we'll be able to kill it."

The amusement left Azure's face. It was strange to see the half-imp so troubled. It certainly didn't help to give him confidence going into battle.

"Here." Lonnell pulled a few of the red health potions out of his Bag of Holding and handed them to Azure. "Just in case I can't get to you in time."

*You have received the following items:*

| **Potion of Minor Healing** | **Quantity:** 3/3<br>**Item Class:** Common<br>**Quality:** Average<br>**Weight:** 0 kg<br>**Uses:** Heals 30 HP |
|---|---|

"Well, that's comforting," Azure muttered, grateful for the gift, but unsettled nonetheless. If nothing else was a clear sign of how dangerous this fight was about to be, Lonnell voluntarily relinquishing the potions to him did the job.

"Are we ready?" Uden asked.

"As ready as we're probably going to be," Lonnell responded, staring at the floor.

Azure blew out a breath, trying to steal himself. “We've come this far. There's no going back.”

"Then activate your Stealth and let's go. We should proceed down the stairs as carefully as possible. No little slip-ups like yesterday." The half-imp glared at Azure. "The dawnflayer will hear us long before it sees us coming. One wrong move will be enough to alert it."

*It didn't move very quickly yesterday*, Azure thought, but he didn't bother to point that out. They were all stressed. The last thing they needed was an otiose argument, so he just nodded in agreement.

Azure began to proceed down the stairs, but the half-imp stopped him by placing a hand on the center of Azure's chest. “There are a few things I need to make abundantly clear to you before we get down there.” The way he was looking at Azure demanded his full attention. “You will succumb to deafness at some point. You will feel panicked and want to run away, but don't. Never before has it been more important for you to trust us. We will do everything in our power to keep the dawnflayer distracted, up to risking our lives. You being able to get close enough to kill it is the most important part of our plan.”

"I've got it," he acknowledged, feeling confident in his comrades' abilities to do what they said they would.

"All right." Uden hesitantly turned away from him, as if he had something else to say but then changed his mind, and continued down the stairs.

Without issue, they made it to the bottom of the stairs. The dawnflayer sat in the middle of the room, cocooned in its wings, an impenetrable barrier to protect it against potential sneak attacks. Uden and Lonnell broke off to one side, staying close to the wall as they made their way around the room. Almost as soon as they did, the creature began to stir.

Azure held his breath as he took cover behind a stalagmite, wondering how well Stealth actually worked against a beast that saw through sound. For all he knew, it may be useless. He peered around the side of the stone structure, curious about what the open wings would reveal. They unfolded slowly, a low rumble coming from the creature's throat. A massive head bent forward, at first just looking like a large flat piece of armored skin. When the head was finally fully exposed, Azure noted the angular shape of it. Like a box with ears. The neck that supported it was equally as thick and bent at a weird angle as if the head was designed to hang in front of the body to protect it. Two beady yellow eyes about the size of dimes peered out aimlessly, so deep set that the only way you could even tell that they were eyes was because of their placement and how they glowed. Now Azure could see why shooting at them would be pointless. The creature opened its jaw and let out a screech that had him immediately covering his ears.

*Holy shit, that was loud.* So loud that some of the bricks in the wall crumbled from the sound of it. So loud that all Azure could hear afterward was a horrible ringing. He expected to see a notice that he had been rendered deaf, but within a few seconds, his hearing returned. He didn't even want to imagine how painful that sound would be at close range.

The ground shook slightly as the dawnflayer continued to unfold, jutting its wings back and revealing massive clawed paws where a regular bat's thumbs would be. They were easily large enough to crush a man beneath them. With a center of gravity low to the ground, the creature's legs were stubby. Azure could see its soft body beneath its head, but barely. Proportionately, the dawnflayer was about thirty percent head, forty percent wings, ten percent legs, and ten percent body. From what he could tell, it didn't have a tail.

He waited for his friends to get into position. Due to them being Stealthed, he couldn't see them, but he knew the signal for him to move would be Uden coming out of hiding. While the half-imp would also be attacking from a distance, he would still need to get close enough for his attacks to connect. His range with his throwing knives wasn't anywhere near as long as Lonnell's would be with Azure's bow.

The dawnflayer seemed to notice the activity around it that was imperceptible to the naked eye. Very slowly, as if moving was intense labor, it began to turn away from where Azure was standing. Again it screeched, and again the horrible ringing followed. Azure quickly decided that he loathed the creature for its deafening ability and that the sooner he killed it, the better it would be for all of them. Uden, with his genetically heightened hearing, was probably suffering most of all. He wondered if the mere sound that the dawnflayer made from a distance was enough to cause the deafening effect to the half-imp. If so, then he now understood why Uden had been so fearful of the creature.

Minutes ticked by like hours as Azure waited, holding his breath and praying that the dawnflayer would keep quiet. He admittedly knew little about bats and how echolocation worked, but if he remembered correctly from biology class, the sound that they made was too high-pitched for the human ear to perceive. That didn't seem to be the case with the dawnflayer. Or maybe he had it all wrong. Perhaps it had been making sounds all this time, and this particular screech wasn't designed for it to see, but for it to startle its foes.

After what seemed like a short lifetime, Azure heard the distinct sound of a bowstring snapping followed by an enormous half-croak/half-screech that made the two sounds that the dawnflayer had made previously seem like a soft lullaby in comparison. Several bricks crumbled in the wall, and a massive stalactite fell from the ceiling, hitting the ground like a dagger and splintering into stone shards some twenty yards away from where Azure was standing.

*Fucks sake, I have to kill this thing as quickly as possible*, Azure thought in misery only a moment before he saw Uden emerge from the far side of the room, daggers in hand.

The creature continued to turn, seemingly unafraid to face its attacker head-on. Azure waited until the dawnflayer's eye was out of sight of him before charging forward. As soon as he left the shadows, Uden started taunting the beast, cursing at it and making all sorts of noise to try to keep its attention. It screeched at him again and began crawling towards him. This forward movement seemed to be a lot faster than its turning had been. With unexpected swiftness, it leaped from the ground, spreading its wings in a fruitless effort to fly, though it did manage to cover a few yards before it fell again. The impact shook the ground enough to knock Uden off of his feet. Stalactites rained down all around them, making Azure turn his attention to the ceiling and have to divert from his beeline path to avoid being hit.

Lonnell cried out from his hiding spot, trying to drag the dawnflayer's attention away from the easy prey now right below its massive jaw. The creature wasn't that stupid, though. While its foes seemed thoroughly distracted by the small earthquake it had caused, it opened its mouth and went in for the kill. Seeing Uden in the path of death, their plan went out the window. Giving up the element of surprise that had been insisted was needed to defeat the beast, Azure used what momentum he had to jump on its back, trying in vain to plunge his blade into the dawnflayer's wing and praying that the pain would be enough to distract it from Uden just in the nick of time for him to escape being devoured.

The effort was wasted. Not only did the creature's skin look like armor, but it worked just as well as a shield, deflecting Azure's blade entirely. In fact, the dawnflayer didn't even seem to perceive him as a threat, continuing the downward sweep of its jaw that Azure was certain would spell the half-imp's demise. His heart clenched in his chest as his eyes shot to Uden's health bar in his peripheral vision while he slid down the beast's body. Somehow, the small red bar didn't diminish or disappear.

Feeling a newfound rage and desperation, Azure threw caution to the wind, ducking beneath the creature's wing to get closer to its body. The scent of its breath was like being in the dungeon with the large bats times ten.

*You have been infected with **sickness**. You will now move 5% slower and will lose one health point per second for the next 10 seconds.*

Nausea roiled through Azure's stomach, but he knew better than to pay attention to it. He heard the bowstring snap again and barely had time to see Uden scurrying away before the creature jutted its head forward and screamed in anger, the force of which was so intense that it created a mirage effect like heat haze on a car's hood. For a moment, the dawnflayer's head had a distorted shimmer to it, as if not made up of solid matter.

*Level 9* ***Dawnflayer*** *delivers 20 damage. You are now* ***deaf.*** *This effect will last for 10 seconds.*

In an environment that had previously been so loud, to hear nothing was unsettling. Azure took half a second to piece together what had just happened before refocusing on his task. Judging by the direction that Uden had run from, he must have managed to roll out of the way before the dawnflayer's jaws clamped down. Relief might have flowed through Azure if he wasn't the one now in the beast's attack radius.

Not wasting another second—because he probably didn't have another one to waste—Azure grabbed the hilt of his blade with both hands and used all of his strength to plunge it up into the dawnflayer's side. Taking the time to search for a vital organ might have been smarter, but a mix of fear and adrenaline were now all that was driving Azure. He assumed that the creature screamed again when he stuck it, and apparently it had because he was met with another notice.

*Level 9* ***Dawnflayer*** *delivers 20 damage. You are now* ***deaf.*** *This effect will last for 10 seconds.*

As soon as his sense of smell returned, it seemed to immediately flee again with a sharp acrid odor and another notice.

*You have been infected with **sickness**. You will now move 5% slower and will lose one health point per second for the next 10 seconds.*

The creature moved, its rock-like body practically dragging him along. He tried to plant his feet, but it was no use. If the blade had hit a vital spot, the dawnflayer was showing no signs. It bent its head towards Azure, but there was no reaching him where he was tucked under its wing. Some safe spot he'd been lucky enough to find. Attacking the beast directly from the front would not have been smart, Azure realized as the neck began to swing around. In an attempt to fend him off, the dawnflayer began folding its wings. Azure struggled to pull his blade free. Everything was closing in around him, and panic started to set in as he realized what the dawnflayer's next move would be. It would crush him to death within its egg cocoon to protect itself since it couldn't reach him with its fangs or claws.

Azure fell to his knees to avoid the dawnflayer's head bearing down on him. He struck at the beast again, driving his blade up into its stomach and then, while clutching onto the pommel of his sword, rotated his body and tugged toward its other side to keep away from its inwardly folding wings. This seemed to have a much greater effect than the first stab. The dawnflayer shook with pain. Just as Azure's hearing returned, it screeched again. Before being rendered deaf, he heard the desperation in its cry.

*Level 9 **Dawnflayer** delivers 20 damage. You are now **deaf.** This effect will last for 10 seconds.*

Sickness seemed to follow in tandem.

*You have been infected with **sickness**. You will now move 5% slower and will lose one health point per second for the next 10 seconds.*

Despite the thickness of the beast's skin, fat entrails began to push through, spilling out toward Azure with a gush of red-black blood. Its wings flared, the force of which threw Azure to the ground. More of its intestines fell from the gash. Azure went to retrieve his sword, feeling that the job of killing the dawnflayer should be nearly done. Again, he found himself having a hard time pulling the blade out. The creature whipped its head back and forth, screaming through the pain. A blow to the side of Azure's skull sent him reeling to the floor again.

*Level 9 **Dawnflayer** delivers 45 damage.*

His sword clattered to the ground, followed by even more of the creature's innards. It stomped its feet, moving way too much, Azure thought, for a monster on death's door.

"Leave it," he heard Uden call to him.

Ignoring his friend, Azure dove for the weapon, narrowly avoiding being hit by the dawnflayer's massive head again. It beat its wings, making it hard for him to keep his balance. Now that he'd retrieved his sword, Azure's only goal was to get away. Leaving the same way he had come from wasn't an option. Dipping beneath the beast's wing exposed him to the possibility of being hit by it, and he was pretty sure it would deliver just as much damage as the side headbutt had. His health was almost seventy-five percent depleted, and the dawnflayer hadn't even managed to get a direct hit on him.

Mustering all of his strength, Azure made a beeline directly in front of the dawnflayer, hoping to avoid the frantic flapping of its wings. He didn't even look back, which he realized had been a big mistake when he felt a hard blow to his back. His body flew forward, his health bar dropping another forty-five points. The next scream he heard wasn't the dawnflayer's, but his own. Pain shot up his legs like nothing he had ever felt before. As he laid on the floor, all Azure could see was red, and that wasn't his health bar blinking rapidly in the corner of his vision as it fell until he only had twenty health points remaining.

While he had plenty of stamina left to move, it was not physically possible. For several moments, Azure just laid there in shock.

"I told you to leave it, you moron," Uden chastised him as he rushed to Azure's side.

The dawnflayer made a pitiful groan behind him, and pain raked through Azure's body again. His vision was fading in and out as was his ability to feel anything. It was a blessing and a curse at the same time. Azure had seen the white lights in his vision before when he had been a preteen in band class and almost passed out from nervousness when he had his first drum solo.

Uden roughly turned Azure's head and emptied a health potion into his mouth. Part of it spilled down the side of his cheek, wasted. “Drink, you stupid son of a bitch, or you're going to die.”

Azure couldn't even concentrate on gulping, but somehow some of the health potion made it in. Enough to raise his health by twenty points and bring the pain back into focus.

Uden looked up and said, “Help me. We've got to get it off of him.”

Azure was so dazed that it took him a moment to realize that the half-imp was talking to his brother. Uden stood and disappeared from his field of vision. There was some barely audible whispering for a few seconds, and then the two men started counting together. Moments later, agony seared through Azure, but also a strange sense of weightlessness.

When Uden returned to attend to him, Lonnell was by his side. The half-imp rolled him over, which made Azure cringe and cry out. Why did everything hurt so much? Glancing down, he had his answer. The dawnflayer had fallen on him as he was running away, crushing his legs until they were nothing but blood and mush. Apparently, the Armor of Light hadn't been enough to protect him from his own stupidity.

"Well, that doesn't look good," he chuckled, trying to make light of a bad situation.

What was worse was that the dawnflayer didn't appear to be dead yet. It stared forward with empty eyes, breathing slowly.

"Just drink." Lonnell uncorked one health potion after another.

As Azure drank them, he felt like an inflatable bed. The healing process was incredibly painful and not without much cursing and wincing, but gradually, his legs began to fill out again, the muscles and tendons and bones repairing themselves with the aid of the magical red liquid. It took five potions to make Azure mostly whole again. As if it had been waiting for him to get well, the dawnflayer finally expired once the last potion was drunk.

*Defeated Level 9* ***Dawnflayer****. 81XP rewarded.*

"That was close," Lonnell said, not sounding happy about it as he helped Azure to his feet and handed him back his bow and quiver of arrows.

"Too close," Uden agreed, walking around the dawnflayer to recover the daggers he had dropped during battle.

"But we got the job done," Azure announced proudly, wondering if there was anything on the dawnflayer that they could loot. "So what are we taking?"

"Well," Uden sighed, staring at the downed creature. "If we could get to its heart, we could take out its monster core. It's a valuable stone used in necromancy to generate a short-lived version of the monster to aid in battle. A dawnflayer's core would fetch quite a sum, but considering that the beast decided to use its last dying moments to try to crush you by landing on its stomach, I don't think we're going to get to it. We would have to turn it over."

"If it's valuable, then we should." He hadn't just gone through all of that pain not to come out at the other end with some sweet loot.

"I'm not sure we could," Lonnell told him. "It weighs at least a ton and is awkward to lift. Attempting it would drain our stamina."

"It will be worth it," Azure assured him. "Don't you think so?" He turned to Uden who shrugged. "Oh, come on. I'm counting on you to take my side on this." Azure's entire body slumped. "We would all split the money, of course."

"I would normally be all for this, but to be honest, I just want to get out of this dungeon. You aren't the only one who almost bit it this time," the half-imp said.

"You didn't even lose any health," Azure argued dryly.

"Because I was lucky. If I hadn't rolled to dodge at the precise moment that I did, I'd be dead right now. Honestly, we were both lucky."

"And we both deserve this." He crossed his arms over his chest stubbornly. "Will the dawnflayer respawn?"

"Not until we leave this area. And it would not respawn for us again. Only if a new group entered its arena."

"Then we have the time to do it," Azure continued to try to convince the brothers that taking the core was a smart idea.

"If we don't take the core, we can keep going and possibly

finish this dungeon today," Lonnell told him, sounding firm. "If we take the core, we're going to have to rest again. There's a chance that Uden and I will go insane. I'm sorry, Azure, but I'm not willing to risk that. If greed is why you are here, then you shouldn't have come."

*Holy shit.* Lonnell had never spoken to him like that before. Did he really think that's why Azure was here with them? Loot had always just been a bonus, but he still hated the idea of not being rewarded for his hard work and almost dying.

"This is bullshit," he grumbled.

"I will do whatever," Uden said, though he wore a tired expression. "I can understand you wanting the monster core, but you must understand that if we take the time to claim it, it could change the outcome of this quest. My brother is right," he glanced over at Lonnell, "staying here for another night puts us at great risk. The monster core is not worth our lives."

"Think about this long-term," Lonnell continued with a much gentler disposition, "you can live today to loot tomorrow, or you could take the monster core, and it could potentially be one of the last things you do."

"Fine," Azure blew out an exasperated breath. He was tired of arguing. This was the dark sprite wings all over again, except on a much grander scale. He was certain that the monster core was worth at least several hundred gold coins. Maybe even enough to buy his Bag of Holding. It pained him to leave it behind, but perhaps there would be greater rewards once they defeated the demon.

"Good. I'm glad you are seeing sense," Lonnell sighed in relief before turning his attention to the back of the room. "Now we must prepare ourselves for what lies on the other side of that door."

"What door?" Azure followed his gaze. To be fair, it had been hard to see anything beyond the dawnflayer, not that he'd been looking. Now that the beast was down, he'd been too focused on its corpse to notice anything else of significance in the room.

"That door." Uden pointed a bony finger at a red door set in the wall. "The dawnflayer was guarding it."

"I'm pretty sure that wasn't there before," Azure insisted.

"It didn't appear until after the dawnflayer died," Lonnell informed him. "There's your loot. The dawnflayer was actually a key."

"That's not the same," Azure mumbled. "So what do you guys think is on the other side of the door?" He secretly hoped it was a treasure room, but that was probably wishful thinking.

"I don't know." Lonnell shook his head.

"Likely a trap," Uden responded behind him.

"It wouldn't be another monster?" Azure asked.

Uden looked at him, seeming nervous. “There's only one way to find out.”

# CHAPTER FOUR

## THE REALM – Day 31

Was this reality? Azure wasn't sure what to believe, but his body had reacted instantly as soon as they opened the door and stepped through.

There was an altar, similar to what Bronna had been placed on when they had first tried to fool the demon into coming out of hiding. Except this time, the demon was already there. The room they had wandered into was ominous and dark. There were no windows and nothing casting light except for the candles placed on the floor around the altar. Instead of inscriptions in the dirt, there were marks made with, what appeared to be, red sand. Azure wasn't really sure what it was. In fact, nothing else in the room existed for him except for the girl on the altar.

Sheila.

How had she gotten here?

She laid on the altar, her eyes closed, her arms crossed over her chest like a vampire in a casket. Azure wasn't sure if she was asleep or not, but when he called her name, she didn't stir. She was wearing a flowy white dress that kissed the tops of her feet. It wasn't like anything he'd ever seen her in before. Not something from her wardrobe. Some type of sacrificial gown, he guessed.

The Dark One stood behind the altar. It didn't even seem to notice the three men entering the room—too focused on the sacrifice it was currently in the middle of performing. A tall, lanky thing made of shadows and darkness, the demon was not as frightful as Azure remembered it being. Its glowing red eyes were trained on the girl before it, and it held a long, curved silver blade in its hand. The dagger was raised, centered above Sheila's chest. Words whispered all around them in some ancient, evil language. It sounded like Latin, but Azure knew it wasn't. The spell had begun. Sheila's body floated up from the table to meet the blade, and the dagger came down at the same time.

Desperation coursed through Azure as he lunged forward. He was screaming the word no, but he couldn't even hear his own voice above the whispers. He ran towards the altar, his legs pumping as quickly as they were physically capable of. He would sacrifice himself to save her. Throw his body on top of hers and feel the blade pierce through him. Do this one last selfless act. It didn't matter that she had dumped him for someone else. He still loved her. It was a strange and melancholy realization—that he was about to die for a woman who had betrayed him.

There was an intense flash of light. So intense that it drowned out everything in the room. It softened and lingered. Everything that had been in front of Azure was gone. He felt a strange sense of calm, like he was floating somewhere in between space and time. Floating without a care in the world. Hadn't he just been panicking? Hadn't he just been trying to stop something horrible from happening? He couldn't remember what. Now he was just floating. Floating, floating, floating in this warm white, airy liquid.

Things began to change again. It was subtle this time. The soft light turned to milk, and the milk started to slowly gray. At first, the difference was imperceivable. But then he noticed it more. The liquid got thicker. It transformed from translucent to opaque and began to cloud. Like a storm lazily blowing in, the gray darkened and darkened. There was a sudden feeling of desperation—like being swallowed up by something—like drowning. Briefly, Azure remembered being dunked beneath the ripples of the raging river when he had tried to escape from The Dark One. He remembered sucking in a lungful of water. This was much the same. He was now drowning in this darkness overtaking everything around him. It closed in on him, invading his open mouth and his nostrils. It consumed him like a giant beast until it was everywhere and he was oh so small.

And then all was black. All was black, and Azure suddenly wasn't afraid anymore.

*Is this death? Is this what death feels like? I don't remember how it happened, but did I die?*

Azure searched his memory and came up empty-handed. All he knew was that he wasn't afraid. Not at peace, but not afraid.

Then, as if vomited out of a dreamless sleep, he was thrust back into reality—a reality that he didn't remember but made sense to him nonetheless. He looked down at Sheila's body as she lay in a casket. Her eyes were closed, her straight dark brown hair resting beneath her head. They had not done her makeup in the right shade. There was no illusion of a sleeping woman. She simply looked dead. The dress they had put her in, a red number with puffed white sleeves, wasn't doing her any favors. Will had only seen her wear it once when she had convinced him to go to church with her family for Christmas Eve Mass. Neither of them had wanted to go. She was only doing it because her grandmother had come down to visit from Florida and Sheila had wanted to make her happy by appearing as much like a family as possible. Will had gotten roped in because he was the new boyfriend and wanted to spend as much time with her as possible. It was not a modern dress. Something that looked like it had come from generations ago. Modest and out-dated. She certainly wouldn't have wanted to be buried in it.

Will looked down at the black suit jacket he was wearing with matching slacks and a white button-down shirt. He didn't remember putting it on this morning. Come to think of it, he didn't remember Sheila dying either, he just knew that she had. Pain coursed through his head, and he reached up to massage his temples. Something was off. Something was wrong he realized, and he began to look around.

The faces of Sheila's family and their college friends stared back at him from the pews. Not so much stared, but glared and leered. Whispers filled the air. Dozens of voices. Somehow, he could decipher and sort them all out. They blamed him for Sheila's death.

"He's such a loser. If he weren't such a loser, this never would have happened," Sheila's mom said.

"Leaving her all alone like that. Of course, the girl would get depressed," one of their friends whispered to another.

"He never cared about her. She saw that," the other replied behind a cupped hand.

"It was his job to protect her. He couldn't even do that much." Her father glowered at him.

"It should have been him. She had a promising future ahead of her. He had nothing," her big brother added.

What was going on? He didn't understand, but the whispers continued. This time, right behind him.

Cold hands touched his shoulders. He felt breath on his cheek and a grumbling masculine voice followed. “You are stupid and lazy and worthless. You went off to pursue a career that everyone warned you against. You thought you were special, above all the rest. But you were always less than average in everything that mattered.

"Sheila was out of your league. But you thought yourself better than you were. You thought yourself worth waiting for. You only cared about yourself. You didn't stop to think about her career, that her life was already starting...without you.

"You were not worth waiting for, but she still cared. So when I showed her that you were in trouble, she came. And now she's dead. All of her dreams, gone. Because you were selfish. Because you couldn't let her go when you should have. You made her suffer because you were selfish. And now she's dead because you couldn't leave well enough alone.

"You are a horrible human being and an even worse boyfriend. There's only one way to atone for this sin"to make up for all of the misery that you caused." The voice switched to his other ear. "You must die."

The words tried to sink in, but they still didn't make sense. Yes, Sheila was lying before Will in a casket, and the voice was implying that he was the cause, but he still had no idea what had happened. Had she killed herself? Had she pushed him out of the way of a moving vehicle when they were walking somewhere? He didn't remember. Pain stabbed at Will's brain again. He winced and grabbed his head.

"Regret," the word boomed in time with his headache. "Repent. Die." A repetition began, growing louder and louder until it felt almost like a physical attack.

Will forced his eyes open, taking in his surroundings. Something was strange. A feeling of deja vu—that he'd been here before. Pews were lined in rows to the back of the funeral home. It could have been any funeral home in the world, but the flowers were familiar. Large bouquets of lilies and roses on metal easels. They were probably the same ones that had adorned hundreds or even thousands of funerals before. Something picked off of a website online. But Will was almost certain he'd seen the exact same ones somewhere before. Maybe in a movie or at a relative's funeral.

"This isn't right. I didn't do this." Will stared down at Sheila's cold, dead body. He should have felt regret but didn't, because somewhere deep down inside, he knew that he was blameless.

The voice had said a lot of truths. He had been stupid in assuming that his relationship would hold together if he moved. Few long-distance relationships ever stood the test of time. But they had both known that before Will had left, and while they were sad to be apart, he doubted that Sheila had ever gotten suicidal over it. She had her family and all of their friends to support her—far more than Will had. Besides, Sheila wasn't the type of woman to kill herself. Two of her best qualities were that she was smart and stable. Unlike most of the girls that Will had dated in the past, she hadn't been prone to mood swings or hormonal outbursts. Sheila approached every problem with logic.

"Failure," the word repeated in his head.

But he hadn't failed. He had simply lagged. Sure, life wasn't perfect. Will wasn't as far along in his career path as he had hoped, but he was still on the right trajectory. Working for Radical Interactive was amazing, even if it was boring most of the time. Someday, they'd see his value, and he'd ascend to a better position. Radical Interactive was good about promoting from within. He had faith that all of his years of schooling would not go to waste. There was no real reason for him to be disappointed in himself.

And then he realized that this was all wrong. He didn't know who was whispering these foul words, but at the same time...he did. There was no fear within him. He was ready to face the monster head-on.

Turning around, a frightfully wicked beast stood before him. Familiar. Like something out of his nightmares. The horns atop its head had a red tint to them. Its jaw had no lips, just two rows of overly long pointed teeth. It stood a few feet away, just staring at him. Challenging him.

"You are a failure," it managed to hiss without even opening its mouth. "Despair and meet your rightful demise."

Will shook his head. Even his name was wrong, he

remembered as he opened his mouth to speak. "No. It is you who is the failure. Your parlor tricks will not work on me."

The scene around them faded away until it was just the two of them standing in the middle of a dark room. Clarity slowly began to return to Will. What he had just seen was not real. And in this world, he was not William Galvan. He was Azure, and he had a job to finish.

# CHAPTER FIVE
## THE REALM – Day 31

"Do not look it in the eyes." It had been a warning that Azure had heard time and time again. The demon's eyes could inflict fear. But for some reason, he wasn't even afraid of that. The Dark One did not have lips to speak. There had been countless times when it could have talked to him, but it never did. That meant this was still just an illusion.

A quick glance back showed Azure that he had been stripped of his weapons. His armor was still intact, though. The Armor of Light was likely what was currently keeping him from being scared out of his wits.

He took a few steps up to the demon, facing it head-on yet staying out of arm's reach, just in case. "Despair," he told it. "For I am coming to kill you."

Just like that, the darkness that was the demon's body began to spread. As if turning into a massive shadow, it swelled, filling the room until it swallowed Azure whole. This was no death. It wasn't even an attack, but something else entirely. He was filled with a sense of calm and resolve, allowing himself to go through the cycle that he had experienced once before; darkness, gray, cloudy liquid, and then clarity.

His eyes flew open, and he realized that he was encased in something. Now there was panic because this was no longer a dream. This was not some illusion that the demon had cast. What he was experiencing was completely real. Drowning in some strange gel.

Azure's eyes widened in distress, and he reached his hand out, his nails raking the surface of a thin membrane and breaking through. As soon as he did, the egg-like sac he was suspended in deflated and birth him out in a wet pile of mucus. Sucking in a lungful of air, Azure coughed and clawed at his chest, desperate for oxygen. Globs of gel fell from his open mouth. It both tasted and smelled of plastic—manufactured—like something out of a science fiction movie.

Once he realized that the threat of drowning was over, he looked around and noticed that he was in a small room. There was another pod beside his. Lonnell floated in the middle of it, suspended within the same liquid that had held Azure captive. His eyes danced behind his lids in a fitful sleep—in a world of nightmares designed to tap into his deepest fears and regrets.

Azure wasn't sure if it was safe to rescue his friend, but that only made him hesitate for half a second. He could not fight The Dark One alone, and Uden was nowhere to be seen. Perhaps he was being held in another room. That didn't matter right now. All that mattered was freeing Lonnell.

Azure dug his nails into the shell of the pod. A wave of gel came spilling out, and he was barely able to catch his friend before they both fell to the floor.

"Wake up," he said, giving Lonnell a gentle shake.

Lonnell opened his eyes, his pupils dilated as if he were on some type of a hallucinogen. He kicked his feet, fighting against Azure for a moment before recognition hit him and he began to settle.

"Calm down. It was only a dream. A trap set by the

demon," he explained.

Lonnell gasped for air again, then turned and vomited on the floor beside them. Clear liquid spilled from his mouth until there was nothing left.

"You're going to be okay." Azure patted him on the back.

"What happened?" Lonnell choked out.

"I don't know." Azure shook his head. "One minute we were in that room with the demon, and the next I was having a nightmare and woke up in that bubble...pod...thing." He didn't know what to call it.

"Where's Uden?" Lonnell's eyes danced around, frantically searching for his brother.

Their party had been disbanded, which was the only good sign that the half-imp might still be alive somewhere else in the dungeon.

"I don't know."

"We have to find him." Lonnell pulled himself to his feet, reaching back to make sure his staff was still affixed to his back. It was. Apparently, the demon had been so confident in its spell that it hadn't bothered to take their weapons.

"What is this place?" Azure asked. It looked like a small storeroom, though there was nothing inside but them. The only light came from the gel that they had been suspended in, which glowed rather brightly. He remembered that same light from the beginning of his dream. It must have started when The Dark One put him inside of the bubble, but everything had happened so quickly that he couldn't be sure.

"I don't know. I've never seen anything like it before," Lonnell confessed, still looking around as if he expected to find Uden tucked in a corner of the room.

"Well, it's a good thing we got out." Azure couldn't help but wonder if this was all part of the demon's plan. They were both confused and disoriented"getting their bearings about them. The conversation he'd held with it in his dream made him think otherwise, though"that the cells were meant to be some kind of prison or sacrificial chamber. Whatever the case, he was thankful he had been able to break free. "Are you all right?" He stood and placed a hand on Lonnell's shoulder.

"I have a headache and a horrible feeling." Lonnell massaged his temples.

Azure could sympathize. Though his health and stamina didn't seem to be affected by what he had just experienced, his brain felt hazy. There was the tiniest throb of a headache in the back of his skull, like a slight hangover. He hoped the feeling would go away soon.

The one door that was in the room didn't give them a lot of options for where to go next. They stood before it, both wondering what they'd find on the other side.

"We need to proceed with caution," Lonnell needlessly told him. "Uden was right. What we encountered before was a trap. What did you see when we opened the red door that made you react so quickly?"

"My ex-girlfriend on an altar about to be sacrificed," Azure responded before glancing over at his companion. "What did you see?"

"Bronna. Same thing," he hesitated for a moment. "I didn't have time to react, though. You were already rushing forward. I glanced over at Uden. He looked panicked, calling out to you. But it was too late. I think you stepped on a rune. That's when everything went white, then black."

"And you dreamed about all of your failures in life. All of your regrets."

Lonnell wrapped an arm around himself as if talking about it made him uncomfortable. "It was horrible. Thank you for rescuing me. I was..."

"Don't worry about it." Azure stopped him from saying anything more. Whilst he was curious as to what exactly Lonnell had seen once in his dreamlike state, this wasn't the time to pry.

A notification popped up.

***Lonnell Namud*** *is requesting to join your party. Will you accept?*

Of course.

***Lonnell Namud*** *has joined your party.*

"Whatever is on the other side of that door, do not rush out," Lonnell warned him. As if Azure would make the same mistake twice. "As we discovered earlier, the demon can cast powerful illusion magic within its dungeon. There may be more traps before we get to it."

Azure grunted and nodded in agreement. Somehow, his last mistake hadn't been fatal, but they may not be so lucky next time.

"Are you ready to proceed?" Lonnell asked him, sounding apprehensive. "We should first focus on finding my brother."

"Yeah. If there's one thing I've learned, we can't accomplish much without Uden," he sighed in resignation to that fact. "He's more perceptive than both of us and much more fearless."

A soft smile crossed Lonnell's lips. "My brother does have

his good qualities."

"They are necessary to our party's success." Azure refused to give the half-imp too much credit. "He's rescued me more times than I can count. Now it's time to return the favor."

# CHAPTER SIX
## THE REALM – Day 31

Blessedly, there was nothing on the other side of the door but a long corridor. It seemed a bit pointless to have only one room at the end of a hall, but what did Azure really know about the construction of dungeons.

The sight that greeted them when they reached the other room was entirely unexpected, and it made them both stop dead in their tracks. Much like it had been in Azure's vision, there was a stone altar at the back of the room. Instead of candles on the floor helping to form the circle for whatever sacrificial spell the demon had cast in his illusion, they lined the walls in plain silver sconces. The room was dark, yet the candles did their job to illuminate what was necessary. Behind the altar stood the demon. At its side was Uden. The half-imp's face was marred with sorrow and distress. The pendant that Azure had glimpsed back at the goblin encampment had tightened like a noose around his neck. Its black stone shard glowed softly.

"I see you broke the enchantment," he said in a voice filled with regret. His emerald eyes glistened in the candlelight. "Of course, you would." A nervous laugh spilled from his lips, and his gaze fell to the floor.

"Uden, what's going on?" Lonnell took a step forward, but the half-imp quickly threw his hand out.

"Stay back!"

"Uden..." Lonnell's voice trailed off.

Azure was speechless. After all they'd been through, he honestly hadn't expected to be double-crossed. Sure, the feeling had been there. The half-imp had been acting suspicious for a while, but Azure had desperately hoped that his hunch wouldn't turn out to be true.

Uden turned his attention to the demon. "We could let them leave. They could leave Crescent Island and never return. And I would stay." Desperation was threaded in his tone.

It was then Azure realized that this wasn't what it seemed. Clearly, Uden didn't want any harm to come to them. Confusion clouded Azure's mind. What in the hell was going on?

The Dark One said nothing. It simply reached for the half-imp with a clawed hand. With discomfort etched in his expression, Uden's gaze followed the hand as it approached him, but he didn't resist as the demon gripped the back of his neck and thrust him towards the altar. His palms molded around the side of the altar, but it did little to keep his body from colliding against it.

"No," the half-imp whispered, his eyes closed as if he couldn't bear to look at his companions. The stone shard at his throat pulsed, slowly changing colors from black to green in a rhythm like the beat of a heart. Then it flashed, and everything changed.

Azure was walking through a forest, his body involuntarily moving forward. There was urgency in his step, but he had no idea where he was headed or why. The forest was like none he had ever seen back on Earth. He must still be in The Realm.

His eyes dashed between the forest floor and his

surroundings as he walked. Was he...tracking something? Azure couldn't figure it out. He had no control over his limbs or anything else.

A glint of green buried beneath a few fallen leaves caught his eye. Normally, it would have made Azure pause, but instead, he continued towards it. Excitement rolled through him as he thought that he had found some type of treasure"maybe a precious stone that someone had dropped while they were wandering through the forest. *Finders, keepers*, he thought avariciously as he brushed the leaves aside to reveal the pendant that Uden had been wearing.

There was a tightness in his chest—an unfamiliar throbbing. Not painful, but filled with foreboding. He immediately recognized the item as something evil, but also something that held great power.

*Should not touch it,* he thought, though he also knew that leaving it was not an option. This was an incredibly valuable item. It would fetch several gold pieces when he sold it to Ruthren. Hopefully, the merchant would be brave enough to take it. He would count on Ruthren's greed to seal the deal. Of course, he would undercut his offer, but what did it really matter. The amount would still likely be enough to buy him passage off of this wretched island. Once he helped his brother and friend get rid of whatever was causing the curse on the island, he was gone. He no longer cared what his father said. The things he had suffered these past few months because Bronna had opened her big, fat mouth...

Azure furrowed his brow. At least, he thought he had. Then he realized that he actually hadn't.

This was not his story. These were not his feelings. And it took him only a second longer before he understood that he was seeing through Uden's eyes, thinking his thoughts, and feeling what he felt. There was a momentary sense of panic, but despite that, the scene continued, and Azure realized that he had no control. All that he could do was watch.

Uden scooped the pendant up with a large leaf lying nearby. He knew that if he touched it, there would be a price to pay. The pendant would connect him with great evil, amplifying his imp DNA. Despite how harshly the people of Cragbell judged him, he had no desire to become the monster they feared.

Uden was just about to place the pendant in his bag when he saw something move in his peripheral vision up ahead. Again, he felt unease stir within him—an innate ability to sense other dark creatures. But this was unlike anything he had felt before. The presence was strong, usurping the evil within him, causing him to reach for the dagger at his hip.

"Come out. I know you're here. If it's a fight you want..." It bothered him that he didn't have the element of surprise. On the contrary, the thing that had obviously been stalking him probably could have attacked him unaware when he was busy examining the pendant. Whatever it was, it had no plans to outright attack him.

The creature stepped from behind a tree, and Uden recognized its countenance instantly. A lesser demon. It Analyzed as challenging to him. Even with his boosted agility, their speed was likely evenly matched. Demons could move with the speed of shadows. It was one of their more impressive abilities. If it decided to attack, Uden wasn't sure what the outcome would be, but the prognosis for him wasn't good.

"Well, I guess I discovered the cause of the curse," he said smugly. Maybe if he faked confidence, the demon would think he had some trick up his sleeve and leave him alone. That was a tough bet though since he knew he Analyzed as an easy target. This was one of those times when he needed his souped-up Luck to do its job. Maybe it already had by keeping the demon from coming in from behind and quickly ending his life.

The demon continued to approach, stopping a few feet short of Uden. The half-imp held his ground, having balls of steel. If he was about to die, then it wouldn't be running. He would fight to preserve himself, even if the effort was fruitless.

"What do you want, ugly?" More bravado. Taunting the beast probably wasn't the best idea, but fuck it.

"Gift," it said through thought transference in a deep gravely voice.

It was odd to hear the word inside his head, but he knew that he shared a telepathic connection with this horrible creature through their blood bond. It was the only way that demons were able to speak; in dreams and through blood.

"Gift?" Uden repeated the word.

The demon turned its fiery red eyes to the item in Uden's hand. “Use gift.”

Hot air blew through Uden's nostrils followed by a haughty guffaw. “You must think me truly stupid if you believe I would fall for this trick. I'm not so uneducated that I don't know what this is.” He gestured to the demon with the pendant.

"Use to save friends. Use to leave. Make deal," the voice said. There was a firmness to it. A hint of a threat.

"Any deal you'd make would be tainted with blood." The half-imp rolled his eyes.

"Much blood. Much death. Offering your freedom in exchange. The lives of your family. A new life."

Uden slipped his dagger out of its sheath. “I'll have my freedom once I vanquish you. It seems easy enough.”

With a flash of movement so quick that it was almost imperceptible to Uden, the demon was behind him. Its hand was on his throat, pulling him back against it. Fear rolled through his body from the creature's touch. He was about to die. He'd never see the mainland—never live his dream of learning magic. Real magic. Not the few menial spells that he had managed to buy from Ruthren. Desperation and sorrow filled him, and the selfish thought rolled through his mind that whatever the deal was, he should have taken it. At the end of the day, did anything else really matter besides saving his family. This island and everyone else on it could burn for all he cared. They had never thought of him as anything but a nuisance anyway.

"Take the gift," the demon's voice was now clearer. More articulate. Perhaps it was the closed distance that caused more clarity. "Use it to protect your family. In return, you will turn your comrades off of my path. No one will know that a demon has come until it is too late. The island will fall under my rule. Everyone who ridiculed you will pay. You will get vengeance without even having to lift a finger. And then you will get to leave this place and live your life on the mainland. It is everything you have ever dreamed of. All you have to do is wear the pendant."

*Well, killing him is obviously no longer an option. If I don't put the pendant on, I'll die. What other choice to do I have?*

"The pendant will bond us and awaken the evil within me." Uden weighed his own words. It was a dangerous thing. There was no telling what would happen to him once he put it on.

"We will be bonded, yes," the demon agreed. "But it will not change you unless you let it."

The demon let his hand slip from Uden's throat, leaving a burning sensation behind. It felt like he was being lightly choked, yet he could still swallow. Perhaps it was the darkness now surrounding him that was causing the constricting feeling. Partly, it felt horrible, but another strange part of it felt like home. Freedom. The ability to be who he wanted to be without fear of what others thought. To be that which was true nature.

The demon reached into Uden's hand and took the pendant, the leaves protecting it from touching his skin falling away. He lifted it to the half-imp's neck.

*I guess this is happening,* Uden thought, feeling a strong desire to run. It was obviously a trap, but at least it meant he would live another day. The only question was, at what cost?

As soon as the smooth black stone touched Uden's throat, there was a flash of green light. Something swirled within him, deep and dark. Horrible urges rushed to the surface—the need to kill and ruin. Uden sucked in a breath between clenched teeth and tried to bite back what he was feeling. This wasn't him. Well, part of it was. But most of it was the trickster blood within him—the malicious part of being an imp. What was worse was that the demon had added a dash of his own evil to the mix. The two of them were now bonded, and Uden knew that this feeling wouldn't go away. It was like everything bad within him had been amplified several times. The wickedness that he normally enjoyed indulging in for funsies—the kind that left farmers wondering where their livestock had gone and women bathing in the river searching for their clothes—turned into pure baleful intent.

*You have received the following item:*

| **Cursed Pendant of Transformation** | **Defense:** +1<br>**Type:** Jewelry<br>**Durability:** 10/10<br>**Item Class:** Extremely Rare<br>**Quality:** Epic<br>**Weight:** 0 kg<br>**Traits:** Can cast **Transform**, allowing the wearer to transform into any creature of equal or lesser level. ***This item is soulbound and cannot be traded or discarded once equipped.*** |
|---|---|

"Enjoy the gift," the demon hissed into his ear. "And remember our deal."

And like that, Uden was left standing in the forest completely alone. It was as if the demon had vanished into thin air. The half-imp no longer sensed his presence, though the evil within him lingered. Feeling a bit foolish for doing so, Uden scanned the trees around him, but the demon was nowhere to be seen.

*A teleportation spell?* He wondered. Or perhaps an illusion had activated the second he had picked up the pendant. Demons were known for having strong illusion magic.

The half-imp reached for his throat to see if what he had just experienced was even real. The pendant hung there, the stone cold against his skin. In vain, he tried to take it off. Soulbound items stayed with the wearer for life or until the item's durability expired. There was no getting rid of them otherwise. He could only hope that once the durability of the item had worn out, it would disappear and he'd be free from the demon's clutches, but that would require using it, and Uden knew that each use would connect him more and more to the demon. Each use would enhance the evil already within him.

"Well fuck," he drawled, tucking the pendant into the front of his tunic.

The vision flashed forward. Azure somehow knew it hadn't gone very far. Maybe a day, at most.

Uden was watching a small group of goblins sitting around a campfire. He stayed close to the camp, listening in on their conversation. When the scout that was supposed to survey the land around his parents' farm left, he followed behind, disposing of the goblin once it was out of earshot of the camp like a silent ninja.

*Defeated Level 5* ***Goblin Scout****. 30XP rewarded.*

*I can use the pendant to transform into this goblin and keep the others away from the farm. That would be the easiest course of action to take. I need to use the pendant to get rid of it anyway.*

And that was exactly what he did. Transforming into the goblin scout, Uden waited for several hours and then returned to the camp to tell the other goblins that the farmers in the area were too poor to be worth raiding. For the next few days, he traveled with the goblins, enjoying their debauchery but keeping to himself otherwise so as not to come off as too suspicious. Not that any of them were smart enough to figure out the ruse.

A larger band of goblins joined up with them to perform the main raid. When they all headed to Cragbell together, Uden made sure to point them in Bronna's direction to be used as a sacrifice to the demon. He hated the bitch, and what better way to get rid of her than when he was unabashedly embracing his evil side. As long as he wasn't the one to slit her throat, he didn't need to feel much guilt over her death. After all, if it weren't for her, none of this would have happened in the first place. She deserved what was coming to her.

Knowing that he had to return to his own life soon and come up with a convenient lie as to his latency in getting back, Uden allowed himself to get injured during his melee with the people of Cragbell, making sure to take on foes that were a much lower level so that he was in no real danger. And also making sure not to kill anyone. Once he'd accomplished his goal of getting believably injured, Uden sneaked off from the fight and headed home, finally transforming back into himself when he was but a quarter mile away.

*Being a goblin wasn't so bad,* he thought, feeling only slightly ashamed for some of the more unsettling things that he had taken part in. If they weren't such a stupid species, he might have been inclined to join them forever.

The scene changed again. This time, Uden was with Azure after their argument about walking in circles. It was strange for

Azure to see himself through someone else's eyes, especially since it was his avatar and not what he looked like in real life. It almost didn't seem like him at all.

The half-imp was panicking internally. The plan had been to procrastinate for as long as possible, then spend a bit of time meandering around before deciding that The Dark One couldn't be found. This was the point where he was supposed to live up to his part of the deal—to make sure that the demon's location wasn't discovered by his companions. It might have worked if Azure hadn't been so damned adamant that they continue searching. Even worse, he had underestimated the human's powers of observation. Once Azure had found the footprints, it was hard to argue.

There had never been any runes or an enchantment, just Uden leading them both on a winding circular path that ended up nowhere. With that plan ruined, the half-imp had to come up with something else to ensure that they'd never reach the demon's lair. The darkness within him had grown since using the pendant for the first time. He had fought many moral battles, and sheer desperation was beginning to make it easier for him to land on the bad side of the coin. They were too close to finding the demon for comfort. Something drastic needed to be done.

If Uden returned without Azure and told Lonnell that he had been slain by goblins, then that would put an end to their quest. There was no way that Lonnell would risk continuing the search for The Dark One if it were just the two of them. As life on the island became progressively worse, they'd have no choice but to leave. Everything would be as the demon had promised.

Guilt filled Uden as he split off from Azure and used the pendant once more to transform into a goblin and alert the others of Azure's presence. The human was alone and vulnerable and would be no match against the higher level goblins.

With that done, he returned home to protect his family. Azure would undoubtedly be used as a sacrifice to bolster the demon's strength. Soon, it would have the power to take over the entire island. Hopefully, Uden would be able to convince his family to leave before then.

# CHAPTER SEVEN
## THE REALM – Day 31

The vision faded away. It was like staring at the sun for too long. There was a brightness, though the light was more green than white, and as Azure's eyes began to adjust, he was back in the room with Lonnell at his side. Uden was still pressed against the altar, his head hung low in shame, his hair obscuring his face.

"Oh Uden," Lonnell said in disappointment. "You should have told us."

"I'm guessing the cook from the camp was the same one at the settlement then. You neglected to show that tidbit." Azure sneered at the demon. There had been a lot left out about the half-imp's betrayals, he thought. He would have liked to have seen it all so that his anger could be fully fueled. At this point, he wasn't sure who he wanted to kill more, the demon or Uden.

"None of that matters now," the half-imp said softly. "This is the end."

The Dark One removed his hand from the back of Uden's neck. When he looked up, the green of his irises had bled into his scleras. Now a solid color, his eyes glowed the same bright shade of green as the pendant around his neck.

"Oh shit, he's going to attack," Azure warned as he watched Uden reach for his daggers.

Both Azure and Lonnell had their weapons drawn before the half-imp was able to make it to them, despite him leaping over the altar to get to them faster.

"I've got this. You take care of the demon," Lonnell told Azure as he blocked the first incoming attack with his staff.

Azure wasn't convinced. He knew that the half-imp was prone to using backhanded battle tactics—tactics that Lonnell wouldn't even think of resorting to. They were all now the same level. Maybe together, he and Lonnell would have a chance.

"You can't fight him alone," Azure insisted, turning to engage Uden as well.

"He's my brother. I'll handle this," Lonnell growled irritably as he pushed Uden back.

*Lonnell probably thinks I would kill Uden, Azure thought. He might be right. More than likely, he's going to try to knock Uden unconscious. Is he even salvageable?*

Azure remembered his battle with the dark sprites. This was another moral dilemma. Killing Uden was obviously the easier path to take but was it the right one.

Deciding to trust Lonnell, Azure turned his attention to the demon. Now at a distance, it was the perfect opportunity to use the imbued arrows that the Tree Queen had given him. Azure drew his bow and nocked. The arrow sailed straight and true, landing in the dead center of the demon's chest. A white burst of light was accompanied by a hellish roar, and when the light faded away, there was a small crater of flesh missing. Dark matter wove together to repair the wound, reminding Azure that he should have gone for a headshot instead.

"Fuck my memory," he seethed under his breath, knowing

that he'd have to get in close to finish The Dark One off. Unless the light magic within the arrows could explode the demon's head, he would have to switch to his sword to cut off its horns. It couldn't hurt to try with the bow first, though.

By the time he nocked another arrow, the demon was already moving around the altar. It sunk down to take cover behind it, though it wasn't long before it came into his view again, proceeding against the wall to where Uden and Lonnell were engaged in melee.

Azure followed it with his bow, loosing another arrow. A quick burst of speed made the demon flash a foot forward, causing the shot to miss. Light filled the room as the arrow exploded and splintered into nothing.

*Do I have enough time for one more shot*, Azure wondered as he drew another arrow from his quiver. The Dark One was quickly approaching his destination, but Azure wasn't sure if it was to join Uden in his fight against Lonnell or to take cover behind them. More than likely, it was the first of the two. The demon Analyzed as orange, so one good swipe should be enough to do the older brother in. Azure needed to act fast.

Desperately, he loosed one more arrow, but his aim was unsteady, and he missed again, though he nearly hit Uden instead when he stepped back to gain momentum for his next attack. Cursing himself for wasting so many of his imbued arrows, Azure quickly put away his bow and unsheathed his sword, rushing in to join the battle.

The Dark One had slipped behind Uden and Lonnell. As Azure circled around the other side of them, he was caught off-guard by a spin attack. Uden made like he was going to charge forward at Lonnell, gripping his dagger for a backhanded strike, then he rotated around, driving the point into the demon's throat, pulling out, and dashing away just as quickly.

Startled by the momentary loss of its grip over the half-imp, the demon clutched at its throat. Azure took advantage, charging in and swiping down with his blade. The blow cleaved through the creature's shoulder, the tip of the sword carving down the side of its cheek. Oddly, there was no blood, just dried up muscle and sinew that magically began to fuse together the very second that Azure drew back his blade.

He almost made a triumphant comment that the demon's spell on Uden had been broken, but then he saw the two brother's fighting again. What had gotten into the half-imp? His eyes were still glowing green with his possession. Was he trying to kill them all?

"I guess it's back to just you and me," he told The Dark One as he swung his blade at an arch, angling it straight for the demon's horns.

It easily dodged, ducking under Azure's sword, and then using another quick burst of speed to move to the side. Azure didn't realize that it was going for an attack until it was too late. With claws outstretched, The Dark One lunged towards Lonnell's blind side. He was so preoccupied with keeping his brother at bay that he never even saw it coming. But Uden did.

Lonnell went tumbling to the ground from the shove. And for a moment after, everything was quiet and still. Azure froze, watching the scene play out in front of him, wondering if he had imagined what he had just seen—if this was all just another illusion. It was hard to make sense of anything after what they'd all been through.

Uden's cough sounded deafening in the silence of the room, the only other noises that of Azure's and Lonnell's heavy breathing. A wet squelching sound followed. The green light faded from the half-imp's eyes, his scleras sucking back in until everything left was just him. Blood dripped onto the dirt, the droplets big and heavy.

Sickeningly, Azure thought of the prompt *Critical hit* and the voice from an archaic fighting video game saying "Fatality."

Lonnell was trembling on the floor, his eyes wide and glistening, his mouth agape.

Weakly, Uden clutched onto the demon's arm, an arm that had gone straight through him like a knife slicing through butter. He looked over at Azure and choked out the words, “Kill him.”

There was no hesitation. Azure raised his sword high above his head. The demon saw their move, but despite all his pain, Uden wasn't letting go. The blade went down, hitting the thick, dark keratin that was infused with the blood of The Dark One's victims. There was a spark and a feeling of resistance, as if the demon was trying to will the horns to stay attached. But Azure's resolve was stronger. So many emotions were going through him that he probably wouldn't have noticed if he drained all of his stamina to get the job done. He yelled at the top of his lungs as he used every fiber of muscle in his body to cleave the horns. Despite their resistance, they parted from the demon with a sickening crack, blowing him back against the dungeon wall, a string of blood following his clawed hand.

Lonnell got to Uden just before he hit the floor, cradling him in his arms. Azure stood there stunned, barely even noticing the prompt that flashed before his eyes.

***Critical hit!*** *Defeated Level 10* ***Lesser Demon****. 100XP rewarded.*

All of the joy was taken out of the defeat by his sense of loss. He knelt by his comrade's side, looking desperately at Lonnell. “We need to give him as many healing potions as we can.”

"It's too late," Uden coughed. "My health is at zero. I am done."

"Then how are you still able to speak?" Azure's thoughts bounced from one thing to another. "There has to be a Resurrection potion or some powerful witch that can make you better."

The half-imp chuckled weakly. “I thought you would have figured it out by now. This isn't a game. People don't,” he winced through the pain, “come back when they die.”

"Hush now, brother. Everything will be all right. You'll be all right," Lonnell told him, though it was apparent by the tears flowing freely down his face that things would not, in fact, be all right for Uden.

"Ah, they were right about me. I'm evil to the core," he ignored his brother's words. "I deserved this for everything I've done."

"That's not true." Lonnell shook his head.

"Just so you're not forever wondering, you were right, Azure. I spared the cook because it wasn't a fighter, and it had a son." The half-imp turned his attention back to his brother. His breathing was labored, and his eyes were beginning to unfocus. "Tell father that I'm sorry I wasn't a better..." his voice trailed off as his last breath left him and his eyes stilled.

"No," Lonnell sobbed, repeating the word over and over again as he clutched his brother's body to his chest. A desperate wail left him in his grief, and all Azure could do was stand there and watch, not knowing what to do, processing everything that had just happened.

This was the first time he'd ever seen a monster one hit kill...one of his friends. He naively hadn't even thought it possible. Everything had gone so smoothly for them up until this point. There was no way this was real?

"It's an illusion," he mumbled. "Another vision. The demon is trying to throw us off." But even as he said it, he knew it wasn't true. There was a palpable clarity to everything around them. No loss of function or confusion. The smell of blood was thick in the air.

Azure's jaw clenched. He could feel his eyes welling up, but he refused to cry. A torrent of thoughts flowed through his mind, memories of the ribbing that he and the half-imp had shared...and then the betrayal. Admittedly, Azure was conflicted over whether or not he should actually be mourning Uden's death, but he couldn't fight that he was sad about it. The fact that the half-imp had allowed the cook to escape because he knew the goblin had a child was proof that he wasn't all bad. Most of his ill deeds these past few weeks had been all due to circumstance. Uden had been trying to fulfill his obligation to the demon, something that had been forced onto him, while keeping them safe at the same time. It was only because Azure and Lonnell had insisted on pressing onward with their pursuit that it had come to this. If they had just left The Dark One alone...

Azure's focus was redirected as he noticed the demon's body starting to quickly deteriorate. Almost immediately, Lonnell took up the chanting of the word no again. A quick glance in his direction showed that the same thing was happening to Uden. Watching the decay before him and being unable to stop it made Azure's heart wrench in his chest. He couldn't imagine the pain of witnessing something so horrific happening to a loved one. Flesh fell away from the half-imp's bones, turning to dust in Lonnell's hands until all that remained was his skeleton. Even his clothing and weapons had decomposed into nothing. Azure didn't understand what was going on. Nothing they had ever killed before had perished like this afterward.

He glanced over at the demon. Not even bones remained of it.

"What just happened?" he asked, wondering if this was like one of those movies where the whole dungeon was about to cave in on them. Instantly, he was on guard, his eyes dancing around.

Lonnell didn't answer. He simply sat there unmoving, staring down at the remnants of his dead brother. The sobbing had stopped. Azure didn't know what to do, but he had a feeling that they should probably leave soon.

"We need to go," he said with a gentle sternness as he bent to collect the demon's horns, the only thing that had been left behind by it.

*You have received the following items:*

| **Lesser Demon's Horn** | **Quantity:** 2/2<br>**Item Class:** Rare<br>**Quality:** Average<br>**Weight:** 0.4 kg<br>**Uses:** Loot. Sell for coin. |
|---|---|

Briefly, he wondered if the horns were as valuable as the monster core would have been. He certainly hoped so. Guilt swept over him as he noticed Lonnell still sitting there. This was not the time to think greedily. His friend needed comfort.

*Congratulations! Quest:* ***Defeat The Dark One*** *has been completed.*

*It took everything you had and came at a great cost, but the demon has been vanquished. All the strife that the inhabitants of Crescent Island have had to endure because of it should now subside. You have lost a dear friend but have gained 210XP.*

Azure scoffed inwardly. Was the prompt mocking his friend's death or trying to be sympathetic? He couldn't really tell. Worse than that, had this been destined to happen from the beginning? If it had been, then this was a cruel joke. He hated that he felt this way—had gotten so attached to someone who he had suspected was evil. He hated himself for having been suspicious of Uden in the first place, his mind and heart still torn over whether or not the half-imp had actually been a villain. He just hated this entire situation.

| **Quest: Bring Uden Home** |
|---|
| There is no greater love than sacrificing yourself for a cherished friend or family member. Uden may have been led astray by the demon, but he proved to be a good person in the end. Honor his memory by returning his remains to his home so that he may have a proper funeral.<br><br>**Difficulty:** Easy<br>**Success:** Return Uden's remains to his parents<br>**Failure:** Die or fail to return Uden's remains<br>**Will you accept this quest:** Yes or No? |

Azure walked over to Lonnell and placed a hand on his shoulder. "We have done what we came to do. We should take your brother back to your parents' farm. I'm not sure what your burial traditions are, but I would like to help with whatever I can. Then we need to go to Cragbell and tell everyone what a hero he was—tell them that they were wrong. Maybe even tell them that they were what caused all of this in the first place and that he was what saved them from it." Wasn't that ironic? Ironic and an injustice. Yes, he felt exceedingly sorry for how Uden had met his demise. It appeared that life in The Realm was equally as unfair as the world he had come from.

With his words of kindness, the prompt disappeared. Of course, he was going to help bring the half-imp's remains home. He owed Uden at least that much...even if the bastard had indirectly tried to kill him.

Lonnell gave a brisk nod, sniffling once before he began to gather Uden's bones. Azure immediately knelt to help, his heart breaking as he watched his friend try to hold himself together. They carefully placed Uden's remains in Lonnell's Bag of Holding and then stood to take their leave.

The sound of stone crumbling alerted them to a new path. Stepping through it led to a tunnel of dark obsidian which Azure could only assume was the first level of the dungeon. Uden had mentioned that once they defeated the dungeon boss, a quick way to the surface would appear.

Silence filled their every step as they walked. Thankfully, there were no foes to be seen. Azure was glad. While he hadn't been injured in the battle with the demon, nor had he lost much stamina, he still felt weak and tired—more emotionally than anything else. Of course, he would do what he had to to survive, but there was no fight left in him for the pleasure and adventure of it. He was just done.

It wasn't until they saw the literal light at the end of the tunnel that another enemy presented itself. Correction. Enemies.

"Oh fuck," Azure whispered under his breath, coming to a stop and reaching back for his bow. He gritted his teeth, too exhausted to deal with this shit.

At the mouth of the cave, two new goblin warriors waited for them. Both of them Analyzed as orange. No doubt, the archer was still perched on the cliff's edge. Even if they managed to draw the warriors into the cave to fight outside of its reach, they would still have to deal with the archer once they made their exit.

*Congratulations! The skill:* ***Analyze*** *has reached Level 5. This skill allows you to see how dangerous a foe is in relation to your own level. Use this skill frequently to avoid getting yourself killed.*

Azure brushed the notification away. There was no time to pay attention to it. He glanced over at Lonnell, who already had his staff in hand. The scowl on his face was a clear sign that he wasn't in the mood for this either.

"Wait!" One of the warriors held a hand up as he watched Azure nock an arrow.

The goblins were not moving towards them, probably trying to stay within the protection of their archer's range. They would, no doubt, venture into the cave once Azure started shooting, though. At this point, the adventurers had the advantage. If the goblin warriors didn't move, he could shoot them both dead where they stood. As it was, he might even be able to do it before they were able to reach him and Lonnell.

"You kill The Dark One?" the goblin half asked, half grunted.

"Yes. It is dead," Lonnell responded.

"You have proof?" the other goblin questioned.

Lonnell glanced over at Azure. Damn him for having put the horns in his bag. He would have to drop his aim to dig for them.

"I've taken its horns," Azure announced, his arms quickly growing tired from drawing the bow for so long.

"You show." The first goblin nodded at them.

"If we show you, will you let us pass?" Lonnell asked, skirting around Azure to start rummaging through the bag at his hip.

The goblins said nothing. They simply stood there with their spears in hand, waiting.

It took Lonnell a moment to locate the horns. Azure wondered how difficult it must be sorting through the dozens of bat wings he had collected. He also wondered how well the recall was while rummaging through someone else's bag. All Azure had to do was think of an item when he stuck his hand into his bag, and he could easily locate it. Maybe it wasn't the same if someone else looked through a bag that didn't belong to them.

Lonnell pulled out the demon's horns and held them up for the goblins to see. One of them grunted and turned to the other to begin whispering in their gruff language. After a moment, they both stepped aside, opening up the cave entrance for the adventures to leave.

"One free pass. Gift for defeating threat to all. You leave, but don't come back or we kill you. This is not a treaty between our people," the goblin to the left told them before stepping out of the cave to shout up to the archer.

Tension melted away from Azure's shoulders as he loosened his grip on the bowstring. He desperately hoped it wasn't a trick. Just to be sure, he leaned over to Lonnell and whispered, "Do you think it's a trap?"

He shook his head. "No. They're not very good at setting traps. He's probably relaying what the chieftain told him. Their job was to keep people from getting into the cave, but since the demon is dead, it doesn't matter anymore. It was taking their people too if they weren't providing other victims, so they're most likely grateful."

Azure hadn't needed that much of an explanation. All he cared about was that they weren't going to get stabbed in the back when they were passing the goblins.

"We will not try to fight you, then," he told them. "Joint celebration gift that this threat is defeated." Hopefully, they wouldn't take offense to that. If he weren't so tired, he would have been tempted to kill them since he did have the advantage. But right now, he just wanted to get back to Manny's farm and rest. The less resistance they faced, the better.

They passed without incident, the two goblin warriors standing like sentinels as they exited the cave. Another tremor of fear and distrust snaked through Azure as the goblins began to follow them once the two adventurers were outside. His entire body was wound with anxiety. When he heard the sound of rocks falling, he immediately turned on his heels and reached for the hilt of his blade.

Azure's heart lurched up into his throat. The goblins furrowed their meaty brows at him, but his gaze quickly shot past them to where the entrance of the cave was beginning to crumble.

Lonnell placed a hand on his shoulder. "Calm down. This is just what happens whenever a dungeon is conquered." He then looked up to address the two goblin warriors who were now clutching their weapons a bit more defensively. "Apologies. My friend here has amnesia, and he did not remember what happens to a dungeon once its boss has been defeated. We will be on our way now." Lonnell bowed his head respectfully towards the goblins and then tugged on Azure's shoulder to indicate that it was time for them to go.

"Apologies," Azure parroted quickly before following his friend.

## CHAPTER EIGHT
THE REALM – Day 36

The adventurers made a detour to Baremire to tell the Tree Queen about their victory, opting to stay the night before continuing on their way. She gave her condolences and told Azure to keep the armor. The rest of their journey was uneventful.

Azure could feel nervousness welling up inside of him as they approached Manny's farm. His heart broke for the man. Even though Uden wasn't biologically his, he knew that Manny loved him like a son.

He stood back and let Lonnell handle things as Manny rushed to greet them from the wheat field, a smile on his rugged face. It wasn't long before his expression contorted into one of extreme grief. They all returned to the house together where Lonnell dropped the grim news on his mother. She fell to her knees in a fit of sobs, and Manny quickly came to her side, though he soon followed suit in tear-shedding. They clung to each other in their grief, and Lonnell joined them, leaving Azure feeling like an outsider—remembering that this wasn't his family or his world.

*Congratulations! Quest:* ***Bring Uden Home*** *has been completed.*

*Uden did a great service to Crescent Island by helping to defeat the demon. You have honored his memory by returning his remains to his parents. You have earned their eternal gratitude and 90XP.*

Due to the sorrow around him, Azure took little joy from having completed the quest. This didn't even feel like it should have been a quest. It was just the right thing to do.

He excused himself and stepped outside, leaving the family to mourn. The sun was still shining brightly, though it would be setting within the next hour. Uden had died, but the world at large seemed unaffected. Life went on, just as it had historically when anyone died. Time stood still for no man. It was not a griever or a forgiver.

Azure spent the rest of the evening walking around the farm, appreciating the glow of the sun as it kissed the field of wheat with hues of gold and yellow. Walking past the garden, he remembered his first lesson with the half-imp. That was back before the demon had gripped him, but even then it had been apparent that Uden didn't quite mind the destruction. It had been a means to an end for him...though certainly, he hadn't expected to have such a final one.

All that Uden had wanted was to leave the island and learn more magic. That fight probably would have gone down much differently if they had some powerful spells at their disposal. A smirk played across Azure's face as he thought about how unstoppable the half-imp would have been with a full arsenal of magic under his belt. Either a strong ally or a formidable foe. It was hard to decide which side of the coin Uden would have eventually landed on. Overall, though, he hadn't seemed like a bad guy. A mix of good and evil, just like everyone else in the world.

Magic, though. Azure sat on a rock overlooking the garden thinking about the small glimpse he'd seen of magic in The Realm so far. Uden's ability to imbue arrows with light magic. Lonnell's small flame spell. All the wonders of Baremire. Azure wanted that. At least, a piece of it. At that moment, he decided that he would still go to the mainland. He would seek out one of these magic schools that Uden had talked so excitedly about and try to learn a few spells for himself. So far, he'd seen no indication that he had to fall in line with a specific class. As a human, he could become a necromancer or a battle mage or anything else his heart desired.

Having decided this, Azure expected to see a quest prompt display, but nothing presented itself. While he had been relieved at first to not immediately have an objective after dropping off Uden's remains, now it was just starting to feel unsettling. He tried not to focus on it, hoping that the system wasn't broken.

As the sun began to set and he headed back towards the barn, he thought about what he would do next. Traveling to the mainland was at the top of his list of personal objectives, but other things needed to be taken care of first, like going to Cragbell to sell his loot to Ruthren and then figuring out how to even get to the mainland.

Part of him wanted to start for Cragbell tonight. Even though the sun had set, traveling had become second nature to him. Azure doubted he would run into any goblins. Now that the demon had been dealt with, the land was no longer poisoned. They had little reason to venture this far for resources.

But he felt it would be inconsiderate to go without Lonnell, and now was definitely not the time to ask. Azure had promised he would stay at least long enough to help with, and bear witness to, Uden's funeral, and he was a man of his word. It would probably do him some good to rest anyway.

With nothing else to do, he decided to settle in early for the night. Tomorrow would be a more appropriate time to speak to Lonnell about traveling to Cragbell. If Lonnell didn't want to go, then maybe Azure could offer to pick up whatever they needed to perform the funeral.

As he was closing his eyes for sleep, there was a knock on the barn door.

"Come in," he said groggily, thinking about how strange it was to even say that. It reminded him of when he was a teenager and his mother wanted to enter his room. He briefly wondered if that had ever even been real.

The door slid open, and Lonnell offered him a soft smile before stepping in. “You look ready for bed already.”

"We've had a long journey." Azure sat up against the barn wall. Straw clung to his armor. Despite being safely back at the farm, he refused to take it off.

"That we have." Lonnell nodded, carrying over a lantern and taking a seat a few feet away. "My father wanted me to offer you Uden's bed. You are a good friend and should not be sleeping out in the barn."

"I appreciate the offer, but I'm fine sleeping here." Those were words Azure never thought he'd hear himself say. Truthfully though, he enjoyed the solitude that the barn offered. A chance to be alone with his thoughts.

"In the straw?" Lonnell picked up a piece from the floor and flicked it. "Awfully uncomfortable."

"A feathered mattress compared to the cold, hard floor we're used to sleeping on." He smirked.

"I suppose so." Lonnell dropped his gaze. It was clear from his solemn expression that his brother's death was still weighing on him.

"Did you want to talk about something?" Azure offered.

"Not really." Lonnell paused for a moment, then snorted. "It kills me that no one will ever know what we went through.

What *he* went through to save the island."

Ah, so he did want to talk after all. Azure was willing to listen. It was his job as Lonnell's friend.

"We will tell them," he said.

"But they won't know. Not really." Frustration was plain in the lines of Lonnell's face. "You can hear a story a million times, but you have to live it yourself to truly appreciate the significance."

"I suppose. But no man can live every story." Azure sighed. "I'm sure that it feels like your brother's death wasn't justified." It wasn't. The people who had created the demon with their hatred should have been the ones out fighting it.

"It all feels so pointless." Lonnell cradled his head in his hands. "They will feel bad that their hatred brought the demon to our island, but they will also be happy that Uden is gone. He was always a trickster"a nuisance to many. Maybe they'll even feel that the end justified the means."

"I would hope not. The last thing we need is another demon to pop up from their hateful thoughts," Azure commented, feeling exhaustion from the idea of having to go through the same ordeal all over again. Perhaps the whole scenario would respawn. That would be horrible. "If that ends up being the case, it can have the island."

"That's not funny." Lonnell glared at him.

"I'm not laughing." Azure countered with a deadpan expression. "If the people of Cragbell are filled with that much hate, then they all deserve to die."

"That's an evil thing to say."

"Well, it's how I feel." Azure looked away, not enjoying the tension between them. "But I digress," he quickly changed the subject, "now that the demon is slain and things will return to normal, what are you going to do?"

Lonnell thought for a moment. “I suppose I'll just continue on as I have been. Help my father with the farm. Save up money to buy a plot of land and start my own.” A smile spread across his lips—the first real smile that Azure had seen Lonnell sport since before they'd defeated the demon. “I think I'm going to ask Bronna to marry me. I'm old enough now to settle down and start a family.”

"Good luck with that," Azure did his best to sound enthusiastic for his friend.

"What about you? What are you going to do?"

"I think I'd like to go to the mainland." Azure shifted his weight, half-hoping that Lonnell would want to join him. That hope had faded since hearing about the possible upcoming nuptials. Even if Lonnell didn't want to tag along, it wouldn't stop Azure from going.

"What business do you have there?"

"Uden talked about some magic school. I'd like to check it out."

"Ah yes. Hawking's School of Land Magic," Lonnell said with a soft smile of remembrance.

"But I have no idea how to get there. No idea, really, about how to even leave this island." Azure gestured around them.

"Well, first you would need to buy passage on a ship leaving for the mainland. There's a small port to the south. You could probably find passage to Squall's End there."

"And how much would that cost?"

"I've never sailed before," Lonnell admitted, "but I would think it would be at least one gold coin."

Hopefully, that was all it would be. There was a lot of loot in Azure's bag. Surely, once sold, it would be enough to get him to Squall's End.

"It's a four-day trip," Lonnell continued. "You likely won't find anything designed for passenger travel. Mostly merchant ships."

"That's fine with me." Azure definitely wasn't expecting any fineries. "And the school is in Squall's End?"

"On the outskirts of it. But it's not free either. I'm afraid you'll find that everything, once you leave the island, is a bit expensive. It's part of the reason why I have no desire to leave."

"If it's too expensive, I suppose I could just buy spells instead," Azure said with a sigh.

"Not if you ever want to become a skilled mage." Lonnell shook his head. "Magic scrolls are actually illegal to sell to the public. The ones that Uden and I came across were black market." He shrunk slightly as he said it, which made Azure grin. Upstanding Lonnell Namud had done something illegal. It was almost unfathomable. "Ruthren smuggled them over. You can often buy them from merchants who sell a variety of...strange things, but only if that merchant trusts you. Still, most of what slips through by illegal means are just low-level spells. To become adept at magic, you have to attend a magic school."

It reminded Azure of the difference between becoming a phlebotomist and a doctor. Phlebotomy is a medical skill, but you don't need to go to college for it. All doctors know phlebotomy, but no phlebotomist can become a doctor without schooling.

"Whatever the case, I want to make it happen." Azure waved away all of the potential roadblocks in his path. "I think it would be what Uden would have wanted."

"Indeed." Lonnell nodded. "I suppose, in that regard, you'll have to carry on in his memory."

"Speaking of which," Azure took the opportunity to change subjects to a more pressing matter. "I was thinking of going to Cragbell tomorrow to sell my loot. Is there anything that you or your parents need for the funeral?"

"Nothing in particular. Uden was not well-liked, so we're not planning for a large service." His expression softened with sadness. "My parents have decided to bury his remains under the tree where he practiced his knife throwing. I feel it's appropriate."

"I'm honestly not sure what to expect from your funeral traditions," Azure admitted. "Do you place flowers on the graves?"

"No." Lonnell gave him a queer look. "We simply bury the body and say a few words of remembrance. The person's belongings are typically divided amongst family members according to what item is most useful or most treasured to that person. Sometimes, it can lead to nasty squabbles."

*That's not too different from my world,* Azure thought.

Lonnell continued, "Uden didn't have much, and what was precious to him was destroyed with his flesh thanks to his imp's blood's decaying skill. It is a bit sad."

*And a bit of a waste.* The decay of Uden's weapons was a loss. Azure felt bad for thinking it, but it was true. If Uden's possessions hadn't been destroyed along with his body, Azure might have gotten some better gear out of it.

"It is sad...and kind of interesting," Azure confessed.

"I suppose it is interesting." Lonnell nodded. "I honestly hadn't known what to expect when he died. It was a strange reminder that he wasn't all human. Truthfully, I often forgot. He looked so much like a human that it was hard for me to believe that he wasn't 100% human."

"I know," Azure agreed, though he still felt there had always been some otherworldly quality to Uden that had separated him from the rest. It was in his eyes and the pallor of his skin and the silent way that he was able to move. The half-imp had been a rather mysterious creature to Azure.

"Anyway, I should let you get some sleep." Lonnell pulled himself to his feet and picked up his lantern.

"Would you like to go with me to Cragbell tomorrow?" Azure asked.

He thought for a moment before responding. “Sure. I suppose there's nothing else to do around here.”

"Good stuff." Azure smiled. "I'm sure you have a lot of things to sell, too."

"I do," Lonnell replied before turning to leave. He took a step and then paused, looking back at Azure. "I never thanked you for coming with me on this...adventure," he hesitated on the word as if pondering if it was the right one. "This isn't your home. You had no stake in what happened here, yet you came anyway.

"I know that Uden often gave you a hard time, and we didn't always agree on things, but I honestly couldn't have done this without you. So thank you." He smiled softly.

"It's the least I could do."

Just then, a notification popped up.

*Your relationship with **Lonnell** has reached **Level 4**. Your relationship has been updated from **Trusted** to **Friend**. You and Lonnell have been through a lot together. His opinion of you is high, and he will not hesitate to help you with anything that you need. Congratulations!*

## CHAPTER NINE

THE REALM – Day 37

The next morning, Azure restocked his supply of arrows from Manny's shed and then collected the rabbit pelts that Meva owed him before heading off towards Cragbell with Lonnell at his side. Upon arriving, he went straight to Ruthren's cart.

"Heyo!" the merchant greeted them, seeming chipper as usual. He glanced at Lonnell, then behind him. "Where's your brother? I just got something in that I think he'll love." Excitement rang clear in his voice.

"Uden died," Lonnell said, not bothering to ease the blow.

Ruthren's smile instantly faded. "How did it happen?"

"It's a long story," Lonnell sighed, "but the short version is that he was protecting me."

"I have time for a long story," the merchant told him, obviously wanting the details.

As Lonnell rehashed their harrowing ordeal with the demon, Azure browsed Ruthren's wares. The Bag of Holding was still there waiting for him. Of course, it was. Who around here could afford such a thing? Somehow, though, seeing it didn't bring about as much yearning as it had before. In all the time that Azure had spent inside The Realm, he'd yet to completely fill his inventory. Sure, he couldn't hold large items in the bag he had now, but it didn't seem to matter as much. Acquiring the Bag of Holding wasn't as important to him as getting off of the island.

Normally, Azure's eyes would have gravitated to all of the shiny weapons with their amped-up stats. But today, he was being practical. Shopping was all about what he needed to survive. Not what he wanted.

"That's some nice armor you've got there," Ruthren commented on his Armor of Light once he had finished talking to Lonnell. "Got any mind to sell it? You don't see a complete set of armor like that around very often."

"It's not for sale," Azure replied quickly, knowing that the armor was one of the most valuable things he possessed. Even if he didn't have enough coin to buy passage to the mainland after he sold all of his loot, selling the armor was out of the question. He doubted he'd come across anything better in a while. He might be wrong, but he wasn't willing to risk it.

Ruthren held up his palms. "It never hurts to ask."

"No, it doesn't." Azure smiled at him. "I do have a lot of other things to sell, though." He unfastened his bag from his waist to begin rummaging through it and placing his loot on the cart.

Admittedly, he had expected a low-ball price for the rabbit pelts and bat wings, but when the merchant only offered him twenty-five copper per demon horn, Azure had a hard time hiding his discontent. "We nearly died to get these. In fact, Uden did die," he pointed out. It would not be beyond him to play the sympathy card in his haggling.

"I'm sorry, kid, but I can't pay you more than they're worth. The smaller the horns, the less they go for, and these are lesser demon horns." Ruthren was unmoving.

“But the item class is rare.” He stared down at the horns, wondering if they were really worth so little.

“Twenty-five per horn is all I can offer you. Take it or leave it, kid.” Ruthren began counting out the coins he owed Azure for everything else.

“I'll take it,” he grumbled, still not happy.

Throwing in the iron halberd, since he didn't think he was going to use it anymore, Azure received four gold, two silver, and seven copper. That should definitely be enough to buy him passage on a ship, Azure thought with relief. Picking up the halberd had been a smart move. He was surprised when Ruthren offered him one gold, four silver, and five copper for it. At the time, Azure had no idea how valuable the weapon was. It felt like one of the few things that had gone right.

Now he wished they had taken the time to kill the two goblin warriors waiting at the entrance of the cave. Maybe their spears would have been worth a lot, too. Oh well. There was no going back to the past. Azure could only look forward and learn from his mistakes.

For his share of shopping, Azure replaced the mortar and pestle that had been taken from him by the goblins and purchased twenty-five empty vials, which left him with three gold, seven silver, and eight copper total (when adding in what coin he already had on him). Being frugal was probably important if he wanted to survive once he got to Squall's End.

“When's the burial going to take place?” Ruthren asked once their business was concluded.

“Tomorrow, shortly after sunset,” Lonnell told him. “Uden hated the sun, so we figured it would be more respectful to do it in the dark.”

“That makes sense.” The merchant nodded. “I'll try to be there.”

“He would like that.” Lonnell smiled softly.

Azure allowed his curiosity to get the better of him. “What was it that you had for him that you thought he would have liked?”

A large grin spread across Ruthren's face as he reached behind his cart to pull out a scroll. He handed it to Lonnell first, who chuckled softly before showing it to Azure. “Yeah, he definitely would have liked this. Is it bad that I'm glad he never got a chance to buy it? I don't even want to imagine what mischief he would have gotten into with this power.”

Drawn onto the front of the scroll in purple was the picture of a hand reaching for some coins on a table. Azure couldn't really tell what the scroll was supposed to be. Concentrating on it brought up the item's details.

| **Spell Scroll:** ***Steal*** | **Quantity:** 1/1<br>**Weight:** 0.0 kg<br>**Mana Cost:** 7<br>**Cool Down:** Ten Minutes<br>**Magic Class:** Necromancy<br>**Uses:** Silently transports items into your inventory from up to 10 feet away. |
|---|---|

Azure's eyes widened in wonder. A spell scroll. This was magic. He never knew how much he actually yearned for it until he had it within his reach.

"How much is it?" he asked quickly.

"Three gold," the merchant replied, causing Azure to cringe internally.

"Is that a good deal?" He raised an eyebrow at Lonnell.

"This is black market, boy. A special item. You pay for the risk of me bringing it here. You can't get this anywhere else but in The Deadlands," Ruthren explained before Lonnell could interject.

Lonnell looked over at Azure. "It would be a good deal if you had no intentions of going to The Deadlands. You would likely be able to buy the same spell at the magic school there much cheaper, but few people who make it to The Deadlands come out alive. That's why it's called The Deadlands. Factor in the cost of transporting it here and the price is actually a steal."

The merchant's grin broadened as he agreed. "Yeah, it's a steal. This kid knows his stuff." He glanced back over at Azure with greed in his eyes. "Are you interested in buying it?"

Azure groaned inwardly. This was yet another instance of the Bag of Holding. Though he could afford the spell, if he spent the money, he definitely wouldn't have enough to go to the mainland. He had a feeling that quests and opportunities to make money would be more plentiful there, so it was probably better to wait. Regretfully, he declined, feeling like he had lost something when he watched Ruthren roll the scroll back up and put it away.

"It annoys me how expensive things are here," he grumbled to Lonnell as they walked away from the merchant.

"It really was a good deal," his friend told him. "Not a very useful spell if you're not into thievery, but still a good deal."

"Yeah. I'm not exactly looking to become a bandit," Azure said with a sigh. "Are you ready to go back?"

"Not yet. I want to head over to the tavern and check on Bronna." Lonnell glanced in the direction of the tavern, and his disposition seemed to perk up.

"All right," Azure replied, not sharing in his companion's enthusiasm. There was a twinge of bitterness in his heart for the squat maiden. Not only did he find her annoying, but it was easy to trace the cause of all of this back to her.

Playing the blame game probably wasn't fair. Honestly, it was more Lonnell's fault for telling Bronna about Uden's heritage in the first place, but he didn't dare to point the finger in that direction. He was certain that Lonnell felt the guilt—the responsibility for his part in his brother's death.

They walked to the tavern and entered. Unlike before, no one glowered at them now that Uden wasn't present. Azure remembered the confrontation they'd had with the barkeep before. He decided that he was glad to be leaving the island. The longer he stayed here, the less he liked the people. Perhaps if he had been dropped into The Realm in another location, Azure would have seen Uden as an evil nuisance, too. But that wasn't the case, and he couldn't help that he now disliked the villagers for how harshly they had treated his friend just because he was half imp. Apparently, the half-human part of him hadn't counted for much.

*Fuck this place,* he thought as he watched Lonnell scour the room for Bronna. Though the tavern was half-full, she was nowhere to be seen. They headed towards the bar where Leland acknowledged them with a nod. He was busy talking to a woman at the end of the bar and seemed to have no intention of serving them.

Lonnell walked over to him. “Has Bronna come by today?”

Leland gave him an annoyed look but pulled himself away from the conversation he was having nonetheless. “No, and she won't be coming by again for a while.”

Lonnell furrowed his brow, and Azure instantly worried that she'd been kidnapped again. The last thing he wanted to do was have to go rescue the hobbit of a woman.

"Why do you say that?" Lonnell asked.

"Esau sent her to the mainland to stay with relatives. He didn't feel it was safe for her here anymore," the barkeep told him and then immediately went back to carrying on his conversation...which it quickly became apparent was more flirting than talking.

"I'm assuming that Esau is her father," Azure commented as they stepped away from the bar.

Lonnell nodded in acknowledgment, looking distraught. "I have to get her back."

Just then, a quest notification popped up.

| **Quest: Find Bronna** |
|---|
| Feeling it would be safer, Bronna's father shipped her off to the mainland. The timing couldn't be worse now that Lonnell has decided to propose. Help him find his lost love.<br><br>**Difficulty:** Easy<br>**Success:** Find Bronna<br>**Failure:** Fail to find Bronna, die, or abandon the quest<br>**Will you accept this quest:** Yes or No? |

"I'm guessing that means you'll be heading to the mainland with me." It was difficult for Azure to hide his happiness about the situation. While he knew this wasn't what Lonnell wanted, he couldn't help but feel selfish. Maybe he'd even be able to convince his friend to stay once they got there.

"I guess I don't have a choice," Lonnell replied with a sigh. "But first I need to find out where exactly he sent her to."

"Does that mean we're going to Esau's?" Azure asked, wondering how far away the man lived.

"It means we're going to the mill. That's where he works." Lonnell pivoted to exit the tavern, and Azure followed suit, having no real idea where they were headed.

They walked until they reached a building on the far side of Cragbell. Having never been inside the structure before, Azure had just assumed it was a dwelling. The walls were made of white stone with a few small windows, but there was no waterwheel or fans powered by the wind to grind grain. The wooden door was flung open to ventilate the building. Lonnell knocked on it twice before stepping inside.

Instantly, Azure's nose filled with an earthy smell. It was like sticking his head into a bag of flour and having a good whiff, but there were other scents mixed in as well. The dark tones of rye and the malt of barley combined with the heat-baked stones of the building and the wood of the roof and the dust of the dirt floor.

The sound of stone crushing grain came to a halt as they entered the dimly lit building. Inside, a man stood behind a large quern-stone. There was a sack of grain to one side of him and a sack of freshly milled flour on the other. He straightened himself and wiped his brow on the back of his sleeve, his expression showing little more than irritation at the interruption of his work. Wisps of white hair clung to his forehead from sweat.

"Lonnell," he said the name with no betrayal of feelings towards it.

"Esau." Lonnell bowed his head respectfully.

"I suppose you're here asking after my daughter." The man hunched over, leaning against the stone table that the quern-stone rested on. He was short like his daughter, standing only about 5 feet tall, with a lean build, and appeared much older than Azure had expected. Clearly, Bronna had been born late in his life, for he had to be in his mid-sixties. Aquamarine eyes rested above a long nose with a hook at the end that concealed part of the lengthy white mustache below it. It extended over his upper lip and was swept messily to the sides. The man was definitely in need of a shave. All around him in the room were sacks of various grains waiting to be milled. It looked like an exhausting job.

"Leland told me you sent her to the mainland. I am here to

tell you that the threat has been dealt with. The curse on Crescent Island is no more, and it is safe for her to return," Lonnell said as if it were just that simple to get her back.

"Is that so?" The man scratched his chin in thought.

"It is as I say." Lonnell nodded in confirmation before glancing back at Azure. "My friend and brother..." he hesitated, heaviness taking over his words, "we defeated a demon that had settled here."

"A demon?" There was surprise in Esau's tone. "I wonder how that got here."

"The town created it," Azure stepped in. It seemed that Lonnell was content on pussyfooting around the topic, but he wasn't. "From their hatred of Uden after finding out that he was a half-imp. He died fighting it to protect the town."

"Is that so?" Esau said more slowly this time, giving Azure a skeptical look.

"That is so," Lonnell replied with conviction. "It was a senseless tragedy all the way around."

"I can't help but feel somewhat responsible." Regret seeped into the miller's voice. Seeing that he was willing to admit his folly made Azure less hostile towards him. "It was not my business to spread ill words about your brother. He was...well, we all know what he was." Was there some hidden meaning behind that? "Whatever the case, I thank you for your heroics and am sorry for your loss. Give my condolences to your parents. I cannot imagine losing a child, which is why I decided to send Bronna away." His gaze fell to the floor. "To be honest, it has always been a great fear of mine that she would get caught up in one of the goblin raids. We are mostly a village of farmers. There aren't any soldiers here, and what fighters we do have come and go. I feel that it was only a matter of time before something like this happened. Crescent Island is no place for an unwed girl with so little protection."

"I was hoping..." Lonnell hesitated, "that I could change that."

"Oh?" Esau perked up with interest.

"I would like to ask for your blessing to marry your daughter. Losing my brother made me realize how important it is to keep the ones that we love close," the inflection in Lonnell's words spoke of his sincerity.

A broad smile swept across the miller's face. “I could not imagine a better husband for my daughter. I would be proud to call you my son-in-law.”

"That's a relief." Lonnell half-sighed, half-laughed.

"But first, I fear you must fetch her." Esau dusted his hands off on his tunic before walking around the table. "I sent her to stay with her aunt and uncle in Roselake. It's a village about five miles to the southwest of Squall's End. Much like this one, but soldiers from the Kingdom of Noseon pass through it frequently, so it's well protected from monsters and invaders."

"Do you happen to have a map of the area?" Lonnell asked.

"No, but it's not very big. Ask for Cristopher Prescott, and I'm sure someone will point you in the right direction. They've lived there for ages."

Lonnell paused as if ready to ask another question, then he simply nodded in thanks. “I will bring her home as soon as I can.”

"That's up to you." Esau gestured absentmindedly as he returned to his post at the quern-stone. "I would understand if you kids wouldn't want to come back here."

"Why wouldn't we?" Lonnell furrowed his brow.

Azure knew why. There wasn't much to do here. He still couldn't understand why Lonnell wanted such a boring life.

"There might be more opportunities for you on the mainland. Besides, even though you dealt with the demon, I still feel like it's safer," his tone showed confliction in his statement.

Lonnell sighed again. "I suppose you might be right. I've lived here my entire life, so I can't imagine anything else. I'll see what Bronna wants to do."

"Just promise me one thing, Lonnell," Esau said as they turned to walk out of the mill. "Keep my daughter safe."

"Of course," Lonnell gave him his word, and they took their leave. Once they were outside, the sound of stone grinding grain continued. He stopped for a moment, his eyes dancing around the village. "Well, I suppose we should pick up what we might need for the journey."

The next thirty minutes were spent wandering around Cragbell and visiting the few merchants that were open for business. Lonnell seemed more lost in thought than interested in purchasing anything. He sold everything he could to help him buy passage aboard a ship as well. The time felt mostly wasted, though, spent window shopping.

Azure hunted on the way back to Manny's farm, taking down a small buck that happened to be feeding in a clearing off the beaten trail. His arrow barely missed a vital area, and they ended up having to track the beast for a good ten minutes before they found where it had fallen. It was worth it, though, because the meat would feed the family for days. Azure equated it to being the same thing as taking a casserole to a grieving family in his own world.

They carried the carcass to Manny's farm where Azure got to work butchering it while Lonnell went to tell his parents about his plan to leave Crescent Island. Without even witnessing the discussion, Azure knew they wouldn't be happy. Since Uden had just passed away, it probably felt like they were losing both of their sons. On the one hand, he felt bad for them. On the other hand, it was far beyond time for the boys to carve out their own lives. Perhaps if Manny had allowed it to happen sooner, Uden would still be alive. It was a sad thought—that a parent could hold on so tightly until they destroyed what they loved the most. Maybe he was overthinking it in this situation, but he'd seen lots of cases in his own world of parents losing their children by either holding on too tightly or not holding on tightly enough. Parenting seemed to be a delicate balance. Briefly, he wondered if he'd ever get a chance to experience it, or if that option had fled the moment he'd woken up inside The Realm. This was real, yet it wasn't. A life he'd gotten used to, yet one he still couldn't entirely accept. He also wondered when his memories of his other life would fade away and this would be all that was left.

They supped on the deer, with minimal conversation. It was evident that Meva and Manny were still dealing with the shock of Uden's death, now coupled with the realization that they were about to be alone. Azure mostly kept his lips sealed, only commenting on how good the stew was that Meva had prepared.

He spent the following day wandering around in the forest outside of the farm gathering herbs and mashing them into minor healing potions. By the end of the day, all of his vials were full, and his Alchemy skill was a little over 80% of the way to level four. He had also received the following notification.

*Congratulations! The skill:* ***Foraging*** *has reached Level 6. Plants collected through foraging have a variety of uses. You can sell them, consume them, or use them to create potions through alchemy.*

After the sun had set, he walked to the house to join the family in preparations for laying Uden's remains to rest. Ruthren also showed up, and they proceeded out to the tree that Manny had picked to bury Uden under. Deep gouges were carved into the bark where it had been struck over and over again by Uden's knives, one of the last remnants of his existence.

They stood together in silence while Lonnell dug a shallow grave for the bones at the base of the tree's trunk. Meva set them delicately inside, holding back her sobs as she did so.

Once they were all standing again, Manny stepped to the edge of the grave to speak. "I found him by the river, but he was always my son. Never did I regret bringing him home. Not for a moment."

He stepped away, glancing at Meva to say something, but she was still too shaken up. She clung to his side, her long flaxen hair hiding her face as she sobbed against her husband's chest. "He was my son," was all that she could manage to get out. Manny petted her soothingly, nodding to Lonnell to say his final words to the deceased.

Lonnell clasped his hands in front of him and cleared his throat before speaking. "He was my brother. My friend. Someone to get in trouble with. Someone to keep out of trouble. Someone to bail out of trouble," he said with a slight smile. "Never did I feel like he was not of my blood. We were very different, yet deep down, we were the same. Both good people just trying to find our way in this world. He will be forever missed."

There was silence for a long moment. Azure wondered if he should speak next, but both Manny and Lonnell were looking at Ruthren. The merchant was staring sullenly down into the grave. It wasn't clear if he was silently mourning or planning what he would say, but he was definitely lost in thought.

Lonnell cleared his throat again, summoning Ruthren's attention.

"Oh!" he said as if coming out of a daze. "I suppose it's my turn." He coughed and shifted his weight, his eyes searching the tree and everything around them for something appropriate to say. When he finally found his voice, his gaze settled on the bones again. "Uden was my favorite customer here on Crescent Island. He always had something witty to say, and he could haggle like no other. If he ever thought I'd taken advantage of him, he'd pay me back by trying to steal something," he chuckled. "One time, that son of a bitch moved my entire cart when I was off taking a piss. I thought I was going to kill him."

Meva glared at the merchant through her hair, quickly bringing the story to an end.

Ruthren shifted uncomfortably again. “He was a trickster but a fun guy. I'll miss him. Your turn.” He reached over and tapped Azure's arm as if he needed the reminder that he was the last one left to speak.

"I didn't know Uden for as long as any of you," Azure began, "but he was one of the most interesting people I've ever met. I felt like there was always a storm brewing inside of him"a constant secret battle between good and evil." He purposely avoided looking at Meva, figuring she wouldn't approve of his assessment of her late son. "There were times I thought he would lose that fight. Times that he almost did lose that fight. But everything he did, he did to protect his family.

"But there was one thing in particular that he did that solidified where that battle ended in my mind. I'm not sure if Lonnell told you guys this or not, but at one point we had a fight with a camp of goblins, and he let one of them go. I had asked him about that goblin several times, and he refused to tell me the truth. But on his deathbed, he confessed that the reason why he had let that goblin live was because it wasn't a fighter and it had a son.

"I don't know much about your world still, but I do know that half-imps aren't innately evil or good. Uden might have done a lot of mischievous things to you," he glanced at Ruthren, "and to the people of Cragbell. But he cared about people. If he didn't care about people, he never would have come with us to help save Bronna. If he didn't care about people, he wouldn't have come to help stop the demon, despite the position he was in. And if he didn't care about people, then he wouldn't have sacrificed his life for his brother. Uden was a good guy that got dealt a bad hand in life, but he played it in the best way he knew how. I will always admire him and his sacrifice."

After the words had been said, everyone gathered around and knelt by the grave to bury the body together, throwing fistfuls of dirt on top of the bones until there was nothing left. Their tears watered the soil. Even Azure felt his eyes welling up from all the grief around him. No one seemed immune.

When they were done, Ruthren, Azure, and Lonnell stood to walk back to the house together. Manny and Meva stayed behind to continue mourning their son and watching over his grave.

"We'll be leaving for Squall's End tomorrow," Lonnell told the merchant.

"I suppose I'll be seeing you there then," he replied, his voice still low and solemn.

"Do you do business there?" Azure glanced at him.

"When I do leave, I tend to hit up all of the little towns along the coast all the way to the Kingdom of Noseon. Speaking of which, I'll be heading that way tomorrow. Maybe we can all board a ship together."

"I think that would be fun." Azure offered him a soft smile. He liked the merchant well enough. Ruthren was a bit hard around the edges, and definitely a strict businessman, but he seemed like a fun guy when he wasn't busy tending to his cart. It might be interesting to see him out of business mode.

"Then you can help us find a ship?" Lonnell asked.

"It's not that difficult," the merchant told him. "Just meet me at the pier when the sun is high in the sky. They typically take off a little past lunch. It's easier for them to pass the sirens at night when everyone is asleep."

"Sirens?" Azure's curiosity was piqued.

"Aye. The deadly, bewitching beauties of the sea." A sarcastic grin took over his face.

"Like mermaids?" Azure wanted to be sure he was hearing him correctly.

"Almost," Ruthren said. "The evil version of mermaids."

"I'd like to see them." Images of gorgeous topless women with long glittering scaled tails flashed through his mind.

"And I'm sure they'd like to see you...falling overboard into the drink," he muttered the last bit. "I never got the fascination. Who wants to yearn for a woman you can't touch?"

Lonnell chuckled, but Azure wasn't getting the joke.

"I've never seen one before. I think it would be interesting," he said.

"Well, they might be able to tie you to one of the masts. I wouldn't recommend it, though. Their song will drive you insane."

"You mean inflict you with Insanity?" Azure raised an eyebrow. That didn't sound like much fun at all.

"No," he hesitated as he thought, stopping with them by the house. "More like make you crave getting to them. Take you down to the likes of an animal. You'd be like a dog trying to go after a bitch in heat. You'd want to stop at nothing to get to them. Men have even chopped off their own arms to break free from their binds to go overboard."

Azure's eyes widened in surprise. “Wow. That sounds intense.”

"So, you see, lad, you're better off not knowing about them." He clapped Azure on the shoulder before turning his attention to Lonnell. "Well, I guess I'll be off. It's best not to leave my cart unattended for too long. There might not be any goblins in the area right now, but thieves are still aplenty, I fear."

"Not on this island, I hope," Lonnell said sincerely.

"One less now that your brother is gone," Ruthren laughed, not realizing that his joke was in poor taste until he saw Lonnell's scowl and coughed to silence himself. "Anyway, I'll see you two tomorrow. And don't be late." He pointed at them as he began walking away. "Those ships wait for no one."

Lonnell waited until the merchant was out of earshot before saying, "I wonder how often he thinks before he speaks."

"It was all in jest, I'm sure." Azure's eyes trailed behind the merchant as he rounded the house and disappeared out of sight.

"Well, we best get to bed. It will be a lazy day tomorrow, but a long one, nonetheless." Lonnell yawned to show his exhaustion.

"Hey," Azure called to him before he could walk away.

"Yeah?"

"There's some other business I'd like to take care of before we leave here."

Lonnell shifted his weight. "Hopefully it's nothing that will take long."

"Ehhh, it might, actually." Azure cringed inwardly at his own delay. This was important, though.

"Well, what is it?" Lonnell tried to hurry him along with the info.

"When I was taken prisoner by the goblins, I noticed that they had several women held captive. I'd like to go rescue them."

Lonnell blew out a long weighted sigh.

"What's wrong?" Azure was surprised that his friend didn't seem immediately on board with the idea.

"Uden told me you were going to bring this up."

"You make that sound like a bad thing."

"Azure...it's not possible to save everyone in the world."

"Excuse me?" His head jutted back almost involuntarily. "I'm not talking about saving everyone. I'm talking about saving three women who are obviously being held against their will and raped repeatedly."

"Those women are slaves. They likely have nowhere else to go."

"Are you fucking kidding me right now?" Azure's anger flared. "Are you telling me that you're willing to just sit idly by while innocent people are being abused? I thought you were better than that, Lonnell."

Now it was Lonnell who raised his voice. "We're not indestructible, Azure. Uden's death should have proven that. And despite what you think, you aren't some mighty hero that can just rush in and conquer all. You're talking about invading a goblin settlement and taking on who knows how many goblins—certainly more than we could handle on our own—to save three women that would then become our responsibility. Oh, and not to mention they're probably all pregnant with goblin babies."

"They're still human," Azure argued. "And we wouldn't have to be alone. I'm sure we could rally some of the villagers to help."

A bitter laugh escaped Lonnell's lips. "Oh yes, a village full of farmers who are afraid of goblins and have no vested interest in these women. I'm certain they'd be willing to risk their lives to save a bunch of slaves when they have families that they need to take care of."

"What is wrong with you?" Azure couldn't believe the words coming out of his friend's mouth. This was a side of Lonnell he'd never seen before. "We don't have to risk everyone"s lives. I could just sneak in and release them. As long as we have backup in case something goes wrong."

"Something would go wrong," Lonnell insisted. "Those women are very heavily guarded. The continuation of that settlement depends on those women being there. The goblins aren't just going to let you come take them."

"Fine." Azure threw his hands up in exasperation. "If you won't help me, then I'll just do it myself."

"You are my friend, but you are an idiot sometimes. I," Lonnell pointed to himself as he spoke, "am getting on that boat tomorrow. You can do whatever you want. Say hi to my brother for me when you get to the other side." He spun on his heels and walked hurriedly away, slamming the door behind himself when he entered the house, leaving Azure out in the cool night air.

| **Quest: Rescue the Goblins' Thralls** |
|---|
| You spotted a large cage with three women inside while you were in the goblin settlement. They are obviously being held against their will and begged you to free them. Honor the vow you made to yourself and liberate them.<br><br>**Difficulty:** Very Hard<br>**Success:** Free all three women<br>**Failure:** Fail to free the women or die<br>**Will you accept this quest:** Yes or No? |

*An overlapping quest*, was the first thing that came to Azure's mind. This was the first time he'd been given two quests at once...which was kind of interesting to him considering that he had been questless for a little while there. Azure couldn't help but wonder if he accepted the quest if it would cancel out his quest with Lonnell. He highly doubted that he would be able to rescue the women and make it to the mainland before Lonnell was able to find Bronna.

The next thing that caught his attention was that the quest was rated as Very Hard. The only other Very Hard quest he'd taken on had been the quest to Defeat the Dark One. That quest had gotten Uden killed. There had been three of them for that one, a party of companions working together to achieve a singular goal. If he accepted this quest, it would just be him. And if anything went wrong, it would likely mean his death.

Saving the decision for later, Azure dismissed the notification and returned to the barn. While the day hadn't been physically stressful, it certainly had been emotionally. The death of his friend still weighed on him, topped off with having a fight with Lonnell, and Azure was in a foul mood. Of all people, he had expected Lonnell to be on his side with the plan for saving the women. Since Azure had woken up in The Realm, he'd considered Lonnell to be the most morally upright person he'd met next to his father. That's why his refusal just didn't make sense. Shouldn't freeing the women be important to him, too?

*Whatever, I'll just do it myself,* he thought stubbornly again, then spent the next several hours pouring over the plan in his head. The cage had been in a central area of the settlement, placed strategically so that it could be watched by not only the guards but everyone else. Sneaking in wasn't going to be easy. It was in a fairly open space, so Stealthing would only work until he got close to it.

There were also the unknown variables that made rescuing the women risky, such as how they'd react when they saw him. If they called out to him or made a ruckus, they would alert the guards, and soon a whole swarm of goblins would descend upon him. Would the women be able to Stealth effectively? He doubted it. They had all Analyzed as blue to him. Being held captive, there was no way for them to level up. More than likely, they didn't possess any skills. And even after the rescue...they would undoubtedly be pursued. Would the women be able to keep up in their fragile pregnant states? Would they even be able to run?

Thinking realistically, it probably wouldn't be long before the goblins caught up to them. With no other backup, Azure would have to face them alone. And if they sent stronger goblins than his level, which they most certainly would, the odds would not be in his favor.

"Fuck," Azure cursed, feeling a ball of anger and guilt forming in his stomach. No matter how he spun it, rescuing the women and making it out alive seemed to be an impossible task. Maybe if Uden was still alive and it was the three of them...But neither brother was on his side with this one.

Despair for the women filled him. If only he were stronger. If only there weren't so many goblins. If only the cage was on the outskirts of the settlement instead of right in the dead center of it. He had no advantage, only hindrances.

*Maybe if I sleep on it, something will come to me in the morning. Something I might have overlooked that would make this easier.*

Discontent but tired, Azure settled down in the straw, hoping that endless scenarios wouldn't keep him awake. If he was to save these women, the last thing he needed was his own body going against him.

# CHAPTER TEN
THE REALM – Day 39

The morning came with no new revelations and little sleep. Azure groaned awake, feeling stiff and cranky. His first thoughts were of the quest to save the women and how overwhelmingly against him the odds were. It bothered him that he couldn't find a solution. Surely, the game wouldn't have offered him the quest if he wasn't capable of completing it.

Azure rolled over and sighed, thinking of some of Uden's last words to him, that this wasn't a game. Uden had died and not come back, but Azure had always suspected him of being an NPC. If that were true, then why had he been so human. More human than Lonnell and Manny. Azure couldn't be sure anymore. Maybe they were all real.

He dragged himself to breakfast and felt the tension between him and Lonnell immediately.

After sitting there in silence for a few minutes, Manny looked between the two friends. "Are you two ready for the big boat ride today?" There was no enthusiasm in his voice.

"I'm not sure I'm going to go," Azure confessed as he

listlessly cut into his eggs.

"Oh?" Manny sounded surprised. "Why not? Want to stay and help me on the farm." He cast a smile at Meva who returned it in kind.

Azure felt guilty for declining, but farming had never been on his list of things to do. “There are some women at the goblin settlement that I'm thinking of rescuing first.”

Manny guffawed. “Look at you trying to be the hero.”

The mockery in his words made Azure scowl. “What's so wrong with wanting to be a hero?”

"You have to be alive to be a hero." Manny turned his attention back down to his plate. "That's a suicide mission."

"I hate to say I told you so," Lonnell chimed in from across the table.

"Uden was a hero," Azure mumbled.

All of the laughter drained from Manny's voice. “And now he's dead.” He gave Azure a pointed look. “Don't go chasing after lost causes. The world is full of wrongs that you won't be able to right.

"Sure, you could save those girls, but what about the hundreds of others held captive in other goblin settlements across The Realm? Where's their rescue? Their justice? And if you did manage to rescue them all, then how would the goblin race survive? No woman is voluntarily going to want to breed with them. You have to think of the ecosystem. Everything has a purpose."

*That's a little warped*, Azure thought, but he didn't say it. "And what's the purpose of the goblins? All I've seen them do is raid, pillage, and rape."

"Goblins can subsist on a lot of aggressive plant and animal life that humans and other creatures cannot. And although they're a nuisance, they also take on other threats, often killing dangerous monsters around their settlements which keeps them from making their way to human villages. Every creature in The Realm has its purpose. It's not their fault that they cannot procreate on their own."

"I personally still think we should kill them all. Or at least most of them," Meva said in a near whisper.

*It's the fucked up circle of life.*

"That still doesn't make it right," Azure insisted.

"No. But it's a necessary balance," Manny told him. "More often than not, the goblins buy women from slaver ships. As sad as it is to say, these are people that no one will miss. Most of them don't have families, and the ones that do probably wouldn't even be able to make it back to them if they were freed."

"Again, that still doesn't make it right," he reiterated.

"Listen, Azure," Manny leaned back in his chair. "If you want to make it your life's work to liberate these women, that's all well and good. But if you're going to rescue them, you also have to be prepared to care for them. To feed and clothe them. That takes money. You also have to be willing to help the ones that want to return home to do just that. That takes money AND time. And while you're busy doing all of those things, the goblins will just keep buying new slaves to keep their race alive. Unless you plan to annihilate them all, in which case you'll need an army. It's too big of a job for one man on his own. So think about that all very carefully before you choose this as your path."

Azure deflated. Manny had a lot of good points, many of which were the same that Uden had made. It just killed him to think of those women suffering. He knew better than to hope that he could commit mass genocide on the goblins and end this problem of women being used for breeding stock. Even if he was able to escape with the women and not die in the process, Manny was right, the goblins would just find more women. The problem was cyclical. Perhaps his time would be better invested in finding a diplomatic solution to the problem...if goblins were even capable of diplomacy. Like scouting out women willing to bear goblin children for a certain amount of coin. Surrogates. But if he were to make it work, first he'd have to find women willing to be on board with the idea. From what he could tell, there weren't many unmarried women in Cragbell. He highly doubted that any that were available would be willing to volunteer for the job.

For a moment, Azure wondered if he should be more outraged that there were slaves in The Realm. That was the perfect way for the goblins to find breeding stock without bringing down the wrath of the human settlements around them by kidnapping women. But even if he were somehow able to end slavery, it wouldn't end the goblins' need for human women.

"So what are you going to do?" Lonnell asked him, interrupting his thoughts.

Azure felt sick. He had vowed to save those women, but it didn't seem possible right now. As long as they were held captive, the quest would wait for him. His joint quest with Lonnell, however, probably wouldn't.

With a long sigh, he submitted to defeat. “I suppose I'll be getting on the ship with you.”

"Good." Manny lightly banged his fist on the top of the table. "I'm glad you've come to your senses."

*Someday*, he told himself, hoping that it wasn't just a lie. There had been many things in his real life that he'd vowed to do that he'd never gotten around to completing. This seemed more important, though. He didn't want it to be the same.

They finished breakfast and then went about preparing for the trip. Azure restocked his arrows one last time, then he met up with Lonnell to head down to the pier. The journey took them in a direction that he hadn't traveled in before, but was rather uneventful.

Eventually, the treeline broke to reveal a small pier built off of the sandy shore. Aside from a rowboat pulled up next to the pier, the only vessel present was a cog about twenty meters long. Its one mast supported a single plain white sail.

Two men were standing on the pier talking, one of which was Ruthren. His cart was nowhere to be seen, so Azure assumed that it must already be on board. Lonnell took the lead as they stepped foot onto the old wooden pier. Neither of the men seemed to acknowledge them, deeply engaged in conversation, until the adventurers approached. Even then, Ruthren's eyes flicked toward them a few times before he deigned to address them.

"Hey. You made it!" He threw up his arms in welcome. "I wasn't sure you would. Captain Gail here was about to leave you behind. I was trying to stall him." Ruthren winked at them.

"Is that what ya were tryin' ta do?" the captain laughed. "Yer usually long-winded, but even I thought this was a bit much."

Captain Gail's long white wavy hair was loosely tied back with a black ribbon yet still appeared wind-beaten. There were strands of color running through it that suggested he might have once been blond or auburn-headed. A thick red bandana was wrapped around his head and tucked under his ponytail in the back. Dark splotches covered his weather-worn face, but Azure couldn't tell if it was a mass of freckles or sun spots. His skin looked rough like leather and had a deep red tint to it. A mix of salt and pepper whiskers blanketed his jaw and neck. Adorning his body was a simple white shirt with a blue captain's jacket and black breeches. On top of those were black boots that went almost up to his knees. He was tall and lanky in build, and while he looked like he could mean business when he wanted to, his dark brown eyes were warm and welcoming.

"Ruthren can talk a lot," Lonnell pointed out with a nervous laugh.

"He tells me ya want ta buy passage aboard my lovely vessel." Captain Gail gestured back to his ship, cutting straight to business.

"We would." Azure nodded. "How much is it?"

The captain looked them up and down critically as if the fee was dependent upon how he assessed them. "For ya gents, one gold and five silver a piece. Since yer friends with ol' Ruthren here, I knocked off a whole silver for ya."

That was a lot more than Lonnell had guessed it would be. Luckily, Azure had budgeted extra just in case. While he wasn't thrilled about the price, there was no way he wasn't going to pay it.

They emptied the coin into their palms and handed it over to the captain. There was no greed in his eyes as he took the fee and placed it in the satchel at his hip. Once he was done, he addressed them again. "I hope ya enjoy your ride on the Shropshire. Now that that business is taken care of, we should set sail. It's a bit of a journey, and I'd like to be deep into The Misty Waters before nightfall."

"The Misty Waters?" It was all Greek to Azure.

"That's what the sea between here and Squall's End is called," Lonnell leaned in to inform him.

"Ya not from around here?" Captain Gail raised a bushy eyebrow.

"I was thinking the same thing of you." Azure smiled, not sure how to explain himself. "Your accent is very similar to his girlfriend's." He nodded toward Lonnell.

The captain guffawed before responding. "No, I'm not from around here. Not many people are from around these parts. I hail from the far north in the Land of Air. And you, sir?"

"He has amnesia," Lonnell quickly butted in. "We're still trying to figure out where he's from."

Captain Gail scratched his whiskers. “Ya have a Patheanian accent, so I imagine yer from around here somewhere. Probably the mainland, though, if no one here can identify ya. Maybe you'll find yer family when ya return.”

*My family?* It was strange for Azure to remember that he had no family here. Strange...and lonely. Though he wasn't sure why it felt lonely. Once he'd moved from Ohio to California for his job at Radical Interactive, he barely saw his family anymore. In fact, he had only spoken to them on the phone once a month. It made him feel like a bad son. Never had he thought he would regret the distance.

"Well, that's enough small talk. Wouldn't want ta run inta the sirens in the daytime just because I was chitchatting." Captain Gail winked again, though Azure was missing the joke...if there was one.

"Ah yes, the sirens," Ruthren said with distaste.

"The sirens." Azure's eyes lit up. "I should like to see them," he told his companions as they walked to board the ship.

"No, ya wouldn't lad." The captain waved his interest away. "They're overrated."

"Sea bitches." Ruthren grunted.

"Sea bitches," Captain Gail parroted with a chuckle.

"Well, I would like to see these sea bitches," Azure insisted.

Once they'd boarded, Captain Gail branched off from them to head to the bridge while Ruthren took them below deck to show them where they'd be sleeping. Before they'd even come back up, the ship was pulling away from the pier. This was it. Azure was finally leaving Crescent Island, and a new adventure was about to begin.

## CHAPTER ELEVEN
THE REALM – Day 39

Azure and Lonnell stayed on deck, leaning over the railing watching Crescent Island get smaller and smaller in the distance as they sailed away from it. Lonnell's expression was unreadable, and Azure could only assume that his friend was having some anxious thoughts.

"We'll find Bronna. Don't worry," he said in the way of comfort.

"I know."

"Your parents will be fine without you, if that's what you're worried about."

"I know that as well."

Lonnell didn't seem to be in a talking mood, so Azure left it at that.

The cog was manned by a crew of ten. All were men except for one, a woman only slightly younger than the captain. She hung out mostly on the bridge, spending her time speaking with Captain Gail. Since she didn't seem to be doing anything particularly productive, Azure assumed that she was likely his wife. There was no ring on her finger, but that didn't necessarily mean anything. On a ship, it probably wasn't very practical to wear such jewelry. Also, Azure wasn't even sure if rings were part of the wedding customs in The Realm.

Once Crescent Island disappeared from sight, the voyage quickly became boring. There was nothing for Azure and Lonnell to do besides stare at the sea or lounge around below deck. It should have been a nice reprieve from all of the walking and adventuring they'd been doing, but Azure found it incredibly dull.

Most of the men were busy helping with running the ship. Ruthren had stowed himself away below deck to drink. Azure planted himself next to the merchant, hoping for a handout and some interesting stories. He stared at the bottle of whiskey in Ruthren's hand, but the man seemed to have no intentions of sharing.

"Do you have any whiskey for sale?" he finally asked, willing to pay for entertainment at this point.

"Libations are not something that I trade in," the merchant told him, still not willing to offer him a drink.

"I should have bought some before we boarded this ship. I had no idea how boring it would be." Azure sighed, leaning against the wall next to Ruthren.

"Aye. There's nothing glamorous about traveling this way. Lots of motionless hours. No fun for guys that are used to being on the run. But your money is probably better spent on something to read than on something to drink. Unless, of course, you plan to drink until you pass out." The merchant raised an eyebrow at him, sniffing for a sale.

"I am admittedly nauseous," Azure confessed, feeling it even as he said it. "Somehow, I've been able to keep from vomiting, but I fear that reading would send me over the edge."

"Then you don't want any of this." He raised the bottle. "It's one of the quickest ways to puking. Actually, your next meal should be quite entertaining."

That wasn't a pleasant assumption. Azure didn't want to make his motion sickness worse, but he knew he couldn't go without eating forever.

"Who is the woman?" he asked.

"The woman?" Ruthren raised a bushy eyebrow.

"The one on board this ship. The only one I've seen."

Understanding hit him. "That's Jade. She's the Shropshire's sea mage."

"Sea mage?" Azure had never heard that term before in any game that he'd ever played. It sounded like a specialized class.

"Yes. That's what they call casters that work on ships like this," the merchant confirmed Azure's thoughts on the matter.

"Ah." He nodded. "What's the likelihood that I'm going to get to see magic on this voyage?"

"Depends." Ruthren cocked his head to the side in thought.

"On what?" Azure pressed him for details.

"If we're attacked by any monsters."

"What's the probability of that?"

"I don't think we're hauling anything that would attract them, and Crosley is pretty good about staying out of their territory. I mean, Captain Gail," he quickly corrected himself. "I think I've only sailed with him once when we've encountered anything more dangerous than the sirens. They're guaranteed to show up, though. Harpies of the sea, they are."

"You really hate the sirens," Azure chuckled.

"I do. Lost a friend to one back when we were young and dumb. Or when I was young and dumb. He never got to become an old goat like me." His expression sagged.

"What happened?"

"Well," Ruthren sighed and shifted his weight, "there are times of the year when the water is just the right temperature for them to venture further inland. My friend, much like you, had wanted to see them. Of course, their beauty is legendary, so any hot-blooded young man would want to catch a glimpse. But it's not worth the danger. We've all heard enough horror stories to know that. Sirens are the main cause of death at sea. Not storms or hydras or any other horrible beast." He took a quick swig from the bottle before continuing. "We all told him it was a bad idea, but he insisted. Said he'd stuff his ears with cotton and tie himself to the boat he was in and he would be fine. He sailed out and never returned."

Azure thought on that for a moment. “It doesn't sound like there's any real proof that it was the sirens that killed him. It could have been a number of things. Maybe he's not even dead. Perhaps he sailed on to someplace else.”

Ruthren gave him an annoyed side-eye. “He's dead. And it was definitely the sirens that killed him.”

"But how do you know for sure?"

"That boat was nothing special. Little more than a rowboat. A school of sirens could have easily tumped it over. That's what I'm guessing happened."

There was no point in arguing with the merchant. He was well-convinced that he was right about this one. And what did Azure really know about the man he was talking about?

"So when will I get to see the sirens?" Azure asked, feeling like it was a somewhat insensitive question after what Ruthren had just disclosed about his friend's demise. Still, the story would not dissuade him.

"We'll be sailing into their waters about the time that everyone beds down for the night. If you're that dead set on seeing them, I'll tie you to the mast. You'll have to plug your ears with cotton when Jade casts Deafening Shriek; otherwise, you'll be affected by it. Then you'll have to take the cotton out of your ears to hear their song. Or rather, someone else will have to do it for you. Kind of hard to do it yourself when you're all tied up."

Azure hadn't thought about that. Hadn't factored in how helpless he would be.

"Would you do it for me?" he asked apprehensively, hoping that Ruthren would be bored enough to humor him.

"Nope." The merchant shook his head. "Just seeing those fishy bitches would make me want to take out a spear. You're on your own with this one."

With a sigh, Azure relented to the fact that he'd get no help from the merchant, either with his personal quest to see the sirens or to get drunk. It was hard not to be disappointed as he pulled himself off of the floor to go find Lonnell. He had been wrong about Ruthren; the merchant was no fun at all.

Azure found Lonnell sitting on a bench above deck with his nose tucked into a thick tome. It was apparent that he had had a better idea of what to expect on the journey overseas than Azure had. Or perhaps he already had the book on him.

"What are you reading?" Azure sat beside him, less interested in the book than in figuring out how to segue into his request.

Lonnell closed the book, using his thumb as a bookmarker. He glanced over the cover as if he didn't even remember himself. It was royal blue with beautiful swirling golden text that Azure couldn't understand. The cover was bordered in ornamental leaves, and the pages had been painted gold on the ends so that when the book closed, it looked like a gold bar beneath the cover. It was the most intricate book Azure had seen since coming to The Realm, not that he'd had too many to compare it to. Probably expensive, he thought.

"It's *The Tales of Arun Pervaris*," he said before flipping the book back open.

"*The Tales of Arun Pervaris*," Azure parroted. "Sounds like a fancy name. Who was he?"

"Arun Pervaris was one of the last wood elves. This book is a collection of the adventures that he went on to try to save his race."

"I'm guessing it didn't succeed if he was one of the last." Azure rubbed the back of his neck.

"No." Lonnell sighed. "It's a tragic tale, really. At the end of the book, he's betrayed by humans. His body was given to alchemists to be used for parts. His race died out a few years later. Or rather, were hunted to extinction."

"That's horrible." He screwed his face. "Why?"

"Elves were some of the most magical creatures to ever grace The Realm. Many of their body parts could be used to make powerful potions. An evil necromancer who was also a master alchemist discovered this. Other alchemists noticed that he was performing magic through alchemy that no one had ever seen before. Once the secret was out, the hunt was on.

"The Realm is filled with alchemists and mages. Elves, in all forms, are a long-lived race. They didn't often reproduce, so they weren't able to replenish the lives that were lost. Humans hunted them to the last one all for the sake of...magic," he said distastefully. "Magic that upset the balance. Magic that was never meant to be."

"But you just said it was alchemy," Azure corrected him.

"It was an abominable type of alchemy. Magic and alchemy married into one. While the process of creating these potions was technically by alchemic means, the results were unnatural. The magic was so unique that the potions were given their own class. They were called Elf Spirits, for it was believed that part of the reason why these potions were so powerful and so magical was because every elven component was made up of a piece of that elf's soul. It was really quite grotesque, if you ask me."

"That does sound horrible," Azure agreed. "So that means there are no elves left in The Realm?"

"None. Both wood elves and high elves were decimated. That was a little over two-hundred years ago."

"Well, that sucks." He was admittedly disappointed, not just acting. Elves had always been his favorite race in most games...unless they were the Keebler variety. They were otherworldly beautiful and seemingly graceful. It was hard to imagine a fantasy game without them. Even the original version of The Realm had them as a selectable race. Azure didn't understand why they'd been taken out. The lore behind it was all well and good, but it was still kind of sad.

"Anyway, that's part of what this book is about." Lonnell lifted it, drawing Azure's attention. "One of the last things that Arun did was defeat the necromancer. Krezor the Plaguebringer, they called him. The cool thing is that their combat was one on one. Elf magic versus dark magic.

"Of course, no one is sure if that's how it really all went down because no one was there. All they know is the story that Arun told before he died. But all elves are innately good and not prone to lying, so there was no reason not to believe him.

"The battle is painted epically in this book. I would have liked to have seen it with my own eyes." Lonnell stared out into the distance for a few moments as if picturing the battle before snapping back to. "You can read it when I'm done, if you'd like."

Azure glanced down at the book. Considering that it hadn't crumbled into dust from Lonnell looking at it, he could only assume that it wasn't something that he could mass digest like the language books he had read before. A book that thick would likely take him more than the boat ride was long to finish.

"I'm afraid I can't read Elvish," he said with false regret. While the tale did sound entertaining, he had never been a big history buff. And if he wasn't interested in reading about history in his own world, then why would he care about it in this one?

"Pity." Lonnell frowned. "That will probably change when you get to Hawking's. Many of the life spells are in Elvish. I assume it will be a prerequisite before you can learn them."

Azure wondered if it would be like college and he'd have to buy the book himself. That would suck, but he'd do what he had to do.

"So," not able to find a smooth place of transition, Azure tried to segue into what he really wanted to know, "are you planning on staying out and seeing the sirens tonight?"

Lonnell snorted. "I have no death wish. Besides, I doubt Bronna would approve of me looking at other women, even if they are the fish-tailed variety."

"Oh, come on. I'm sure Bronna isn't that uptight. She seems like a fun gal." Azure elbowed him playfully, but he wasn't smiling.

"No. If that's what you're into, more power to you and have a blast, but whenever the sun goes down, I'm going to bed."

"Well, that sucks." Azure's entire body sagged. "I was hoping you would at least stay on deck and help me watch."

Lonnell lifted an eyebrow. "How am I supposed to help you watch?"

"Ruthren said I would need someone to pull the cotton out

of my ears once Jade finishes casting Deafening Shriek, because my hands will be bound to the mast."

"And how am I supposed to do that if I'm also tied up?"

"I had assumed you wouldn't be."

Lonnell chuckled and shook his head.

"What?" Now it was Azure giving him a strange look.

"You really don't know how things work, do you?" When Azure didn't deign to respond, Lonnell continued. "Sirens emit a...frequency of sorts. Seeing one is enough to make you crave getting closer. Imagine two magnets held really far apart, but not so far that they lose their magnetism. The closer they are together, the stronger the pull. You'll feel the pull as soon as you see a siren. As it approaches the ship, that pull will only get stronger. What I'm trying to tell you is that just seeing one is enough to make you want to jump overboard. Only the strongest of men can resist.

"Hearing a siren, on the other hand, will drive you mad. You will not be able to resist the compulsion at all. You will stop at nothing to get free to get to the siren. That is where their real power lies."

"So what you're saying is that even if you were unbound, you wouldn't be able to escape their spell?" Azure simplified.

"Yes." He gave a curt nod.

"But what if you didn't look? What if you just focused on me?"

Lonnell sighed. “It's entirely too risky. Not worth it when one wrong glance could spell the end for me.”

It was understandable. This wasn't something necessary, just something that Azure wanted to do. And it was seeming less and less like it was actually going to happen.

"So wait." His head perked up in thought. "If what you're saying is true, then how does the captain steer the ship when there are sirens?"

"He doesn't," Lonnell replied, casting his gaze at Jade where she stood at the bow with her arms wrapped around herself. "The sea mage does. It's the most important job on the ship next to being the captain. While the sirens are out, she will be making sure that we stay on course. If any drunk idiot happens to wander on deck, it's her job to protect them with her spells."

"Oh." Azure was admittedly impressed. "But what about her? Wouldn't she fall prey to the sirens as well?"

"Most women are immune. There's a very small percentage who are not, and you can probably guess where their sexual appetites lie."

"Interesting. That makes sense though, I suppose." He stared at the woman while she stared out at the sea, presumably watching for sirens and other potential threats.

"Having said that, she'll be the one who cares for you while you're tied to the mast, if that's still what you want."

Azure felt a bit guilty for being selfish enough to still want to see the sirens. If Jade was going to be the only person on deck once the sun went down, it would probably be a pain in the ass for her to tend to him. He didn't want her to dislike him, but at the same time, he wasn't sure when or if he'd ever get a chance to see sirens again.

"I suppose I should go speak to her then," he said, pulling himself up from the bench.

"Go on then." Lonnell shooed him off, eager to get back to reading his book.

Trying to figure out how to approach, Azure paused for a moment. When he thought he was ready, he took apprehensive steps, wondering if Jade would even accept his request. He was sure she'd tell him he was being foolish like everyone else had.

Jade turned before Azure was able to reach her, looking lost in thought. She smiled softly at him. A gust of wind caught her long fading auburn hair, sweeping it into her face, and she quickly moved to brush it out of the way.

“Hey there,” she said in the way of greeting.

"Hi. I'm Azure." He held his hand out.

Jade glanced down at it for a moment before turning her eyes back to the sea. “Nice ta meetcha, Azure.”

"And you're Jade?" He hesitantly stepped up beside her, following her gaze to see what she was looking at. The deep blue water rolled in the distance but seemed relatively calm. All that could be seen for miles was the ocean, a vast wasteland of unforeseen wet dangers.

"I am," she replied, keeping her answers short.

"Ruthren told me you're this ship's sea mage."

"I am," Jade said again.

"How does one become a sea mage?"

Her eyes shifted to him, dark brown and narrow beneath thin eyebrows. She assessed him, much as Captain Gail had before he had told them their fee for boarding the Shropshire. “Ya couldn't become one, so what does it matter?”

"Why couldn't I become one?" Azure furrowed his brow, trying not to be offended.

"Because yer a boy. Only women are sea mages."

"Oh..." He shifted his weight. "I suppose that makes sense...with the sirens and all." There was a long uncomfortable silence between them. It quickly became clear to Azure that she was a woman of few words. "Speaking of sirens..."

"No." She turned away from him abruptly, heading towards the bridge.

He gave chase. "Please. I've never seen them before."

"And the better ya are fer it." Jade didn't slow. "Ma brother told me ya would ask this, and I already told him no."

"Why not?" Azure asked stubbornly, realizing that it almost sounded like whining.

Jade spun on her heels, and he practically ran into her. "Because this isn't an entertainment ship. If ya want ta see sirens, there's a vessel in Chaman Bay that takes men out ta see the sirens fer a fee."

"Where's Chaman Bay?"

"In the Kingdom of Noseon," she told him before continuing up the stairs.

Azure hesitated, feeling like he would get in trouble for going onto the bridge, but then he decided to continue up anyway. It wouldn't be long before the sun faded over the horizon, and he wasn't about to let this go. "But I'm not planning on going to Noseon."

"That's too bad for ya, then." Jade took the wooden steps two at a time, seemingly in a hurry to get away from him.

They reached the top where Captain Gail was manning the helm. Thankfully, he didn't seem angry when he saw Azure trailing behind Jade. In fact, a broad smile took over his face.

"Ya asked her, didn't ya?" His grin grew wider.

"You knew she was going to say no." Azure glared at him.

"She always does." He laughed.

Jade had reached Captain Gail's side and turned to flank him. He placed a hand on her shoulder, giving her an overzealous side hug as if they'd both just played a big joke on Azure.

"If you knew she was going to say no, then why didn't you tell me to begin with?"

"Because she's my sister, and I love antagonizing her." Captain Gail leaned away from Jade to look at her, and she quickly slapped his chest, pulling out of his grasp.

"Yer an ass." She glowered at him.

"Yes, I am," he replied, clearly proud of it. "All joking aside, though, ya should let the boy have his fun. Ya only see a siren fer the first time once."

"And it's often yer last time, too," Jade grumbled.

"It will be fine." The captain waved her worry away. "You'll keep him safe."

"That shouldn't be my responsibility." She crossed her arms over her chest.

"There are no obstacles in The Misty Waters. The ship practically steers itself. You'll have time ta tend ta him and steer the ship," he argued for Azure. Perhaps Captain Gail was on Azure's side after all. Or maybe he had just been wanting to annoy his sister. Whatever the case, as long as things fell in Azure's favor, he didn't care.

"The last thing I want ta have ta do is blow through my Mana potions just because this kid wants ta see sirens," she said irritably.

"Perhaps I can compensate you?" Azure dug into the satchel at his hip. At that, her eyes lit up. "How does two silver sound?" That was about twenty dollars in his world. Probably what he'd pay for the same experience in real life. Maybe? He'd never been sightseeing on a ship before.

Jade took the coins from him, but she didn't smile as she looked at them, her face still stuck in a half-frown.

"Look there, Jadie. He's even willing ta pay ya." Captain Gail nudged her, sounding excited for his sister, though Azure couldn't tell if it was genuine or fake enthusiasm.

"This isn't even enough ta cover two Mana potions at the market," she grumbled before sticking the coins in her purse.

"Oh, don't act like that," Captain Gail chastised her. "Ya make yer own potions anyway."

"If I didn't, I wouldn't be able ta afford ta eat with what ya pay me." She glared at him.

"Ya act like *you* pay fer them. It's a business expense."

It looked like the two were about to start fighting, so Azure decided to take his leave. “I'll come up when the sun goes down, yes?” He held both of his thumbs up, hoping to interrupt them long enough to get confirmation.

"Come back up in about an hour," Jade told him, still not looking happy.

"Good stuff. See you then." He waved to the siblings as he turned to walk away, listening to them squabble over finances until the wind drowned them out.

With nothing left to do but wait, Azure walked over to the railing and looked out onto the sea. Somewhere not far away, beautiful maidens were waiting for him. Could they even be called that if they weren't human? Sirens, he silently corrected himself.

Having something to look forward to made the hour pass incredibly slowly. Azure could tell when it was getting close to time, though, because the men on deck finished their duties and then headed below.

Captain Gail came by to pat him on the shoulder before retiring to his cabin for the night. “Ya don't cause my sister too much trouble now. Ta be honest, this isn't normally something I would force her ta do, but I know ya just lost a comrade and a friend. My condolences fer that. Just don't let the sea bitches trick you inta following them inta the drink after him.”

"I'll be tied up, so there's nothing to worry about." Azure wasn't sure if that was a statement or a question.

"Aye. You'll be fine, mate." Captain Gail gave his shoulder a final pat before taking his leave.

Once everyone was gone, Azure expected Jade to come retrieve him. She stayed on the bridge though, looking out over the sea. It seemed to be an obsession. There was something eerie about her, like she was always lost. Seeing her standing on the bridge, her hands draped over the helm, she reminded Azure of a ghost. Her long hair blew in the wind, silky and fine, and her baggy clothing beat against her body. She wore a simple white shirt and brown pants, both of which seemed to be several sizes too big. A variation of the tall boots that Captain Gail adorned were on her feet as well, though hers didn't go as far up her legs.

After waiting for what felt like fifteen minutes, Azure finally pulled himself away from the railing and went up to the bridge. The sun had already receded over the horizon, making the surface of the ocean even darker. Blue waters were turning purple and would soon be black as night set on top of them.

"I hope you didn't forget about me," he gave a nervous laugh.

"I didn't forget about ya, lad." There was no joy in her voice.

They stood there silently together for a while before Jade finally left the helm and motioned for Azure to follow her down the stairs. The next several minutes were awkward as she made him stand against the mast while she affixed him to it. Azure figured she must really hate him for this, because she looped the rope over him several times, tying it so tightly that it hurt. He half expected to see his health bar drop, but it didn't.

When she was done, Jade walked to the railing and waited.

Azure had only thought that the hour before had passed by slowly. Though, he hadn't been in extreme discomfort then. It seemed that as soon as Jade had finished tying him up, his nose began to itch. Of course, Azure wasn't about to ask her to scratch it for him. As it was, he already knew he was being a nuisance.

Azure's discomfort seemed to increase as time marched on. Soon, he was wondering if this was even worth it. He was pretty sure that his blood circulation was being cut off by the ropes. There would definitely be a bruise across his torso from where Jade had tied him when this was all done.

Just when he was about to tell her that he had changed his mind and wanted to be let go to join the men below deck, there was movement on the water. Only a ripple at first.

Jade stepped to the side so that she wasn't blocking Azure's view. Then she pushed herself away from the railing and approached him. “Are ya ready, kid? Here they come.”

He barely even heard her words, his eyes were so fixated on the water. A splash was heard in the distance, and then light broke onto the surface of the sea. There was the flash of a tail, the fins long and practically translucent, a glittering shade of pale purple. For some reason, he was able to see it clearly in the darkness. And finally, he saw the crown of a head. A literal crown of shells and pearls before the actual head popped above the water.

Something surged within him from the sight of the first siren, and it only increased with each new one that broke through the water's surface. There was a glow to them, reminding him of that of an anglerfish. Illumination used to lure in prey despite the darkness of night. They looked like women but at the same time didn't. Their skin was pale with a soft shimmer to it. Wet, like that of a dolphin or seal coming out of the water. Large eyes took up most of the real estate on their faces, reminding Azure of something he'd see in an anime—larger than life, framed with long, thick black eyelashes that seemed to fan in a come-hither fashion. Their noses were tiny, barely dots on their faces, but their lips were full and fleshy looking. Desirably kissable, all set in a sexy pout as if they were sad that he was on the ship and they were stuck down in the water.

They made no noise at first, simply staring at him. Their eyes darted from Azure to Jade, and he could sense that they saw her as a threat of sorts. Silent hunger washed through the air. Azure felt it as something sexual, but he knew that the siren's hunger was for a different kind of flesh.

If his erection wasn't already apparent just from looking at them, there was no denying it when they started pushing their bodies out of the water. It was unlike anything Azure had ever expected to see. They seemed to be able to propel themselves until they were a little more than waist-height exposed. All of their human flesh was on display for his enjoyment, only the V from the beginning of their tails still peeking out of the water, that of which extended down to very human vaginas, their mounds completely hairless and slick like the rest of them. But that wasn't half as titillating as their breasts, Azure thought. Coming in all shapes and sizes, each one had a tiny starfish over their nipples, leaving nothing else to the imagination. And each starfish pulsated as if it was sucking on the nipple that it covered. It was incredibly erotic, and Azure found himself wishing that his mouth was those starfish.

It was strange to Azure that he felt so compelled to have sex with a creature that was clearly not human, but the magnetism that Lonnell had spoken about was definitely there. He wanted to get closer, and the closer that the sirens came to the ship, the more he felt the pull to be near to them. Lecherously, his mind raced, and he knew he would be ashamed of his thoughts once this was all over. They were only sex objects to him. He saw them as nothing else. Dolls to indulge in selfishly, though he had an irrationally strong feeling they'd enjoy it. It's like they were beckoning to him with those oversized eyes, speaking a silent language that only he could hear. It said, “Come to us. We'll take care of you. You'll never want for anything again.”

Azure was in turmoil, knowing that the sirens' beauty was an illusion of his mind but being unable to tear his eyes away now that he'd seen it. No other women existed anymore. Nothing was ever so attractive as the smorgasbord of finned Goddesses before him.

Desperately trying to fight the need within him, Azure tore his eyes away only to look down and see that his hands were already fretting with the ropes. How had he not noticed that he was pulling at them? Were the sirens making him lose control of his entire body?

And then the most beautiful and painful thing he'd ever experienced happened. They began to sing.

It wasn't just one voice that rose up from the ocean, but a choir of voices all in perfect harmony. A choreographed song, weaving a wickedly peaceful melody that only made his desire surge.

"Sailor at sea so far from home.

You travel on water, The Realm you roam.

No fair skin you touch, your bed is laid bare,

but I have the cure if only you dare.

You've been fed a tale, that's all a big lie.

They say if you enter the water you'll die.

But all that I want is to share my warm kiss.

If you enter the water, my promise is this.

I'll give you my love, and I'll protect your life.

I'll bear your children and become your sea-wife.

You will never want for anything more.
I can be your lover and also your whore.
So come to the water. Ignore what they said.
The dangers they warned of are all in your head.
Come see for yourself. I'll show you the way.
I'll love you for life. In my arms, you will stay."

They seemed to be singing in multiple languages, several of which Azure couldn't understand, but the song blended beautifully, and he was reasonably sure they were all singing the same thing anyway.

The world around Azure disappeared. Suddenly, nothing mattered but being with the sirens. Their song conjured images of a life at sea. Not at sea, but in the sea. He was a king surrounded by a harem of sirens, all tending to his most devious sexual desires. It was then that he realized his one purpose in life. To make that vision a reality.

"Let me go," he growled maliciously at Jade while trying his best to wriggle free of the ropes.

She replied to him, but he couldn't hear it. All his ears would allow to enter was the sirens' song over and over again. But she was smiling at him. A knowing smile. A mocking smile. That bitch was keeping him from everything he'd ever dreamed of. He'd rip her to shreds when he got these cursed ropes off. Rip her to shreds and then join his loves in the sea. Anyone who kept him from them deserved to die.

Struggle as he might, Azure couldn't free himself. The desperation inside of him reminded him of what a cocaine addict must feel like coming down from a high. Except it was constant. Constant pain from needing to be with the sirens. What was worse was that his whole body was feeling the effects. His ears were filled with nothing but their song. His head swam with a barrage of images of what he was missing out on. He knew he was tearing the skin of his hands away fighting with the ropes. The red, wet tint left behind was proof of that. But he couldn't feel it. Not that pain, at least. What he was acutely aware of was the aching in his balls. It was like he was being edged over and over again, and the only thing that would give him release was getting to the sirens. It was the most miserable, wonderful torture he'd ever experienced. But there was no reprieve from it.

The song carried on for hours as the sirens followed the ship, gazing at Azure longingly—willing him to break free from his bondage and join them. At some point, Jade went back up onto the bridge to check the helm, but she was back some fifteen minutes later to make sure that Azure hadn't somehow freed himself.

All he could do was beg for her to untie him. Tears fell down his face in a pitiful display. Squirming and pulling at the ropes was getting him nowhere, but he wasn't about to give up.

"Ya wanted this," she told him. "Now deal with the consequences."

Azure tried everything to get her to let him go, all the way up to claiming that he was having a heart attack. She would not budge, though. The stubborn old woman had likely seen every trick in the book when it came to men trying to get free to be with the sirens. Even if his lie had been true, he doubted she would have released him.

Finally, the sirens gave up and receded beneath the sea's black surface. Darkness surrounded them except for the few lanterns aboard the ship. It was almost as if Azure felt his entire body sigh with relief as soon as they were gone, and a near crippling exhaustion followed. The pain he had experienced from intense longing had been replaced by the realization that his hands were now raw from tugging at the ropes so much. His stomach ached from pressing against them. Any bruises he'd have now couldn't be blamed on Jade. If it had been humanly possible, he probably would have sawed himself in half to get to the sirens.

"Are ya satisfied?" she asked mockingly. "I bet yer right sore from all that fitting."

"Are you sure it's safe?" Azure continued gazing at the sea. Even though he was beyond tired and filled with physical hurt from his exertion, he knew that if the sirens came back and he was free, he'd rush forward and jump overboard to get to them. Of that, there was no doubt in his mind.

"We should be out of their range by now. If not, I've got ya. Sirens are dangerous, but they're not smart enough to set traps. Usually, when they disappear, they're gone. Not always the case," Jade cocked her head to the side, "but most of the time."

Azure preyed that was the case. He couldn't be held responsible for what he'd do if he saw them again.

"I was so enthralled that I didn't even bother to cast Analyze," he thought out loud.

"They're weak," she told him, which was easy for her to say since she Analyzed as orange to him. All of the crew, including Captain Gail, Analyzed as either yellow or orange. That made sense though since they were on the sea all the time where horrible monsters lurked below. "It's their songspell and numbers that are the problem. A level one siren can easily take down a level one-hundred man if he's dumb enough to succumb to her charms. It's happened before."

That was rather surprising. He supposed that level didn't matter much after all, depending on your opponent's abilities. The sirens were definitely deadly despite their beauty and vulnerable, exposed bodies.

Just as the last of the ropes had been loosened, a light appeared on the horizon. Azure held his breath, already knowing what it was and that he shouldn't look, but he couldn't help himself. He just had to see the sirens again. He'd had his eye on a particularly innocent-looking red-headed one. Despite knowing it was wrong, he had to see if it was her. If she, specifically, had come back to charm him.

It wasn't the red-headed one, but that didn't matter. In an instant, Azure was pushing Jade away. She fell to the ground with an, "Oomph!" Before she even had time to stand, Azure had freed himself. Though there was only one siren this time—a raven-haired beauty—she started her song again. Other sirens popped up beside her to join in.

Azure made a run for the railing. His goal had been renewed. Now nothing was stopping him. He would get to the sirens.

At least, he thought he would until he heard a sound so loud that he thought his eardrums had been pierced by it. A status notification immediately popped up in his field of vision, but he quickly brushed it away so that he could continue towards his goal.

*You are now **deaf.** This effect will last for 50 seconds.*

Azure was almost to the railing. Just before he was about to place his hand upon it, a blue cloud appeared in front of him. He didn't even have time to react as it descended upon him with the speed of light, burning his eyes and throwing him onto his back.

***Jade Gail** delivers 25 damage. You are now **blind.** This effect will last for 25 seconds.*

Azure wailed and clawed at his eyes, feeling trapped in a dark, silent void. Panic washed over him as he realized he had lost two of his most important senses. If it weren't for the fact that he could still feel, Azure would have thought he was dead.

He didn't have time to process anything else that was going on. Someone reached for him, and his fear spiked as he worried that he had somehow made it to the edge of the ship and one of the sirens had gotten a hold of him. How stupid he had been for wanting to see them, Azure realized with despair. Now he was quite possibly about to be dragged to his death—a watery grave at the bottom of the sea. What was worse was that the sirens' spell had been broken, so he wouldn't even be able to enjoy it.

Momentarily, Azure thought about fighting whoever or whatever was gripping at him, especially when it began to drag him. His arm reached for the assaulting appendage, and he was relieved to find that it wasn't wet. It had to be Jade pulling him away from the edge. Didn't it?

Too afraid and shocked to stand, Azure allowed himself to be dragged, trying to calm himself by counting down to twenty-five. Only then would he be certain of his safety. But as soon as he got to the bottom of the countdown, he was only allowed a flash of sight.

This time, when he opened his eyes and his vision returned, there was no blue cloud preparing to descend and suck all the moisture out of his eyes. It was simply Jade standing in front of him with her palm outstretched. At least he knew it was her who had him now...seconds before she blew a handful of glittering dust into his eyes that rendered him blind again.

*You are now **blind.** This effect will last for 10 seconds.*

It was a different spell from the last time. Blessedly, he took no damage, and the effects wouldn't last as long.

Jade helped Azure to his feet. As soon as the ten seconds counted down, he was blasted in the eyes with sand again. This continued until they reached the stairs and she was able to safely get him below deck...which was a struggle when he also couldn't hear her to tell him when to step. Once his hearing came back, she shrieked at him again. Apparently, it wasn't safe for him to listen until they were well within the cargo hold. Finally, Azure's hearing and sight returned to him. It was more of a relief than he could have ever imagined.

Smack!

The sound was almost as startling as the sting to his cheek.

"Ya damn fool!" Jade chastised him, keeping her voice low so as not to wake the other men who were already sleeping, though it was a wonder that any of them had been able to fall asleep with Ruthren's loud snoring. "Are ya satisfied? Ya about went over the edge, and if that would have happened, I likely wouldn't have been able ta fish ya out."

He did remember the sirens rushing towards him just as quickly as he had rushed towards them. The magnets had been too close, ready to meet in the middle and bind together in blood and death. Azure shuddered to think about what would have happened if he had gone overboard. While he had no idea how the sirens actually killed or what they did with their prey, he imagined it was probably gruesome. Behind those soft, supple lips were rows of jagged shark-like teeth. He had noticed when one of them had smiled at him. At the time, it hadn't mattered. The sirens had him well convinced with their song that they'd never harm him—only give him pleasure beyond his wildest dreams. It was crazy how bewitching they were.

"Thank you for saving me," he told Jade with all sincerity.

"That was more trouble than it was worth. Now I'm going ta have ta drink a Mana potion," she grumbled, digging into the satchel at her side to extract one and drink it right in front of Azure as if he needed proof.

He was a bit confused as to whether or not she was expecting further compensation, but he didn't want to part with what coin he had left, especially since he knew that magic school was going to be expensive.

"You hurt me," he mentioned dryly.

"Ya were out of range of my Dirty Move spell. I had ta cast Blinding Winds on ya instead. It's a higher level spell and can't be cast without dealing damage. In that situation, it couldn't be helped," she told him. "It was either that or let ya jump overboard and die." She placed the empty vial back in her bag. Thankfully, some of the anger had dissipated from her voice, probably from the guilt of having to harm Azure to save him.

"While I did almost die," Azure said, glancing at the floor ruefully, "I am glad I got to experience the sirens. Now my curiosity is satiated."

"Curiosity killed the cat," Jade reminded him.

"I didn't even know there were cats here." He certainly hadn't seen any on Crescent Island.

"There wouldn't be any on the ship." She looked at him like he was daft.

He had meant in The Realm, of course, but didn't bother correcting himself. She wouldn't understand. But he knew that saying had come straight from his world. It was too coincidental not to.

"Anyway," Azure rubbed the back of his neck, "I'm exhausted. I think I'm going to hit the hay."

"The what?" Jade quirked her head back.

"Two can play the idiom game." He grinned at her before walking away to find a clean spot on the floor to lie down.

"Idiot," she mumbled before turning around to head back up to the deck.

## CHAPTER TWELVE
THE REALM – Day 42

Azure thought he was going to die of boredom before they reached the mainland. He got so bored that he even asked Ruthren what books he had for sale. Pickings were slim. His choices were *Arenas of The Realm, Dungeons of Chaos,* and *The Tale of Enzio Huxley*. Apparently, *Tales of* books were popular in The Realm, mostly being an accounting of history.

While Azure was most interested in the *Arenas* book, it carried an unreasonable price tag of two gold coins. Ruthren told him it was because the book was a rare item, but Azure thought that was bullshit. *Dungeons of Chaos* was six coppers while *The Tale of Enzio Huxley* was only one copper. Being a cheapskate, Azure went with Enzio Huxley, but regretted it when the merchant handed him what should have been called a pamphlet instead of a book.

*You have received the following item:*

| **Book:** ***The Tale of Enzio Huxley*** | **Quantity:** 1<br>**Durability:** 1/1<br>**Item Class:** Common<br>**Quality:** Average<br>**Weight:** 0.1 kg<br>**Uses:** Map |
|---|---|

It took him an hour to breeze through the book, which was basically about this guy who had gone in search of all of the Gods in The Realm. There was really no adventure to the journey, or if there was, it had been left out of the book, to Azure's disappointment. What the book mainly contained was a collection of geographic descriptions of each region where the Gods could be found as well as a rough sketch of each God. There was a crude map at the back that marked their general locations. For a while after reading the book, Azure thought about selling it back to Ruthren but then decided on keeping it. While he doubted he'd ever want to travel the entire planet to see all of the Gods, he never knew when the map might come in handy.

After several hours of doing nothing, Azure considered going back to Ruthren to buy *Dungeons of Chaos* as well, but he didn't want to have to break a silver to do it. If there was one thing he'd learned, it was that coin was hard to come by in The Realm. The merchant likely wouldn't repurchase the book at the same price either. It just wasn't worth it.

The rest of his time was spent meandering around the ship, making small talk with the crew and his travel companions, and sleeping. Eating wasn't a fun event, seeming to always make Azure's motion sickness rear up. And he was embarrassed when the captain guffawed at him for puking overboard on the second afternoon. By the time land finally came into sight on the fourth day, Azure decided that he absolutely hated sailing.

He hadn't been sure what to expect of Squall's End, but as

they approached, it quickly became apparent that it was much more than just a pier with a few small buildings. Seeing it get closer and closer made Azure feel like he was finally reaching medieval civilization. This was a town. A real town. Too bad Uden had never gotten to see it, he thought dolefully.

Azure felt like a dog waiting for its master to open the door. As soon as the gangway was put out, he practically sprinted across it to get to land. If it wouldn't have caused such a scene, he would have thrown himself onto the ground and kissed the dirt. This was freedom and adventure and everything else he'd missed.

Lonnell smirked at him as he followed along. “I never thought I'd see someone so happy to get off of a ship.”

Azure turned and stopped to wait for his friend. “I never thought it was possible to actually die of boredom, but I'm pretty sure it would have happened if I had to stay on that ship one more day.”

"It's because you don't know how to keep yourself properly entertained." Lonnell tapped his Bag of Holding, and Azure knew he was talking about the giant tome he had brought along.

"Reading isn't for everyone," he told his friend. "Hell, even the little bit I did while we were on board made me nauseous."

"Where are you boys headed to now?" Ruthren came up behind them, wanting to say his farewells before they went their separate ways.

"I suppose we're going to make the journey to Roselake now," Lonnell told him as he stretched and yawned.

It was early afternoon, but Azure felt exhausted as well. Sitting around doing nothing had somehow drained him of energy.

"That's a good walk. You boys best get going soon if you want to reach Roselake before nightfall."

"Five miles, give or take." Lonnell gave a curt wave of his

hand.

"Well, have safe travels. I'll be heading back up towards Noseon. I'm not sure when we'll cross paths again, but I doubt this will be the last we'll see of each other."

"I certainly hope not," Azure said with a smile. "You have safe travels, too." He clasped wrists with the merchant and then Lonnell did the same.

"Well," Lonnell turned toward the bustling town and took a deep breath, "I suppose we should get going."

As they walked through Squall's End, Azure was taken in by the wonder of the place. He had never seen such a variety of people in all his life. Women and men of all shapes, sizes, and skin tones, shorter stocky humanoids with thick plaited beards and muscular bodies that were obviously dwarfs. He even saw a miniature version of a dwarf talking to one of the shopkeepers.

Azure tapped Lonnell's shoulder, trying not to draw attention as he whispered. “What is that?”

"Hm." His gaze volleyed around, trying to see what Azure was talking about. "Ah. That is a gnome."

"A gnome," Azure parroted gleefully. The stout little man stood about two feet tall. He had a thick white beard and a bald head. Covering his eyes were a pair of black goggles with green lenses. Adorning his body was a tight white shirt beneath red suspenders. He looked like a steampunk miniature Santa Claus.

Lonnell slapped Azure's chest with the back of his hand. “Don't stare. It's rude.”

"Oh, right." Azure coughed, forcing his eyes away, though he kept the gnome in his peripheral vision.

Squall's End was awash with sights and smells and sounds. The entire town was surrounded by a wall of stone with lookout towers on the corners. There was only one entrance in and out and a dirt path that seemed to split the town in two until it reached the official buildings in the middle. At least, that's what Azure assumed they were because they were much larger and ornately designed than any of the other buildings. Just beyond the official buildings, the traveling merchants had set up their carts and were announcing their wares and their associated prices. Few of the buildings had any lettering on their signs. Most just had pictures of what they were. Against the walls were the permanent merchant shops. Though they didn't explore enough to see it all, Azure could make out a forge, a cobbler, and a bakery.

There were other buildings without signs. The first time Azure saw someone emptying a chamberpot out of the window of one, he realized they were residences. That would explain the stench of piss and feces that seemed to permeate the place. In all honesty, it mostly smelled horrible. A mix of animals and sewage and the sea.

*This is going to take some getting used to*, Azure thought. While he wanted to look around more, he knew he would be coming back here so there would be time for that later. Squall's End was the closest town to Roselake, and it was also next to Hawking's School of Land Magic, which he could hardly wait to visit. But first, he needed to help Lonnell find Bronna and complete the quest he had already committed to. Everything else could wait.

They stopped to ask someone for directions to Roselake before leaving the town. With a general idea of where they were headed, they passed through the gates and continued on down the dirt road. The land around them had a more country feel to it, devoid of the tropical trees and flora that dotted Crescent Island. A plain gave way to softly rolling hills. It was a comfortingly familiar topography, reminiscent of what Azure had seen in many games before.

After about a mile, they came to a fork in the road with a signpost. While it gave no direction as to what lay ahead, to the left, it read Hawking's, and to the right it said Roselake. At least now, Azure knew how to get to the magic school, he thought as they took the path to the right.

There was something incredibly wonderful yet boring about following a path. Back on Crescent Island, Azure had been used to traveling through difficult terrain. More often than not, Lonnell had been in the front hacking away with his machete at the foliage that blocked their way. There had been no human-made paths to Baremire or the goblin settlement.

Where they were now seemed well-traveled. Azure could see a good ways behind and in front of them, making him less cautious and fearful of being taken unawares. He wasn't naive enough to think that there weren't enemies in this part of The Realm, but he felt relatively safe following the path.

The forest grew in patches, giving way to fields of tall grass that blew in the breeze. As they continued on, the scenery slowly began to change, and it wasn't long before they found out how Roselake had gotten its name. A southern bend in the path revealed a lake to the west. Bordering its shore were hundreds of rose plants of various colors. It was unlike anything Azure had ever seen before, and he had to take a moment to pause and stare at it in wonder.

"Beautiful," he whispered.

Lonnell was less enchanted. He merely glanced at the lake but kept going. The village could be seen not far in the distance. It was clear that he just wanted to get there.

Roselake was a lot less streamlined than Cragbell had been. There was a path going through it but a wide berth between what few buildings were there. They seemed to dot the village in random places as opposed to being right next to each other, though they all faced the path that cul-de-saced at the end of the village.

"I'm guessing that's the tavern." Lonnell gestured to a building with a cup on its signage. "Best place to start as any."

Upon entering, Lonnell walked straight up to the bar to consult the barkeep about Cristopher Prescott. Azure would have liked to have sat down and had a drink—take a load off after all of their traveling, but his friend was a man on a mission.

The bartender pointed them in the direction of Cristopher's, and they set off again, finally leaving the path to traverse through the fields and forest. About a quarter mile to the southeast they stumbled upon a large wooden fence. Letting themselves in through the gate, they found several cows grazing inside. A small dwelling sat at the back of the property. While there was no arable land, there was a large animal pen to the right of it where about half a dozen pigs rooted through the mud for whatever scraps they could find. Two horses whinnied from a barn to the right, and a whole brood of hens clucked noisily from a hutch next to it.

Smoke billowed out of the smokestack of the house, carrying with it the scent of burning logs, though it was highly overpowered by the stench of the animals. It might have been a welcoming sight if not for the fact that there was a rooster standing in their path. If roosters were capable of narrowing their eyes, Azure would have been sure it was glaring at them. It took a few steps towards them, scratching at the ground before making a ruckus as it charged.

Azure knew he shouldn't be afraid—after all, he'd faced far worse than this—but he couldn't help but panic. He held up his hands and immediately started walking backward. “Oh, God. What do we do?” he said only a second before the rooster jumped to attack. Instinctively, he ran from it, causing Lonnell to burst out laughing. “Dude, this isn't fucking funny. Get it off of me.”

For some reason, the rooster didn't seem to have any interest in Lonnell.

"Some mighty warrior you are," he continued to laugh.

"I've never dealt with one of these things before. I don't know what to do. We can't kill it." Was that a question? The rooster Analyzed as blue, but damn was it ever aggressive.

Lonnell simply shook his head and ignored Azure, continuing on towards the house. The front door began to open, the occupants disturbed by the noise outside. A woman poked her head out before her body followed. She was short at only 4'10, with olive skin and curly brown hair that went all the way down to the small of her back despite being pulled back into a ponytail.

"Oh Red," she said in a southern drawl that was completely unexpected in comparison to all of the other accents Azure had heard so far, "why don't you leave those boys alone."

"Evening, ma'am," Lonnell greeted her. "We were wondering if this might be the residence of Cristopher Prescott."

"It is." She walked over to retrieve the rooster, giving Azure a reprieve from its attacks. He had already worked up a sweat from running from it. "What business do you have with my husband?"

Lonnell seemed relieved by the news that they were in the right place. “No business with him, ma'am. I came to see Bronna. Her father, Esau, told me that he'd sent her here to live with you. I was...kind of her beau back on Crescent Island.” He scratched the back of his neck nervously as he said it.

Before the woman even had time to respond, Bronna pushed past her and rushed into Lonnell's arms. He lifted her into the air and spun her around. It was, Azure thought, disgustingly cute how happy they were to see each other. He decided to ignore them, approaching the woman instead, though keeping a safe distance because that bloody rooster was still eying him murderously.

"Hi, ma'am. My name's Azure. And you are?"

"Owe," she replied almost absentmindedly, her gaze fixed on the two lovebirds, obviously not sharing in their happiness. If anything, she seemed concerned.

"Owe?" Azure asked, wondering if she was ignoring him

completely.

"Yes, Owe," she repeated.

"Are you all right?"

"Owe is my name," the woman clarified, finally realizing that Azure was confused.

"Ohhh. Owe," Azure parroted, tasting it as a name instead of a word. It seemed odd.

*Congratulations! Quest: **Find Bronna** has been completed.*

*You traveled over land and sea to help Lonnell track down his lost love. Bronna seems to be in good health and glad that you came. What the lovers do next is up to them. You have earned 90XP.*

*Congratulations! You are now **Level** 7! Your base stats have been boosted. You have earned 3 points to assign to your characteristics. Please note that adding points to some characteristics(Vitality, Intelligence, and Strength) will further boost your base stats. You may also advance any 1 skill of your choosing by 1 level.*

Finally! It felt like forever since Azure had last leveled up. Not that he'd really been doing anything that was too productive. He could hardly wait to assign his characteristic points, but he knew he was about to be dragged into a conversation at any moment, so now wasn't the time.

"Let's go inside," Owe suggested, opening the door wider for them to enter.

Lonnell slung his arm around Bronna's shoulder. As soon as they were all inside, Owe released the rooster to go back to its apparent duties of protecting the property from strangers. Azure kept his eyes glued on the door, not feeling safe until it was closed behind them.

The inside of the dwelling was much the same as Manny and Meva's place. There wasn't much in the way of furniture except for a table, a few chairs, and some cots. While there was a fire burning in the hearth, there was no pot bubbling over it. Azure's stomach gurgled in disappointment, wondering when the mealtime would be.

Lonnell led Bronna to a chair, pulling it out for her to sit down. The second she did, he knelt before her, taking her hands in his. “I know this is sudden, but when I returned to Cragbell and realized you weren't there, I thought about how much I didn't want to live without you. Bronna Prescott, will you marry me?”

The hobbit-like woman's face lit up with excitement, and she jumped into his arms again, knocking him back onto the floor as she chanted yes over and over again.

Azure wasn't sure if he should be happy for his friend or uncomfortable at what he was witnessing. Seeing as how Owe was displaying the latter of the two, he decided to side with her. This all seemed way too sudden. I mean, he hadn't even taken the time to tell her that Uden was dead.

Slowly, a soft smile crossed Owe's lips, and she shook her head.

Azure's thoughts were elsewhere. He had expected to feel a wave of depression"had thought that he'd be assaulted by all of the fading hopes and dreams he'd had about marrying Sheila someday. But they were just that. Fading. Even if he could have made things right, he'd likely never see her again. Besides, she had replaced him, so what did it matter. They were practically dead to each other. Maybe he even *was* dead. Whatever the case, it was time to move on. No more dreaming about a life that no longer existed.

"That's all well and good, you lovebirds," Owe broke them all out of their current personal fixations, "but what are you going to do to support yourselves? Do you have land?" she asked Lonnell.

He and Bronna looked up at her from the floor. “Well no...” Lonnell replied hesitantly.

"A house to call your own?"

"No."

"Do you even have a job?" She placed her hands on her hips.

"Well...no, but all of that will come in time." He waved her concerns away, smiling at his bride-to-be.

"Poppycock. All of that needs to come before the wedding," Owe insisted. "I am not letting you take this girl out of here until you can put a roof over her head."

"What?" Lonnell seemed startled by the news.

"You heard me. I didn't stutter. Bronna's father placed her in our care, and I'm not about to let her wander off with some penniless farm boy."

Damn, this woman had attitude. While Azure felt bad for his friend's spontaneous plans getting ruined, he couldn't help but like Owe for her protective nature and realistic view on the situation.

"I'll take her back to Cragbell," Lonnell told Owe, pulling himself from the floor.

"Do you have enough money to buy passage on a ship back to Cragbell for the both of you?" She eyed him skeptically.

A sheepish look took over his face. “Well, no.”

"Ey don't wanna go back ta Cragbell," Bronna whispered against Lonnell's arm as she stood and clung to him.

"It's the fastest way for us to be together. My parents would let us move in with them now that Uden's..." his voice trailed off, and his eyes roved over her face showing guilt.

"Did Uden move out? Is he here with ya?" She sounded way too excited by the prospect.

Lonnell turned to Bronna and gently held her by the shoulders as if he expected she would crumble from the news. “Bronna, Uden is dead.”

She gasped, drawing a hand up to her mouth. “Dead?”

"Yes. He died fighting The Dark One. He died...protecting me."

"Oh. That's horrible. I'm so sorry, Lonny." Bronna wrapped her arms around him for comfort.

"While I'm sorry for your loss, that doesn't change the fact that you don't have the coin to get back to Crescent Island," Owe told them.

Bronna looked up at Lonnell beneath a mask of sorrow. “Ey don't want ta go back ta Crags, Lonny. It's so boring. Der's no lyf fer us der. Here,” she gestured to encompass everything around them, “we have da world at ar feet. We can do whatever we want.” Her face lit up as if she had already completely forgotten about Uden's sacrifice.

Lonnell's expression was unreadable, but it was clear that he was deep in thought. Azure stayed silent, not having a horse in this race. No matter what the two of them decided to do, he was going to Hawking's School of Land Magic. If this was where they parted ways, then so be it. Azure felt he knew enough about The Realm now to be able to navigate it without Lonnell by his side, and what he didn't know, he could learn.

"Well, no matter what you decide to do, you're going to need money," Owe said.

Lonnell looked over at her. "Are there any farms around here that are hiring? I know how to plant and sow and harvest."

"I'm afraid not. Most of the people around here are too poor to take on workers."

It sounded much like things on Crescent Island. You either got your family to help you for free or you did it all on your own.

"What about you guys? I could help with the animals." Lonnell nodded towards the door.

"We can't afford to pay you either. It was hard enough taking on another mouth." Owe glanced over at Bronna.

"Ey could work at tha tavern in Squall's End," Bronna suggested quickly.

"You most certainly will not," Owe insisted. "Our job is to keep you safe, and we plan on doing just that. The tavern is no place for a lady.

"The only thing that I can suggest is the Adventurer's Guild, if you have the metal for it." She noted the staff strapped to Lonnell's back.

"Adventurer's Guild?" This piqued Azure's interest. It sounded like a fun way to make money.

"Yes. The locals submit quests there. Stuff they either can't take care of on their own or just don't want to deal with. Payment is usually dependent on the difficulty of the quest."

This was a familiar concept to Azure. He'd seen the same system used in many games before. The thought of finally being able to earn a decent amount of money was exciting.

"That sounds perfect, doesn't it?" Azure asked Lonnell,

who didn't seem anywhere near as thrilled as he was.

Lonnell sighed. “I suppose there's no other choice.”

"No, there's not," Owe agreed. "I won't let you marry Bronna until you can afford to put a roof over her head. If adventuring isn't your thing, then you can always just do it long enough to be able to afford some land and start a farm of your own."

"Speaking of farming, where is Cristopher?" Azure asked.

"He's in Squall's End running his shop. He's not a farmer. He's a cobbler. I'm the farmer." She smiled proudly.

"And apparently, I'm just a girl that sits around doin' needlework all day." Bronna glanced at an embroidery hoop sitting on a chair in the corner of the room with distaste.

"It's a good skill for a woman to have," Owe told her before returning her attention to Lonnell and Azure. "You're welcome to stay for dinner. After that, though, you have to be on your way. I'm sorry, but we can't afford to take on two extra mouths right now." Her hand went to her stomach, and for the first time since seeing Owe, Azure noticed a small bump. She was pregnant.

"We understand," he told her, wondering if it was hard for her to tend to the farm all by herself while her husband was in Squall's End. It was clear that she didn't want that to be any of their concern, though. More than likely, she set Bronna to the tasks that she didn't feel like completing. Some hard labor would probably do the girl some good. From what little Azure knew of her, it seemed as though Esau had spoiled Bronna rotten and allowed her to run wild.

Lonnell's mood seemed to sink by the second. “I suppose we'll have to find somewhere to stay then, too.”

"There's an inn in Squall's End. They rent rooms nightly, monthly, and yearly, depending on how long you plan on sticking around," Owe suggested.

"That sounds perfect, ma'am," Azure thanked her for the information.

Supper was served late, and most of the time before that was spent with Lonnell and Bronna occupying one corner of the room discussing their plans for the wedding and the future, Owe outside tending to the animals, and Azure tasked with the chore of plucking the chicken she had slaughtered for their dinner. He figured that his cooking skill would go up from the work, but no dice. At least, the task afforded him the time to go over his character sheet and assign his characteristic points.

He brought up his stats to analyze them and see where improvement was needed the most.

**Name:** Azure

**Race:** Human

**Level:** 7, 4% of the way to next level

**Health:** 210 / 210

**Mana:** 170 / 170

**Stamina:** 210 / 210

**Vitality:** 14

**Intelligence:** 10

**Strength:** 14

**Agility:** 13

**Dexterity:** 12

**Charisma:** 10

**Luck:** 12

**Skills:** Archery Lvl 3; 50% of the way to next level

Stealth Lvl 3; 57% of the way to the next level

Analyze Lvl 5; 46% of the way to next level

Cooking Lvl 5; 50% of the way to next level

Alchemy Lvl 3; 83% of the way to next level

Foraging Lvl 6; 3% of the way to next level

One-Handed Weapons Lvl 5; 6% of the way to next level

Tracking Lvl 1; 80% of the way to next level

Two-Handed Weapons Level 5; 0% of the way to next level

**Languages:** Common Tongue, Sprite, Goblin-Tongue

Azure felt pretty comfortable with his Health and Stamina. He doubted he would be facing any incredibly powerful foes anytime soon. Starting magic school was his top priority, and to be able to cast all of the spells he planned to collect, he would need

Mana. Worrying that he was being perhaps a bit too overzealous, but deciding to be reckless anyway, Azure placed all three of his available characteristic points into Intelligence, raising his Mana to 200.

In regards to leveling a skill, he faced the same conundrum as last time. Both his One-Handed and Two-Handed Weapons skills were at the start of a new level. But Azure didn't foresee himself picking up another two-handed weapon anytime soon, and he'd already sold the iron halberd. That made his decision much easier.

*Congratulations! The skill:* ***One-Handed Weapons*** *has reached Level 6. This skill enables you to use all manner of one-handed weapons to defeat enemies. What you do with your other hand is up to you.*

Cristopher returned from Squall's End just after the sun had set. Taller than his brother by a few inches, Cristopher was a barrel of a man. His hair was dark and stringy and swept to one side. Pinched eyes and plump cheeks framed a wide nose. No one would probably be able to tell that he was related to Esau if they didn't know.

He gave the boys a warmer welcome than his wife had, interested in the tale of how they had crossed The Misty Waters and guffawing at Azure's foolishness for having wanted to see the sirens. When he asked if they were really as beautiful as he'd been told, Owe gave him a slicing gaze. That didn't keep him down for long, though.

They finished their meal in merriment that Azure hadn't expected. Cristopher even offered for the boys to sleep on the floor, to which his wife quickly whispered to him, audibly enough for everyone to hear, that they weren't a house of charity. His expression sulked, and it soon became apparent who wore the pants when it came to making decisions in the house. Azure figured that the only reason Bronna had even been allowed to stay was that she was kin. At least, Owe seemed to have a strong sense of family. That was admirable.

"I'm sorry we can't do more for you boys," Cristopher told them as he walked them to the door. He lacked the accent that Bronna shared with the captain and his sea mage. More and more, Azure wondered if she was adopted. Physically, though, she seemed in line with the two brothers.

"You've done more than enough," Lonnell replied graciously as they took their leave.

"I really hate to send you out into the dark with all of the wolves and goblins and orcs running about," he said loudly, throwing a half-glance over his shoulder. Owe wasn't budging, though. "Sorry, I tried," he whispered.

"It's quite all right," Azure assured him with a chuckle.

"Seriously, now, you two take care. It's a long way back to Squall's End. I wish we had an inn in Roselake, but the village is too small to support one. It's rare that people come here for any reason other than to settle down or fish the lake."

"We'll be fine," Lonnell said, waving a final goodbye to Bronna.

"It's almost pitch black out here," Azure mentioned as soon as the door was shut behind them.

"I know." Lonnell continued staring at it as if he hoped that Owe would have a change of heart. "Not the ideal conditions for travel."

"I wonder if he was being truthful about the wolves and goblins and orcs or if he was just saying that to try to convince her to let us stay." Azure pivoted, remembering the rooster and raising his guard. For now, it was the most threatening thing that might attack.

"I'm sure there are wolves and orcs and goblins here. And thieves," he added. "Towns like Squall's End tend to attract the less savory. I would feel none too comfortable about staying on the path tonight."

"My feelings are much the same. I think we should travel a ways and make camp in the forest. It's no worse than we had to do back on Crescent Island."

"Agreed." Lonnell nodded before looking down at his fist and clenching it to cast Small Flame.

Azure filed in behind him as Lonnell led the way to the gate. Thankfully, Red never made a reappearance. Apparently, he had gone off somewhere to roost for the night. Silently, Azure hoped he'd never have to come back here again, even though he really had enjoyed Cristopher's company. The cobbler had been one of the lighter spirits that Azure had encountered in The Realm so far. Perhaps he'd pay the man a visit at his shop in Squall's End from time to time once he got settled.

Despite saying they weren't going to travel very far, Lonnell lead the way to Roselake then continued on down the path back towards Squall's End for about a quarter mile before breaking off into a grove of trees. He handed his machete over to Azure to hack away at any foliage in their path. When they were a good ways from the road, they stopped to make camp.

Sleeping somewhere new felt strange to Azure. The ground wasn't really any different than anywhere they'd been before. It was the unknown dangers that kept him awake at night. Many of the sounds were unfamiliar to him. Insects and animal grunts that he hadn't heard on Crescent Island. By the time morning came, he had barely gotten a wink.

They continued on in the early morning. Lonnell was never one to waste time. When Azure asked if he'd like wild hare for breakfast, Lonnell countered that they should forage instead. That led to an hour-long detour wandering around a field looking for things to eat.

| You have harvested: **Fireweed** | **Uses:** Alchemy component |
|---|---|
| You have harvested: **Wild Onion** | **Uses:** Alchemy component, Restores +5 HP if eaten |
| You have harvested: **Blue Mushroom** | **Uses:** Alchemy component, Restores +10 MP if eaten |

Azure found seven of the fireweed, fourteen wild onions, and ten blue mushrooms. Lonnell assured him that it was all edible, but a tasty meal it did not make. He ate half of his supply and kept the other half, still feeling hungry afterward. It just wasn't enough food for someone who burned so many calories. It also didn't satisfy Azure's craving for a hot meal.

They made their way back to the path and didn't stop again until they had reached the fork. Well, Azure stopped. Lonnell continued right on walking towards Squall's End.

"Hey, wait up," Azure called to him.

"What?" Lonnell turned.

He pointed at the sign to Hawking's, and his friend stared at it for a moment before understanding hit him. “Oh, yes, you wanted to go to the magic school.”

"That's the plan," Azure told him.

Lonnell blew out a breath, and his expression changed with thought. “We should return to Squall's End and secure a place to stay first.”

"Maybe the school has a dorm?" Azure suggested, hopeful.

"What's a dorm?"

"A place where students stay while they're going through school. It's typically free."

Lonnell laughed and shook his head. “That's the craziest thing I've ever heard of. Free room and board.”

Azure sulked. “Your parents let me stay in their barn. That was free.”

"That was different. Schools here aren't prone to charity."

"It never hurts to check." He shrugged.

"And even so, where would I stay? I'm not planning on attending magic school. I need to be making coin, not spending it." Lonnell gave him a serious look.

Tension filled the air between them. It was like a silent game of tug-o-war.

"You don't even want to check it out with me? Uden probably would have liked you to see it." Azure tried to persuade him to come along.

"I can see it after I'm settled." Lonnell glanced in the direction of the school. "Right now, I need to start making coin so I can buy some land."

It was clear that their goals no longer aligned and that they were at an impasse. “I guess this is where we part ways then,” he said, feeling a bit ill about it. Yesterday, he had told himself that if this was how things had to be, then so be it. Now, facing the thought of losing his only friend in The Realm, he didn't seem so sure.

"I guess this is." Lonnell took a few steps towards him with a soft smile before stopping and gazing up at the sun. "If only

Uden could see us now. Both on the mainland. You going off to study magic and me preparing to make this my new home."

"If only." Azure tried to force a smile as well.

"We'll see each other again. I'm sure of it," Lonnell told him. "If this dorm of yours doesn't exist, you'll end up in Squall's End looking for shelter. And if magic school proves to be too expensive, you'll have to find some way to pay for it."

"Yeah..." Azure's voice trailed off. Part of him was upset that he had gone through so much to help Lonnell and the guy wouldn't even give him a few hours of his time to check out the magic school. That was very dick of him.

"Well, it's been fun. Good luck at the magic school." Lonnell extended his arm so that they could clasp wrists.

"Good luck with your...marriage," Azure replied awkwardly. What else was he supposed to say? Maybe good luck finding some work would have been better, but he was admittedly in a bitter mood right now.

Lonnell turned from him and walked away, never looking back. As if to add insult to injury, he began whistling a merry little tune. Azure gave his backside the finger before turning to face the direction that Hawking's School of Land Magic was in. It was finally time to start an adventure of his own.

## CHAPTER THIRTEEN
THE REALM – Day 44

The path to the School of Land Magic was unlike any that Azure had walked before. At first, it was just the regular brown dirt beneath his feet, his sides flanked by fields of grass and the occasional thickness of the forest. But as he continued down the path, things began to change. Dirt turned to gravel then turned to cobblestone. The fields began to change in color, their flora growing more diverse. Azure couldn't identify even a fraction of the plants that he saw, and when he tried to go off the path to harvest some, he ran into a wall of nothingness. Outstretching his hands to touch the transparent surface, he felt like a mime. There was obviously some type of barrier in place.

The trees grew taller, their trunks wider, the closer to the school that he got. Deep brown was their wood, and emerald green was their foliage. Some of them entwined, coupled like lovers as they reached toward the heavens. Birds danced between their branches, their plumage bright with the colors of a rainbow. Striped deer sauntered through the forest, munching on the buffet around them without a care in the world. For a few moments, Azure thought about trying to shoot one, but deep down he knew that the barrier was there for a reason. This was a protected area. A menagerie. Maybe even a zoo of sorts. There was no way for him to tell until he reached the school. All that he did know was that he didn't want to get kicked out before he even got there by disturbing something he wasn't supposed to mess with.

The school itself was about a mile off the main road. Azure had expected some giant university, but what greeted him was far different from anything he could have imagined. The building was made up entirely of trees clustered together. There was an archway between two of them that served as a door, and gaps between the trunks that were used as windows. Azure couldn't tell if it was a single-story structure or made of multiple levels. The trees reached up at least forty feet into the sky before branching into a large canopy of leaves. In front of the building on a free-standing metal sign were the words Hawking's School of Land Magic in elaborate cursive.

A few young people, whom Azure could only assume were students, were sitting outside of the building reading. Azure smiled at them as he passed, letting himself in since there was no one at the door to greet him or tell him that he couldn't enter otherwise. Surprisingly, for being made entirely of live trees, the building was sectioned off rather well. Upon entering, there was a small room with only a stone desk and a woman sitting behind it. She wore thick horn-rimmed glasses, glancing up at him over them.

“Hi,” he said in the way of greeting as he strode up to the desk. “My name is Azure, and I'm here to enroll in your school.”

She cocked a thin eyebrow at him as if he was crazy, seeming none too enthusiastic to start dishing out information. “Do you have an appointment?”

“I wasn't aware that I needed one.” He frowned.

She closed her eyes and pressed her fingers to her temples.

“Are you casting a spell?” Azure asked excitedly. “Telekinesis, perhaps.” He wanted to impress her with what little knowledge he thought he had of magic.

"No. I have a headache." The woman looked at him like he was stupid, and Azure instantly felt that way.

"Oh..." Maybe it was best if he just kept his mouth shut.

"What are you wanting to major in?" She sifted through some papers on her desk.

"Major?" This really was like college back in his own world. He hadn't taken the time to think about it, and asking her what he could major in would make him look like even more of an idiot. "Land magic," Azure replied hesitantly, making it sound more like a question than a statement.

She continued looking at him like he was a moron for a few seconds longer before finally saying, "I'll go get Elise."

The woman stood and left her post, entering a walkway to her right and disappearing around the corner.

Had he said something wrong again? Azure wondered as he stood there waiting with his wrists clasped behind his back.

Two students came out from the same walkway, chatting amongst themselves. He greeted them politely. They merely looked at him and smiled, not bothering to say anything in return. Several moments later, one of the people who had been sitting outside reading came back in. It was then that Azure realized he'd been waiting for an excessively long time. Still, he had nothing left to do, so he simply paced slowly around the room, searching the walls for points of interest, though there was nothing notable.

Finally, after what seemed like forever but was probably closer to twenty minutes, the woman returned. She looked startled to see him still standing there, as if the whole point of being gone for so long was to drive him off. As she took a seat at her desk, she said, "Elise will see you now," offering no further information.

"And where do I find this Elise?" Azure stepped back up to the desk to ask.

"Third door to the left." She gestured to where she had just come from without even glancing at him, her eyes focusing again on the stack of papers.

"Thank you," he replied courteously before heading down the walkway.

*Well, she's a pleasant one,* he thought sarcastically, hoping that the rest of the staff wasn't quite so rude.

Much like the opening that served as the door into the school, there were large spaces between the tree trunks that denoted rooms. The first door Azure passed seemed to open into a classroom. Desks sprouted from the floor in the form of deformed trees. He could only assume that they'd been magicked to look that way. Several students were sitting about either eating or studying. They were all facing away from the door, so Azure couldn't really tell.

The next room appeared to be an office. It was empty except for a stone desk and a few chairs, also made from trees. When he came to the third room, Azure was pleased to find it occupied. In all honesty, he hadn't been sure that it would be. The receptionist's reaction to him still being there hadn't given Azure a vote of confidence that she cared whether or not he found Elise.

"Azure." The woman stood to greet him.

He was surprised to see that she was a dwarf, her features wide and squat. While her skin was smooth with the youth of a woman in her early adult years, everything about her seemed chubby. Chubby for a human, that was. Proportionate for a dwarf. Her long red hair was braided away from her face, running down the length of her back. Bright blue eyes welcomed him and, for the first time, made him feel like he wasn't out of place. The outfit she had on reminded him of that of a headmistress. She wore a white long-sleeve blouse buttoned all the way to the collar and a black pencil skirt and heels. A thin black ribbon was tied around her neck.

"My name is Elise Smith. I'm a professor of land magic here at Hawking's. Have a seat." She gestured to the chair in front of her desk.

"Thank you." Azure nodded in respect before moving to sit across from her. The chair felt firm and honestly wasn't very comfortable. He took note of the tiny leaves sprouting from the armrests, doing his best not to touch them.

"Miss Ogden told me that you're interested in enrolling. Do you have any prior experience with land magic?" Elise folded her hands on top of her desk, looking nothing but professional.

"I'm afraid not. I've never done any magic before." Was that the right way to phrase it? After that conversation with the receptionist, Azure was worried that everything that came out of his mouth sounded stupid.

"That's perfectly fine." She smiled at him. "May I see your credentials?"

"My credentials?"

Just then, a notification popped up.

***Elise Smith** has asked to join your party. Will you accept?*

"Oh, of course," Azure stuttered, immediately accepting her request.

Elise's name displayed at the bottom right of his vision. She stared at him for a moment, her eyes glazing over. Azure could only guess that she was casting some silent spell that would allow her to see further into his stats. He would not make the same mistake twice by assuming he knew what was going on.

After a moment, she disbanded from him, her smile

returning as she seemed to come back to life. “I have good news and bad news. Which do you want to hear first?”

"The bad news." Always the bad news first. It usually made the good news that much better afterward.

"The bad news is that you don't speak Elvish. Elvish is a prerequisite for taking any of our courses here."

"My friend told me something along those lines." Azure sulked, thinking back to what he and Lonnell had spoken about on the ship.

"The good news," Elise perked up, "is that I can help you with that."

He sighed in relief, letting a soft chuckle escape. “You got me there.”

"The other good news is that you are a high enough level to start novice lessons here." Things were looking better by the minute. "Do you know how our lessons work?"

"I do not, ma'am." Azure settled into his seat, preparing for what he knew would likely be a lengthy lecture.

"Miss Ogden told me that you were primarily interested in learning land magic, but I'd like to give you an overview of how things work here before we get down to the business of assessing your finances and selecting the courses that would be the most suitable for you." She took a breath before continuing. "I'm not sure how much you know about magic schools, but as you have probably already guessed, land magic is our specialty. Here at Hawking's, we teach all levels of land magic from novice to master. We are the only school in all of The Realm that teaches every land magic spell known to man, gnomes, dwarfs, and elves. I, myself, am a Master Land Mage," Elise told him proudly. "Having said that, we also teach novice fire, water, air, and life magic. The only thing we don't teach is necromancy." She paused as if waiting for him to be disappointed.

"Why don't you teach necromancy?" Azure asked hesitantly, feeling like she was sniffing for the question.

"Because it is evil," Elise replied plainly. "You will not find necromancy spells anywhere except for The Deadlands unless they've been smuggled in."

Now he was intrigued. "Is necromancy forbidden?"

"It depends on the spell. Most of them are outlawed, and generally, necromancy is frowned upon. Teaching necromancy in the element countries is illegal. The only place where it is taught publicly is in The Deathlands, but few people are willing to venture there due to the high level of monsters and other perils. Besides, what's the point if you can't use it anywhere else."

If Azure remembered correctly, the Steal spell that Ruthren had tried to sell him was of the necromancy class. Now he kinda wished he would have forked out the money to buy it. He hadn't realized exactly how rare it was at the time.

"Moving on," Elise cleared her throat before continuing. "Here at Hawking's we also teach all levels of battle magic, enchantment, and alchemy. Alchemy can be learned separately from everything else. We have had many students that have come from around The Realm just to take our alchemy courses.

"While this does not apply to you, I feel I must tell you that if you had come with the intentions of learning any other field of magic besides land magic, you would still be required to first take one land magic course before we would be willing to teach you anything else.

"Spells here are divided between five different levels: novice, apprentice, adept, expert, and master. You must meet the level requirements of each before moving on to the next. Novice spells are taught to those between level three and twenty-four. Apprentice spells between the levels of twenty-five and forty-nine. Adept spells between the levels of fifty and seventy-four. Expert spells between the levels of seventy-five and ninety-nine, and

Master level spells are only taught to those level one-hundred and above. Either your character level or your skill level in that magic class must meet the requirement for you to be able to acquire the spells within that level. For instance, a level five character with a level fifty in land magic would still be considered an adept Land Mage and would be able to learn the spells within that level range."

Azure nodded, doing his best to follow along until Elise stopped speaking. “How many spells are in the novice level of land magic?”

"Three."

That was disappointing. He had expected there to be much more.

"Now we should probably talk about how you plan to pay for your lessons," Elise began the subject that Azure was the most nervous about. "We have two options for payment. You can pay for your novice semester in full or one spell at a time. Either way, learning land magic will be cheaper here than at any other school within The Realm because that is our specialty. If you pay for your semester in full, it will cost eleven gold, six silver, and one copper. If you pay one spell at a time, each course will cost you three gold, eight silver, and seven copper. How would you like to pay?"

Azure thought his asshole was going to suck up the seat beneath him. Many had warned him that magic school was going to be expensive, but this was an absolute outrage. How could anyone possibly afford to attend at those prices? Now that he thought about it, the students he had seen did look wealthy. Their clothes had been nice and their appearance kempt.

Azure inhaled deeply, his expression unable to hide that he didn't have the money. Just one class cost more coin than what he had on hand. Hawking's School of Land Magic was starting to make that Bag of Holding look cheap.

A short laugh passed between Elise's lips, and she dropped her gaze to the papers on her desk. “I've seen that look before.”

"I didn't realize that magic school was going to be so expensive," Azure confessed, feeling like he had just wasted her time. While he still wanted to attend, it didn't seem like it was going to happen anytime soon.

"Why do you think there aren't many mages in The Realm? Magic is a rare and precious thing."

"I still want to learn. I just have to figure out how to get the money together. Do you happen to have a price sheet I can take with me? I want to know exactly how much I'll need to save up to learn everything that I want to learn," he tried his best to sound eager.

She nodded before taking the top paper from the stack on her desk and handing it to him.

Azure's eyes scrolled over it. For supposedly being the cheapest school for land magic in all The Realm, the land magic classes were the second most expensive next to air magic. Air magic classes had a whopping price tag of four gold, four silver, and three copper a piece. Water spell classes followed close behind land magic at three gold, three silver, and two copper a piece. The cheapest classes on the list were for life magic, which were only nine silver and five copper a piece, followed by battle magic which were one gold, six silver, and six copper a course. Alchemy classes were priced the same as battle magic classes.

Azure quickly decided that if he could just jump over the hurdle of being able to afford his first land spell that he'd switch his major to life magic and work his way through all of the least expensive classes first. While he had no interest in taking on a cleric role, it would be good to be able to heal himself without needing potions.

*Well, shit. It looks like I shouldn't have invested all of those points into Mana just yet after all.* Azure thought as he placed the sheet of paper in his bag and thanked Elise for the information. As she walked him to the door, he turned to her, hoping there would be at least some silver lining to dropping so much money on magic school.

"Do you guys have a dorm here?" he asked, optimistic.

She gave him a puzzled look. “What's a dorm?”

# CHAPTER FOURTEEN
## THE REALM – Day 36

It was difficult not to feel hopeless. Nothing in The Realm came easy, it seemed. The parallels between his own world were a bit annoying. If this was really just a game, then wasn't it supposed to be fun? Radical Interactive needed to dial down the difficulty level of earning coin.

Oh well, maybe he'd get exactly what he was looking for at The Adventurer's Guild. It was his only hope right now. If he was lucky, he'd qualify for some decent paying quests. Azure knew from past experience with other games that there would be a hierarchy to what quests he would be allowed to take. That would put a cap on how much he could earn until he grew stronger. Much like life in his own world, living in The Realm could be a slog sometimes.

As he was about to reach the gates of Squall's End, he was surprised to come upon Lonnell walking in his direction. Seeing his friend instantly brought a smile to Azure's face. A strange comfort after suffering a minor defeat.

"Hey there, stranger. I didn't expect to see you again so soon," Azure said.

Lonnell smiled back at him in greeting. “I told you our paths would cross again.”

"Where are you heading?" Azure stopped to talk to him.

"To find you, actually." His expression changed, the smile fading.

"Miss me that much already?" Azure elbowed him.

Lonnell drew his tongue over his bottom lip, hesitating. He opened his mouth to speak and then stopped again. It was then that Azure realized he was about to be asked for a favor. “Does the magic school have a dorm?”

"No. Why?" Azure waited for him to get down to business.

"I just came back from the inn," Lonnell rubbed the back of his neck, looking nervous. "It's a bit pricey. Four silver for a night. Two gold and four silver for a week, and eight gold for a month."

Azure sucked in a breath, feeling his hope dripping away again. Why was everything here so damned expensive?

From that short conversation, he already had a pretty good idea of what Lonnell was going to ask him.

"It looks like we won't be sleeping easy for a while." Azure tried to force a smile. "Are we going to argue over who gets first watch?" he tried to make a joke of it.

"I'm not really sure what we should do." Stress was apparent on Lonnell's face. "I am really tired of sleeping in the forest. It feels more dangerous here than on Crescent Island. At least there, we didn't have to worry about bandits. Here, we could save up a bunch of money only to be robbed in the middle of the night."

"Then we best find a good sleeping spot." It was definitely a concern. During their brief walk through Squall's End, Azure had noticed some unsavory characters wandering about.

"I was thinking more along the lines of us rooming together," Lonnell suggested.

Azure wasn't sure why he hadn't thought of that. Perhaps because he was so desperate to keep the money he already had on him. Paying for a roof over his head and magic school seemed like an impossible task. Maybe it was beyond him. Something meant for only the wealthy.

"I wonder if they have grants here," he mumbled under his breath, already pretty sure of the answer to that. Handouts in this world would be few and far between.

"What are grants?" Lonnell gave him a queer look that quickly turned hopeful.

"Don't worry about it." Azure dismissed the question. "I think we should go to The Adventurer's Guild first. It would be a good idea to gauge how much money we're going to be bringing in before we dig ourselves into a hole spending what we already have on us."

"That sounds like a good plan." Lonnell nodded, seemingly lost in thought. It was strange to see him so panicked, but he was obviously internally freaking out over their situation. Azure honestly wasn't sure what Lonnell had expected to happen when they reached the mainland. Maybe that Bronna would willingly return to Crescent Island with him and that her relatives would have been generous enough to pay for their passage. No dice. He was going to have to work just like everyone else.

They headed back into town, walking the straight path that led to the building they were pretty sure was The Adventurer's Guild. It had been one of the more impressive buildings in the middle of Squall's End. On its sign was a shield with two swords crossed in front of it. That either had to mean it was The Adventurer's Guild or an excessively large smithy.

They ascended the two steps to reach the wooden door that led into the building. Upon entering, they saw a long bank of windows. Half of the space in the building seemed to be dedicated to the front office, which made sense because the lines were looong. Thankfully, each window was labeled accordingly. Azure didn't know what they all meant. Five of the windows were marked with letters of the alphabet: A, B, C, D, and E. The other two windows were labeled Quest Submission and Registration.

"I'm assuming we need to be in the Registration line," Azure whispered to Lonnell. Unfortunately, that was one of the longest ones.

They shuffled in behind the six people ahead of them. Not wanting to waste any more time than necessary, Lonnell tapped the guy standing in front of them on the shoulder to ask if they were in the right place. He was an energetic youth, excitedly acknowledging that this was, in fact, the line that you needed to be in to register as an adventurer. Then he proceeded to tell them his entire life story and how all he had ever wanted was to be an adventurer. When Azure Analyzed him, he showed up as blue. It was nice to know that he wasn't the smallest fish in the pond in Squall's End. He also realized that he could probably power level his Analyze skill if he picked a spot in the town to just people-watch all day. With that thought, he spent the rest of his time in line Analyzing the other fifty-three people in the room.

*Congratulations! The skill: **Analyze** has reached Level 6. This skill allows you to see how dangerous a foe is in relation to your own level. Use this skill frequently to avoid getting yourself killed.*

Yup. He'd definitely found a loophole in power leveling the skill. Azure made a mental note to plan some time where he could just hang around the town Analyzing people.

Finally, after nearly two hours of waiting, it was their turn. Lonnell and Azure walked up to the window together, and the lady that was manning it gave them a disapproving look.

"One at a time," she said in an irritable tone, shooing Azure away. "Get back behind the line." She pointed to a line drawn in chalk on the floor, making him retreat further. Apparently, Azure wasn't supposed to be listening in on what they were talking about.

*People here are rude*, he thought, recalling the receptionist at Hawking's School of Land Magic. Maybe the mainland wasn't as great as Uden had made it out to be. Briefly, he wondered if the half-imp would stand for such treatment. He'd probably either have a witty counter or be complaining loudly.

Being next in line made the time pass by even more slowly. There was a lot of talking, head nodding, paper shuffling, and writing going on. After close to twenty minutes, Lonnell finally stepped aside and the woman motioned for Azure to come forward.

"I'll wait for you outside. I'm going to take a look around the market," Lonnell whispered to him before passing by.

Azure simply nodded, not wanting to keep the cranky clerk waiting. She held onto the annoyed expression even as he approached.

"Name," was the first thing she barked at him.

"Azure," he replied quickly.

She cocked her head to the side, giving him a look that said, "Really?" What came out of her mouth next though was "Full name?"

Azure's mouth dropped open. He hadn't really thought of a last name for his gaming moniker. And her expression spoke that he didn't have a lot of time to decide on one.

"Galvan," he belted out, startled that he had used his real last name. Well, Azure Galvan sounded all right anyway. It had a bit of a heroic ring to it, so that should be fine. Much better than William Galvan.

"This is your first time registering for The Adventurer's

Guild? Any Adventurer's Guild?"

"Yes."

"Let me see your credentials," she said dryly before a notification popped up.

***Ferne Clifton*** *has asked to join your party. Will you accept?*

He quickly accepted, and she began jotting down his information on a sheet of paper. Azure stared at Ferne while she worked, fascinated by the deep mocha of her skin. Long hair cascaded down her back in dreadlocks. Blue glitter dotted her eyelids, going perfectly with her bruise-colored lips. She would be quite beautiful if she would just smile, Azure thought.

"All right," Ferne began after setting down her quill. "This is how The Adventurer's Guild works. Quests are divided into five groups by letter. Since you're new, you'll only be able to accept quests designated as E for now. Once you've completed your prerequisite quest, you'll be able to go into the E line to acquire new quests. That is also where you will report into to collect your rewards.

"The receptionist in the E line will give you up to four different quests to choose from. There are four types of quests available: gathering quests, monster quests, bounty quests, and miscellaneous quests. Gathering quests will require you to collect certain items or materials for a client. These items will be delivered back here, and then we will give them to the client. Monster quests typically involve you eliminating some pest monsters that are bothering the client. Bounty quests involve hunting down an individual or group of individuals that are causing trouble. The reward for them is usually better than the other two because those quests are often submitted by law officials or other members of the government. They also tend to be more dangerous. Bounty quests don't just involve people but also sometimes involve high-level monsters which will require you to enter dungeons. Miscellaneous quests are just that. They can involve anything from being protective detail to a traveling merchant to delivering a message.

"If you want to take on a quest with more than one party member, know that whoever the quest is assigned to will be the person that has to collect on it. We do not divide the rewards, so you would have to do it amongst yourselves. Do you understand?" Ferne gave him a pointed look.

Azure nodded, and she continued, “Before you are allowed to become an official member of The Adventurer's Guild, you must complete a preliminary quest. This is to make sure that you actually have what it takes to be an adventurer. This quest must be completed alone. If you are found to be partying with someone else, you will be banned from The Adventure's Guild...forever,” Ferne emphasized the word, staring at him to make sure he understood. Azure nodded again, and she quickly shuffled through her paperwork. “Let's see here,” she said to herself, briefly skimming a few of the papers on her desk before selecting one and sliding it over to him. “This should do.”

As Azure's eyes began to read over the paper, a notification popped up.

| Adventurer's Guild Quest: An Author's Dream |
| --- |
| Enno Berkeley is a renowned angler and has decided to write his own book on the best fishing spots in Patheana. Unfortunately, he fears that his fishing ability is far superior to his writing ability. Seek out Enno in Roselake and give his book a read. You will be required to fish in one of the spots in his book. Once you are done, report to The Adventurer's Guild about your experience and to collect your reward.<br><br>**Designation:** Prerequisite<br>**Type:** Miscellaneous<br>**Difficulty:** Very Easy<br>**Deadline:** 14 days<br>**Success:** Fish one of the spots in the book<br>**Failure:** Cancel quest<br>**Reward:** Acceptance into The Adventurer's Guild<br>**Will you accept this quest:** Yes or No? |

Azure's eyes bulged. A two-week long duration and no monetary reward? What the fuck?

He lifted up the paper, pointing at the Reward field. "Am I to assume that I won't be paid for this quest?"

"Prerequisite quests have no compensation requirements. There will be a reward, but it won't be monetary. The main reward is that you gain admittance into The Adventurer's Guild and will then be able to accept paying quests.

"Prerequisite quests are non-optional. You have to accept whatever quest I give you or you will not qualify to be an adventurer. Once you are an official adventurer, you'll have much more leeway in choosing which quests you want to accept and decline. Having said that, any quests that you accept must be completed by the deadline displayed on them. We have a three strike policy here. You can cancel any quest that you accept by the deadline up to three times. On the fourth time, your membership to The Adventurer's Guild will be revoked. If you fail to complete more than three quests by their deadline, same thing. The moral of the story is that we don't want adventurers who are not capable of honoring their contracts."

"So you're saying I'm not getting paid for this quest...a quest that says it will take me two weeks to complete," Azure reiterated.

"No," she replied plainly. "I know it sucks, but that's just the way that things are. This is how we separate the chaff from the wheat. The people who really want to be adventurers from the ones who aren't serious about it.

"The silver lining is that the deadline is usually a broad estimate. Most of our quests can be completed way before their deadline. For instance, with this one in particular," Ferne gestured for him to hand her back the quest form. When he did, she scanned it over again quickly before continuing, "Roselake is only a few hours away. It would probably take you half a day, at most, to find Enno. Depending on how quickly you can read, it might only take you a day to read his novel. Since Enno is from Roselake, I'm going to take a good guess that Roselake itself will be one of the fishing spots in his book. You can spend the day fishing it to see how accurate his information is. All in all, I'd say this quest will take you three days tops. The extra days are given in case you are a slow reader, have a business to run, or have other duties that would get in your way of completing it quickly."

"Ah." Azure nodded. That was a relief. But there was another issue that he had with this particular quest. "I don't own a fishing pole. Will I have to buy one beforehand?"

"No. Everything you need to complete this quest will be provided to you," she informed him.

"Good. Good." Well, that was at least some good news.

"That's it." Ferne folded her hands on top of her desk. "Complete your quest and you'll be made an honorary adventurer."

"Thanks," Azure said before taking his leave. As he walked away, Ferne disbanded from him.

Before he reached the door, Azure noticed a bunch of people standing around staring at a cork board on the wall. He paused to see what they were all looking at. Affixed to the board were several quest papers. Without removing one, Azure focused, and the details of the quest popped up before him.

| **Adventurer's Guild Quest: Defeat The Bower Boys** |
|---|
| Outlaw James Bower has brought his despicable Bower Boys to Squall's End. They've been robbing people along the various roads leading into the city. These menaces need to be dealt with...permanently. Find them, kill them, and bring James Bower's severed head to The Adventurer's Guild as proof that the deed is done.<br><br>**Designation:** C<br>**Type:** Bounty<br>**Difficulty:** Very Hard<br>**Requirements:** Character Level 50<br>One-Handed or Two-Handed Weapons Skill Level 59<br>Agility 55<br>**Deadline:** 7 days<br>**Success:** Kill all 7 members of The Bower Boys<br>**Failure:** Cancel quest<br>**Reward:** 11 gold<br>**Will you accept this quest:** Yes or No? |

Holy shit! The reward was almost enough to pay for an

entire semester at Hawking's School of Land Magic. It was more than a month's worth of rent at the inn for only a week's worth of work. This board was probably where the real money was at. Unfortunately, he didn't qualify for the quest.

Speaking of which, this was the first time he'd ever seen requirements for a quest before. Azure took several moments analyzing the quest before moving on to the next. Every quest he looked at was either hard or very hard. They all paid a lot, too. Unfortunately, he didn't meet the requirements for any of them.

His eyes scanned up to the title of the cork board. It said Open Quests. That didn't tell him too much, so he looked to one of the other people staring intently at the board and asked, “What's this?”

The guy's eyes flicked over to him before returning to the board. “It's the Open Quests board,” he replied plainly.

"I know that, but what are Open Quests?" Azure tried not to sound annoyed. Maybe he should have waited to ask Lonnell, though he wasn't sure that his friend would know the answer either. They were both new to this Adventurer's Guild thing, after all.

Without turning from the board, the man told him, “Open Quests are quests that have either been repeatedly failed by the adventurers who have accepted them before or have not been accepted by anyone for a certain period of time. They are open to any adventurer or group of adventurers that meet the requirements.”

"Interesting." Azure scratched his chin. "Do they pay more because they're basically rejects?"

"Usually. It really depends on the level of difficulty and how many people have died trying to complete them already."

How many people have died? Jesus. Judging by how much the Bower Boys quest was worth, Azure could only assume that it got to be on the board because many people had tried and failed at it. Killing seven experienced outlaws seemed like a lot.

"Thanks for the info, friend," Azure said before turning away. His head was swimming with greed. If only he and Lonnell could qualify for some of those quests, their financial troubles would be over. It was a pipe dream, though. The Open Quests were all incredibly difficult, and he and Lonnell were still pretty low level. More than likely, the Open Quests board wouldn't be an option for them for a long time.

With a sigh, Azure headed outside and down the stairs. Thankfully, Lonnell was waiting for him there. He was half-worried that he'd have to track down his friend.

"How'd it go?" Lonnell asked.

"Probably the same as it went for you. We both have to complete a prerequisite quest before we can even think about making money."

"Yeah." He frowned. "Luckily, mine was easy."

"Mine's easy, too. Just time-consuming." The thought of wasting time on a quest that wasn't going to pay him made Azure grumpy.

"I already finished mine. I just need to turn it in for my reward."

"What?" Azure's mouth fell agape for a moment. "How did you manage that? It's only been twenty minutes."

"I got a gathering quest. Instead of going out and foraging, I just bought the required items at the market."

Azure gawked at him. “Isn't that cheating?”

"No." Lonnell shook his head. "As long as you don't party with someone else, it's not cheating. And don't worry, I asked before I did it. If you don't have time to complete a gathering quest, you can buy the materials. Your compensation for the quest likely won't cover what you spent because of inflation and what not. After all, most clients are either trying to find rare materials or materials at wholesale pricing. Luckily, these prerequisite quests don't require any rare materials to complete. If you got a gathering quest, you could probably buy what you need to complete it, too."

Damn, that lucky bastard. Why couldn't Azure have gotten a simple gathering quest? Ferne must have really been pissed off at him for coming up to the window with Lonnell initially.

"Unfortunately, my quest is going to take a bit more time. I have to go to Roselake to meet with this fisherman author and read his book. Then I have to fish at one of the spots in his book and report back about how accurate the information in the book is." Just explaining the quest made it feel like a giant time-suck.

Lonnell hummed in thought. "That might be fun. And you don't have the fishing skill yet, so there's that."

Azure fought the urge to roll his eyes. "It's really not something I want to have to waste my time on right now. Coin is more important. Speaking of which, what are we going to do about the inn?"

Lonnell sighed. "Let me go collect on my quest and grab a new one. Then we'll have a better idea of what kind of coin will be coming in when we're doing this full time."

Azure decided to wait outside while Lonnell went back into The Adventurer's Guild to complete his prerequisite quest and pick up his first real quest. About ten minutes later, he came back out with a sheet of paper in his hands.

"So, what's the verdict?" Azure asked, leaning over to peek at the quest.

"Not all bleak," Lonnell admitted, though he still didn't sound happy. "This quest pays two gold, five silver, and seven copper, but it's going to take a lot of footwork. I just chose it because it seemed like it paid the most for the least amount of time."

"A gathering quest," Azure noted. He also noticed that it required multiple different items, and they weren't anything he'd ever heard of before.

"I'm definitely going to get my exercise in," Lonnell said with an inhale. "I won't be able to find this stuff around here."

"The quest has a seven-day duration. Do you think it will take you that long to complete it?" Azure looked at him.

"I'm hoping I can knock it out in three days. None of these places are close together, from what I can tell."

"So that's two gold, five silver, and seven copper for three days worth of work," Azure started doing the math. "If you can take two quests like this on per week, that's a little over five gold per week. More than enough for room and board and saving up money, especially if we're splitting a room."

"That's the silver lining, isn't it," Lonnell replied with a soft smile before rolling up the sheet of paper and sticking it in his Bag of Holding. "For as eager as I was earlier, I don't feel like getting started on this today. It's been a long, stressful day. Broke or not, I need a drink."

Azure couldn't help but chuckle. He'd never heard Lonnell sound so worn out before. “I suppose we should find the inn then and get settled. I'm sure we're both looking forward to a night of restful sleep where we don't have to watch each other's backs.”

"You can say that again." Exhaustion rang clear in Lonnell's voice.

They made their way to the inn and purchased a week's stay, splitting the rent. It was no Marriott, Azure thought as he took in the one cot that they had to share and a bedside table with a lantern. But it was better than possibly getting robbed and losing what little money they had left. Or worse, ending up dead.

"You can have the bed tonight," Azure offered.

Lonnell just nodded in agreement, and they headed downstairs to the tavern. At first, Azure had planned on saving his money, but as soon as he saw the beer wench place a pint in front of Lonnell, he couldn't resist. Two coppers poorer, Azure was surprised when an item notification popped up.

*You have received the following item:*

| **Pint of Beer** | **Quantity:** 1/1 |
|---|---|
| | **Item Class:** Common |
| | **Quality:** Average |
| | **Weight:** 1.0 kg |
| | **Uses:** Makes your worries feel less harrowing. |
| | **Effects:** Increases strength by 3% for one hour |
| | Decreases attack of all weapons and magic by 20% for one hour |
| | Decreases Agility, Dexterity, Charisma, and Luck by 3 points for one hour |

Azure guffawed. Seriously? It was funny to see how dangerous alcohol was in The Realm. It was basically battle ED.

"I'm guessing these effects stack with each drink?" he asked Lonnell.

"That's correct." His friend nodded.

"Well then, it looks like my limit is five before I'm absolutely useless. Such bullshit," Azure grumbled.

"Less than that depending on how much Agility and Dexterity you have. The other two don't matter as much," Lonnell reminded him.

"Ah. Yeah. True," Azure replied as he raised the beer to his lips and took a sip.

*Congratulations! New skill learned:* ***Drinking*** *Level 1. Life sucks sometimes and you need a reprieve. Be careful when and where you decide to relax, though, because danger lurks around every corner.*

This made Azure laugh again. He could only assume that the more he drank, the less his decrease of attack would be and the higher his strength would grow. That still made Drinking a useless skill, though.

"I can't even enjoy a drink without worrying about shit," Azure mumbled, feeling that the text in the notification was contradicting. He turned his attention back to Lonnell. "Did you happen to see that board on the wall that everyone was standing around in The Adventurer's Guild?"

Lonnell glanced up in thought for a moment. “I can't say that I did.”

"Well, when you go back next time, have a look at it. It's called the Open Quests board. It's basically a place where hard quests are posted that either no one wants to do or that people have had difficulty completing. I saw a quest on there for some guys called The Bower Boys. Apparently, they've been robbing people along the road to Squall's End. There are seven of them. The reward is big." Azure's eyes widened as he thought about all of that gold.

"How big?" Lonnell's voice went all serious.

Azure shook his head. “It doesn't matter. We're too low level to accept the quest.”

"What if we combined our levels?"

"What would that matter?" Azure gave him a queer look. "Whoever accepts the quest has to meet the level requirement of it."

"That might not be true." Lonnell paused to take a quick gulp of his beer. "The receptionist told me that sometimes they'll make exceptions for a party if your party's level adds up to the requirement, but it's judged on a quest by quest basis. Either way, she said it's not smart to accept a quest that's higher than your level. Super risky, but might be worth it if the money is good."

"Well, the two of us do not a level fifty make. That was the requirement."

"Yeah." Lonnell seemed to deflate a bit.

To Azure's surprise, his companion drank three beers. By the time they left the tavern, Lonnell was slurring his words and teetering to the point that Azure had to help him walk. He forced his friend to eat some bread, but that was one thing that didn't work like in the real world. The bread didn't sober Lonnell up at all.

Azure helped Lonnell up to bed and made sure he was all right. As soon as Lonnell's head hit the pillow, he was snoring loudly. Azure couldn't help but smirk.

*Damn, he must really be stressed out. And who can blame him? If it weren't for the fact that we're on a very fixed budget, I probably would have gotten wasted too.* But he hadn't gotten wasted. Having a feeling that he would need what money he still had, Azure kept to only drinking one beer. It admittedly gave him a pretty heavy buzz, far more than one beer would have ever caused him in his world. Somehow, his tolerance had gone to shit.

With a sigh, Azure bedded down on the floor. For having told himself that he was used to sleeping on hard surfaces, it was particularly uncomfortable. Perhaps he had lied to himself. Then again, he was used to sleeping on hard earth, not on wood. He could have always rolled to find a soft patch of grass or somewhere with fewer rocks. The wood floor was just...stiff. It reminded him of how much he'd hated being on the Shropshire.

Hopefully, the alcohol would do what it typically did in his own world and help him find sleep faster despite all of his discomforts. For as much as he hoped, though—for as much as he finally felt safe, sleep wouldn't come easily. The noise of the tavern was an unwelcome distraction. Never had Azure thought he would miss Crescent Island, but living in the city kind of sucked. This was worse than his apartment on Earth had been. It wasn't uncommon for him to hear his upstairs neighbors or the occasional party. But here it seemed he'd be listening to a party every night. Music and laughter and voices ascended through the window. He wanted nothing more than to shut them all out, but he knew that wasn't possible. Perhaps he would have gotten a better sleep in the forest, but there was no going back now. At least not for this week. Their money was gone, and it was safer here. Wasn't it?

## CHAPTER FIFTEEN
THE REALM – Day 45

To Azure's surprise, Lonnell was already gone when he awoke the next morning. Then again, he may have slept all day if not for the rays of the sun beating on him through the window and filling the room with an uncomfortable heat. Azure groaned as he rolled away from the light, his arm sore from having laid on it all night. He was definitely looking forward to getting the bed tonight.

Azure smacked his lips, feeling unusually dehydrated and knowing it was because of the beer he'd had the night before. There was the tiniest hint of a headache stabbing at his temples, too. He didn't even want to imagine how Lonnell must feel. Then again, Lonnell had spent a good amount of time at the tavern in Cragbell thanks to Bronna working there, so his tolerance might be higher.

Just wanting to get the quest over with, Azure immediately set off for Roselake. Traveling the main road to Squall's End alone made him feel somewhat insecure now that he knew the Bower Boys were out there robbing people. Out of fear of having bad luck, Azure had decided to leave half of what coin he had left in the room at the inn, not that it was probably that much safer there.

The door didn't have a lock on it, so anyone could wander in at any time. Knowing that beneath the mattress would be the first place that he would look for coin if he were snooping around, Azure decided to hide it behind the bedside table legs instead. Hopefully, that wasn't a mistake. It would piss him off if he returned and found he'd been robbed. The more he thought about it, perhaps he would have been better off keeping all of the coin on him after all. Oh well. He didn't want to waste time going back for it.

Turning off on the road to Roselake made Azure feel a little bit safer, though he wasn't sure why. It made more sense for the Bower Boys to be waiting on an offshoot of the main road than to be on it. From what Azure understood, soldiers from Noseon patrolled the main road from time to time. Any smart bandit would avoid it.

Staying ever vigilant, Azure reached Roselake without incident. Knowing it was the best place to start his search, Azure first went to the tavern to inquire about Enno's whereabouts. While he was there, he went ahead and Analyzed everyone in the bar, wanting to try to level the skill as quickly as possible so that he could see more details about his foes and companions in the future. The barkeep pointed him to a small residence, not surprisingly, next to the lake. Azure had to trudge halfway around the lake before he reached it, and there was no question about the identity of the man who stood on the shoreline with a fishing pole in hand.

"Enno Berkeley?" Azure asked as he walked up.

The man looked over at him and smiled. “That would be me,” he announced before reeling in his pole and setting it down to clasp wrists with Azure. “And you are?”

"Azure. Azure Galvan." It felt so strange using his last name. "I was sent by The Adventurer's Guild to read your book."

"I figured as much." Enno started walking back towards his house, and Azure followed.

For a fisherman, Enno seemed well-off. He wore a long tan

tunic and blue pants with a red bandana tied around his neck and a brimmed hat to keep the sun off of his face. Round spectacles covered his blue eyes, resting just below bushy eyebrows. His hair was cut neatly above his eyes, a natural salt-and-pepper that was mostly pepper. A man in his late forties or early fifties, he seemed fit for his age, no doubt from a life of being active.

"I was wondering when The Adventurer's Guild would send someone," he said excitedly. "I had half expected that they'd just toss away my request." He set the pole down on a bench before turning to Azure. Enno's house looked different than any Azure had seen in The Realm before. It was small but built more modernly than the other residences. Light blue trimmed the windows and adorned the columns that held up the front awning. The rest of the house was white. This guy definitely had money. It made Azure wonder why his quest didn't come with a monetary payout. "After all, this probably seemed like a quest of vanity to them," Enno continued.

"I don't mean to be rude," Azure began, "but if you're famous, then why didn't you just have one of your fans read the book?"

"Well that's simple," Enno said as if Azure were daft. "My fans would have given the book a glowing review. I need an unbiased opinion. Someone who doesn't know me or what I do. You don't...know me, do you?" He eyed Azure suspiciously.

Azure chuckled. "Sir, I am the most unbiased opinion you're going to find. I have never heard or you, and I've also never been fishing in my entire life."

Enno gasped. The shock stayed on his face for half a second before joy took over. "Well, we'll certainly have to change that, my good lad." He placed a hand on Azure's shoulder, walking him up the steps in front of his house and pausing again before reaching the door. "Now, you stay out here, and I'll go fetch my book."

Azure nodded and then simply stood there looking out over

the lake while Enno went inside. It was a gorgeous view. Glistening from the rays of the sun, the surface of the water was calm. The roses ringing the lake gave it a rich, ethereal feel. While Azure was certain that this wasn't the height of luxury in The Realm, it did seem like one of the nicer lives that money could buy. Maybe someday, he'd have something similar.

To Azure's appreciation, Enno didn't dawdle. He was only gone for about five minutes before returning with the book in hand. It had a thick green, hardback cover with golden type on the front.

*You have received the following item:*

| **Book:** ***Fishing Patheana*** | **Quantity:** 1<br>**Durability:** 1/1<br>**Item Class:** Extremely Rare<br>**Quality:** High<br>**Weight:** 0.7 kg<br>**Uses:** Map |
|---|---|

Azure took the book from him, noting how pristine it was. “I thought you hadn't published this yet.”

"It's my personal copy," Enno admitted. "I wanted to see what it would look like when it was complete, so I went ahead and had the manuscript bound."

*Money*, Azure thought again. *This guy obviously has a lot of it to waste. Perhaps he'll tip me after the job is done.*

Looking specifically for a map of the locations that he had to choose from to fish at, Azure flipped open the cover and skimmed through the pages. A smirk crossed his face when he found Roselake. “Well, I suppose I should hurry up and read this so that we can get to fishing." He closed the book.

"Oh, you won't be fishing here." Enno shook his head.

Azure gave him a queer look. "Why not?"

The man laughed, outstretching his arms. "How are you to learn from the book if you're taking lessons from the master?"

"Roselake is in this book as one of the locations," Azure pointed out, doing his best not to sound annoyed.

"Here." Enno motioned for him to hand the book back. Once Azure did, he flipped back to the map and tapped his finger on top of one of the locations. "I want you to fish here at Jade Pond. It's a good starter pond about sixteen miles away. Better for a beginner, like yourself. You won't have to worry about reeling in any monsters."

Azure cocked an eyebrow. "You can reel in monsters when you fish?"

"Yup. That's why I carry my trusty Betty Sue with me." Enno patted a machete at his hip that Azure hadn't noticed before.

"Hm," Azure hummed in thought. *Who woulda thunk.*

"Now, I have a few more things for you before you head off." The fisherman thrust his book into Azure's hands before heading back down the stairs and around the side of the house. Azure wasn't sure if he was supposed to follow or not, but he decided to stay planted.

When Enno returned, he had a fishing pole in one hand and a small box in the other. Azure just stared at him for a moment, feeling like he was running out of hands.

"You might want to put the book in your bag." Enno nodded towards Azure's bag, and he did as he was told before taking the two items from the fisherman.

*You have received the following items:*

| Starter Pole | **Attack:** 3<br>**Range:** 1<br>**Durability:** 10/10<br>**Item Class:** Common<br>**Quality:** Average<br>**Weight:** 1.3 kg |
|---|---|
| **Box of Basic Bait** | **Quantity:** 10/10<br>**Durability:** 1/1<br>**Item Class:** Common<br>**Quality:** Average<br>**Weight:** 0 kg<br>**Uses:** Must be used with a pole. Used to catch fish. |

The first thing Azure noticed was that the pole was not historically accurate. It was simple enough, made from bamboo, but it did have a reel that he could use to bring the fish in. If he remembered correctly, medieval fishing poles were merely just a stick with a string and a hook attached. This pole was much more modernized.

“Should I assume that if I reel in a monster with this pole, I'm supposed to then beat it over the head with it?” he chuckled to himself, thinking of the pole's attack stats.

Enno gave him a wry look. “You should know better than that.”

Truthfully, Azure didn't.

“It does have attack stats,” he pointed out.

“The attack stats on a pole wear the monster down as you're reeling it in. Nothing more. Once it's onshore, you'll have to fight it in the traditional sense,” Enno explained.

How dangerous could a fish out of water be? It was no matter. Enno had promised that Azure would encounter no monsters at this new fishing spot.

“Well, I guess I'll learn it all when I read your book,” Azure told him with a smile. “Thanks for all the stuff. I'll get to it then.”

“I hope you enjoy my book,” Enno called to Azure as Azure walked away.

*I highly doubt that I will*, Azure thought, not looking forward to reading it.

Once he reached the road heading back to the village of Roselake, Azure paused to figure out his next course of action. Since he was close to the village, it made sense to carry out his reading at the tavern there where he would have a comfortable place to sit and could drink some water. Having made up his mind, Azure diverted to the village, finding a quiet corner in the tavern to sit. He pulled out the book and sighed as he flipped it open to the first page, wondering how much time it would take to get through the entire thing.

The answer was...over five hours. By the time Azure was done, the sun was beginning to set. This presented a new set of challenges. Should he press on to find the pond and try his luck at night fishing or should he go back to the inn and work on this tomorrow? The book had said that night fishing was a thing. Different fish could be caught at night than in the daytime. If he did choose that route, Azure would still be able to fulfill the requirements of the quest. But while the book had spoken volumes about the types of monsters that you could catch while fishing in Patheana, it said nothing about the monsters that lurked on the land. Considering that Azure hadn't encountered any yet, he wasn't confident that he would out-level any of them. Besides, he didn't have the Small Flame spell that Lonnell had. If he wanted to venture about at night, he'd need a torch, which he would have to buy. It just seemed like more trouble than it was worth.

With a sigh, Azure pulled himself up from the bench he was sitting on and made the long trek back to Squall's End. Staying in a town afforded him more time for nighttime activities. Azure parted with two copper coins to take a drawn bath at the inn. It seemed like a luxury after having bathed in rivers for so long. For two more copper, he could have had one of the 'women of the night,' as they were called, scrub him down, but that just seemed like a waste of money. The service was obviously designed to coax him into renting a prostitute, and while it was something that he was incredibly curious about, now was not the time to spend his money on excessively frivolous things.

After bathing, Azure went to the tavern for dinner. He sat there for a little over an hour, Analyzing people as they came and went. Most of the men were a higher level than him, but that made sense considering that The Adventurer's Guild was nearby. Once the urge to purchase a beer became too great, Azure retired to his room, immediately kneeling down to check and see if his money was still where he had left it. To his relief, it was. Azure placed it back in his bag, deciding that he wouldn't leave it again tomorrow.

As time ticked on, Azure found himself growing increasingly worried about Lonnell. It was well after dark, making the roads more dangerous. Hopefully, he had found somewhere to hole up for the night.

Trying to distract his mind, Azure pulled *Fishing Patheana* out of his bag again. He flipped the book open and looked at the map, tracing the distance between Squall's End and Jade Pond with his finger. He regretted not asking Enno more questions about where the pond was located. More than that, he was annoyed that the game didn't have a better mapping system.

Closing his eyes, he thought to bring up a map of the area.

To his surprise, his vision filled with a large map, most of which was completely black. Only a tiny sliver had any color to it at all. There was a blue blinking light that Azure could only assume marked his location.

Why hadn't anyone told him about this before?! It would have made things so much easier.

Azure concentrated on zooming in. Most of the black disappeared. He could now see Crescent Island, Squall's End, and Roselake. Surprisingly, there were quite a few areas on Crescent Island that he hadn't explored, not that he cared much about that now that he was on the mainland. What he was more interested in was the yellow blinking marker on his map. Focusing in further, Azure could see that it notated the location of his current quest objective, though it was pretty far into the black below Squall's End. Concentrating further didn't bring up any more details. More than anything, Azure was hoping to get an idea of how far away the pond was, but no dice. He wasn't much better off than before, having to take a guess that it was some twenty miles away from his current location.

This quest was going to take longer than Ferne had anticipated, Azure realized with a groan. He really regretted not going before Lonnell in the line at The Adventurer's Guild now. There was nothing to be done about it, though. Azure was stuck with the quest. Whether he liked it or not, he would have to waste at least two more days on it, one night of which he'd likely spend sleeping in the unknown. That thought frightened him. Maybe being an adventurer wasn't going to be so much fun after all.

# CHAPTER SIXTEEN
## THE REALM – Day 46

Lonnell didn't return that night. Thankfully, worrying about him hadn't kept Azure awake. After analyzing his own quest, he realized that there would probably be a lot of times that they would be sent so far out that returning to Squall's End for the night wouldn't be possible.

Trying to see how well Azure could navigate on his own, he resolved not to ask for directions to Jade Pond. Instead, he pulled up his map about every thirty minutes and used it as his guide, deciding not to venture off of the main road until it seemed that he had no choice.

With his meals being provided by the inn, Azure didn't bother wasting any time on hunting. Nor did he spend time foraging, just wanting to get to the pond and complete the task.

He walked for six hours down the road leading away from Squall's End before his map told him to divert to the left. The man-made path he found was a pretty good indication that he was headed in the right direction. About a half mile further, he came upon the small body of water that had undoubtedly gotten its name from its color. It was no wonder that the path leading to the pond was well-worn either. Three other people were already set up around the pond with their poles in the water. They cast a smile in Azure's direction in greeting as he approached.

Jade Pond wasn't more than fifty yards across from its two furthest points. Shaped like a teardrop, there wasn't much fishing real estate. Azure was glad that there weren't more people around. It already seemed a bit overcrowded.

Feeling awkward from his lack of fishing experience, Azure tried to get as far away from everyone else as possible. He fumbled as he attempted to bait his hook with one of the fat squirming worms that Enno had given him. If a creature could have a skill for avoiding being pierced, Azure was pretty sure that this particular worm would be maxed out. His finger felt the sharpness of the hook long before the worm did. Azure was just about to rip the damn thing in half before he finally got it.

*Critical hit!* He thought smugly, then immediately felt guilty. The worm had just been trying to survive like everything else. Azure doubted it had ever hurt anything in its entire life, yet here he was skewering it for the sake of the quest.

Remorse should be the furthest thing from his mind though when he was in such a hurry. Azure pulled his pole back and flung the line forward. It didn't go as far as he had hoped, but he didn't feel like trying again. The distance was good enough.

As soon as his bait hit the water, a notification popped up.

*Congratulations! New skill learned:* ***Fishing*** *Level 1. Give a man a fish and you feed him for a day. Teach a man to fish and you feed him for a lifetime. As long as he has enough bait, that is.*

Fishing proved to be, as Azure had feared, incredibly boring. It seemed like the fish were craftier than the fisherman, stealing his bait time and time again. If not for the fact that no one seemed to be catching much except for this one guy at the far end of the pond with a souped-up pole, Azure would have thought he was doing something wrong.

After twenty minutes and four casts, he finally felt something tug on the line. His exhilaration lasted only as long as it took to reel the fish in.

*You have caught:*

| **Jade Catfish** | **Level:** 1<br>**Item Class:** Common<br>**Quality:** Average<br>**Length:** 2 cm<br>**Weight:** 0 kg<br>**Uses:** Cooking, Restores +1 HP if eaten |
|---|---|

*You've got to be kidding me,* he thought as he saw the tiny thing dangling from his hook. It looked like something you'd buy at a pet store. Tiny. Barely a morsel.

"Pathetic," he mumbled as he went to unhook the fish and stick it in his bag.

Azure spent the next forty minutes going through the rest of his bait to no avail. He quickly decided that he was not a fan of fishing. Perhaps it would have been more entertaining if he could have reeled in a monster, but that wasn't the case. At least, he was one step closer to completing his quest.

Azure groaned at the setting sun. He also groaned at the fact that his stamina had been nearly halfway depleted from his fishing efforts. Each cast cost him ten stamina points. It seemed a bit excessive for something that really didn't take much strength. His arms were sore, and he worried that it might impact his ability to swing his sword efficiently, should he have to fight.

The man with the souped-up pole was setting up camp on the far end of the pond. Azure spied him erecting a tent. While he wasn't really in the mood to make a new friend, there was definitely strength in numbers. The guy Analyzed as orange, so sticking around him would probably be the safest way to get through the night.

“Hey there, friend,” Azure said to him in the way of greeting as he approached. “Would you like some help with that tent?”

The man stopped, giving Azure a wary look as he wiped his hands on his pants. “And what would be in it for you? Few people offer to help without wanting something in return.”

A smile crept across Azure's lips. “You got me there. I have a room at the inn in Squall's End, but I won't be making it back tonight. Or I'd rather not try. There are some unsavory characters on the road—The Bower Boys, they're called. Also, I just moved here from Crescent Island, so I don't know much about the monsters in this area. I'd feel much safer if I were camping near someone familiar to the area. I'm not asking you to share your tent or your food. Just that you don't mind if I stick nearby.”

The man looked Azure up and down, seeming to be assessing whether or not he was a threat. After a moment, he continued setting up his tent. “I saw you fishing across the pond. You new to this?”

Not sure what to do, Azure just stood there and watched him. “Yeah. Today was my first time trying out fishing.”

“How'd you like it?”

Azure shifted uncomfortably, hoping he wouldn't offend the guy by not sharing in his love of the sport. “It's...not really my thing."

The man laughed. "A game of patience, it can be."

"I suppose. Are you sure you don't want any help?" He watched the man continue working.

"Nah. I've done this hundreds of times before. Got a routine down."

"My name is Azure, by the way."

"Goddart," the man replied, though he didn't stop to clasp wrists with Azure in greeting.

"That's a fancy pole you've got there." Azure nodded down at the pole. It appeared to be made of metal.

"Your last name isn't Bower, is it?" Goddart eyed him suspiciously.

Azure snorted. "Trust me, man, I'm not interested in stealing anything you've got here. I genuinely am just looking for somewhere safe to camp. If you know of somewhere better nearby, I will happily piss off." It was clear to him that Goddart didn't appreciate his company. There was no point in making them both miserable while he still had enough light left to travel a bit further.

The fisherman sighed as he finished staking his tent and stood before dusting off his hands again. "Apologies. Unfortunately, unsavory characters are abroad in this part of Patheana. It seems like some of the worst of Noseon come to Squall's End to make it their home. Some asshole tries to rob me at least once a year. It's hard to know who to trust."

Azure's eyes widened from Goddart's assessment of Squall's End. Hadn't Esau sent Bronna to Roselake to keep her safe? From the way it sounded, she might have been better off staying on Crescent Island. Perhaps that was the real reason why Owe didn't want to let her out of her sight.

"I had no idea," he said softly.

Goddart offered him a small smile. "You seem like a good lad. But I've run into those who seemed good before, and they weren't. I suppose I could take you, if need be, but I honestly don't feel like sleeping with one eye open.

"While I can't stop you from camping near the pond, I'd rather not share my campsite with you. Sorry if that makes me sound like a dick, but I've been burned one too many times."

Lad? Goddart didn't appear to be much older than Azure. Maybe thirty, but he highly doubted it. He wore an orange shirt with brown pants. A mop of light brown curls framed his head and face, merging into an equally curly beard. A sock cap rested on his head with several hooks affixed to it. Goddart didn't look particularly wealthy, but judging from his fishing pole, he wasn't poor, either.

Azure stood there in thought for a moment, and Goddart continued working around him, carving out a spot in the dirt to make a fire. It was obvious that he wanted Azure to leave, but Azure wasn't giving up just yet.

"While I don't feel like I have the coin to part with," he grumbled under his breath, "I'll offer you a silver if you allow me to share your fire."

Why wasn't bribery a skill in this game? Azure sure felt like he was using it a lot.

Goddart guffawed. "Wow. You are desperate." He picked up some logs stacked haphazardly next to his tent and began building a fire. "But I suppose a thief wouldn't offer to give me coin. Could be wrong." Goddart cocked his head to the side. "You said you're from Crescent Island. What are you doing on the mainland?"

"I came here to attend magic school, but it proved to be more expensive than I can afford, so I'm working as an adventurer to save up for it." Azure frowned, thinking about his predicament and how this quest wasn't paying him anything at all.

"And how's that working out for you?"

"This is my first quest, actually. My prerequisite quest," he admitted.

"You know that you can buy the fish from this lake at the market in Squall's End. There's a fishmonger there. I take him my catch sometimes," Goddart informed him.

"It wasn't that kind of quest." Azure decided to sit down. While he still didn't quite feel welcome in Goddart's campsite, it didn't appear that the fisherman was trying to chase him off anymore, and Azure had been standing for hours. He was exhausted.

"Then what kind of quest was it?"

"Have you ever heard of Enno Berkeley?" Azure asked.

He snorted. "Who hasn't heard of Enno Berkeley?"

"I hadn't until I came here," Azure confessed. "Anyway, he's written a book about fishing. He submitted a request to The Adventurer's Guild for someone to read it and fish one of the spots in it. I'm supposed to report back on the accuracy of the information inside. To be honest, after using all of the bait he gave me, I'm still not sure how accurate that information is. I mean, fishing in The Realm doesn't exactly seem like rocket science. I only caught one fish the whole time I was here, and most of the others didn't seem like they were having much luck either."

"Rocket...science?" Goddart raised an eyebrow at him.

Azure waved his confusion away. "It's just a saying from where I come from. Ignore me. It basically means that I don't think fishing is difficult."

"It's not," Goddart chuckled. "Fishing is twenty-five

percent skill, twenty-five percent the pole you're using, twenty-five percent your bait, and twenty-five percent your level in the skill. Everything gives you a different advantage. The reason you weren't catching anything is because you just acquired the skill, you're using a shit pole, and I'm guessing just basic bait too. Am I right?" His eyes lit up, already knowing the answer to the question.

"That's right." Azure nodded.

"It's a lot less boring when you get everything right. I'm not sure if you were watching or not, but I was pulling in fish like I was draining the pond of them," he said proudly.

"I did notice," Azure acknowledged.

Goddart straightened himself, placing his hands on his hips. "That Enno Berkeley ain't got nothin' on me. The only reason he's so famous is because he has the money and time to travel all over The Realm. Speaking of which, would you mind if I took a look at that book you were talking about?"

Azure shifted uncomfortably. Would it be all right? He was pretty sure that he wasn't supposed to be showing the unpublished manuscript to anyone, but he also knew that if he didn't hand it over, Goddart would likely think him a liar.

Hesitantly, he turned to pull the book from his bag. "I really don't think he wants anyone to see this yet."

"I promise that there likely isn't anything in that book that I don't already know," Goddart told Azure, gesturing for him to hand it over.

Despite feeling like he might be making a big mistake, Azure let Goddart look over the book. Goddart thumbed through it, humming to himself. When he walked away with it, alarms went off inside of Azure's head.

"Can I have it back, please? It's Enno's personal copy, so I have to return it to The Adventurer's Guild tomorrow." He tried not to seem panicked.

"If you're going to be sharing my campsite, then there's no harm in letting me read it." Goddart winked at him.

Azure was seemingly forgotten once Goddart had his hands on the book. For as insistent as he had been on doing everything around the camp himself, he relinquished all duties the second that Azure had handed the book over. He barked out orders, setting Azure to the task of lighting and tending to the fire. Then he made Azure cook them dinner from one of the fish he had caught.

*You have received the following item:*

| **Jade Lungfish** | **Level:** 5<br>**Item Class:** Uncommon<br>**Quality:** Good<br>**Length:** 85 cm<br>**Weight:** 8.25 kg<br>**Uses:** Cooking, Restores +5 HP if eaten |
|---|---|

Azure's eyes bulged from the size and weight of the fish. It was hard to believe that Goddart had caught such a large fish from such a small pond. Surely, the fish had to be worth a considerable sum at the market.

Carefully, he placed it on a spit and set it over the fire, hoping he had done it right since he had never cooked a fish like this before. He was rewarded with the following notification:

| You have cooked: **Burnt Jade Lungfish** | **Uses:** None. You wouldn't feed this to a troll you were trying to kill. Because the troll would know you were trying to kill it and would likely kill you instead. |
| --- | --- |

Uden must be laughing from his grave, Azure thought dryly.

“Is this your first time cooking, too?” Goddart looked over the book. Azure didn't even need to see the rest of his face to know that he was scowling. His voice said it all.

“My cooking skill is level five,” Azure replied in a half-assed attempt to defend himself.

Without further argument, Goddart put the book down long enough to extract another fish from his bag and cook it himself. After that, hours passed with nary a word between the two men, though there was much humming, nodding, frowning, and head shaking from Goodart's side of things, thoroughly engrossed in the book that had nearly bored Azure to tears. When he finally pulled the book away from his face, Azure asked, “So, is it accurate?”

“Eh, it's nothing special,” the fisherman replied, finally handing the book back. Then he disappeared into his tent and didn't come out again.

## CHAPTER SEVENTEEN
THE REALM – Day 47

When Azure awoke the next morning, Goddart was already standing on the shore of Jade Pond with his line in the water. How he hadn't woken Azure while he was moving around camp was a miracle. For some reason, Azure had slept hard these past few nights. Perhaps because he didn't have Lonnell around to nag him into action. That was a small benefit to being set on a different path from his friend.

"Morning," Azure said as he walked over to Goddart, stretching and yawning.

The fisherman pressed his index finger to his lips. “Shh. You'll scare the fish.” He didn't even turn to acknowledge Azure's presence.

Azure snorted. It was clear that he was no longer welcome. Their nighttime camaraderie had disappeared the second he had gotten the book back from Goddart. Oh well. What did it matter? They'd likely never see each other again anyway, and Azure needed to return to Squall's End to turn in his quest.

"I'll be off," he called overly loudly, smirking as he saw

Goddart cringe. The fisherman shooed him away with a wave of his hand.

At least Azure hadn't had to part with the silver coin, he thought as he walked away. Once he had told Goddart about the book, the bribe took on a new form.

The walk back to Squall's End was blessedly uneventful. Azure had pep in his step knowing that his prerequisite quest was almost complete and that he was about to start making some real money. As soon as he got to Squall's End, Azure made a beeline for The Adventurer's Guild. A sigh left his lips as he saw how long the line was. Six deep again. *What a slog*, he thought as he filed in at the end to wait his turn.

Two hours later, he was standing before Ferne. While he was smiling from the triumph of having completed his quest, she still didn't seem happy. It was late afternoon, though, and she'd likely had a long day.

"Here is the book," he said, pulling it out of his bag and placing it on the table. "Here is the fishing pole that Enno let me borrow. Here's the fish I caught as proof that I completed the quest." Azure wasn't sure if she wanted that, but it was better to be safe than sorry. "And here is my report. Do you want me to be honest or to lie?"

A small chuckle left her lips, and Azure grinned at the fact that he had *finally* made her smile. "I suppose I'll take the honest truth first."

"I still don't know shit about fishing, it was a miserable experience, and I have no idea whether or not the stuff in this book is accurate or not. It seemed a bit blown up and long-winded. What I did learn is that fishing is twenty-five percent skill, twenty-five percent the pole you're using, twenty-five percent your bait, and twenty-five percent your level in the skill," he rehearsed what Goddart had told him, because he did believe it to be true. "The map in the book was useful, as was the list of fish that could be caught at each location." Azure had enjoyed that, but it was a small portion of information compared to the rest of the book, which mostly covered Enno's fishing adventures in each location. “Honestly, I think this should be split into two books. One that is just the maps, the list of fish at each location, and the bait to use. The other should be Enno's memoirs. I don't think the two marry together very well.”

Ferne sat back in her chair and nodded, a strange expression on her face. “I'm impressed. That's a much better report than I had expected. It proves that you read the book. I had honestly thought you'd skip it and just go fishing to complete the quest.”

“Do people actually do that?” He raised an eyebrow. If Azure had known that, he might have tried to get away with it. Reading the book had been a giant time suck.

“You would be surprised the shortcuts that people try to take,” she said with a sigh.

“I'm sure you've seen them all.”

“I have,” she admitted. “Having said all that, congratulations. You are now an official Adventurer!” Ferne picked up a stamp from her desk and pressed it against his quest sheet. When she pulled it away, the word 'Complete' was left behind. Immediately, a notification popped up.

*Congratulations! You have been granted the title **Adventurer: Rank E**. Complete more quests with The Adventurer's Guild to raise your Adventurer Rank.*

*Knowing that you are an Adventurer will automatically raise people's trust in you. This will open up more quests that previously were not available.*

*Congratulations! Quest:* ***Adventurer's Guild Quest: An Author's Dream*** *has been completed.*

*You came, you read, you fished. Enno will be happy knowing that he has received an unbiased opinion on his book. He may not like your opinion, but that doesn't matter. You have earned 105XP.*

"And now for your reward," Ferne continued. "You may keep the fishing pole that Enno let you borrow as well as the fish you caught. He also gave me the following things to give to you." She left her desk for a few moments and returned with a large box in hand, sliding it across to Azure. He peered inside.

*You have received the following items:*

| | |
|---|---|
| **Sardine** | **Quantity:** 10<br>**Level:** 1<br>**Item Class:** Common<br>**Quality:** Average<br>**Length:** 10 cm<br>**Weight:** 0.12 kg(each)<br>**Uses:** Cooking, Restores +1 HP if eaten |
| **Box of Basic Bait** | **Quantity:** 10/10<br>**Durability:** 1/1<br>**Item Class:** Common<br>**Quality:** Average<br>**Weight:** 0 kg<br>**Uses:** Must be used with a pole. Used to catch fish. |

Azure wanted to be grateful, but he was almost out of inventory slots. What he was more grateful for was the experience he had earned from the quest. That made it seem like less of a waste of time.

“You will have to thank him for me,” Azure said politely.

“Tomorrow, you can step into the E line to start accepting quests,” Ferne informed him.

“Why not today?” Azure gave her a queer look. He distinctly remembered Lonnell being able to get his first quest on the same day that he had turned in his prerequisite quest.

“Because we're about to close for the evening, and there's no way you'll make it to the front in time,” she replied.

Looking over at the E line, Azure realized she was right. Why were the lines so long? He groaned internally. There were five people currently in the E queue.

“I suppose I'll come back tomorrow then,” he said, feeling a bit defeated, despite the day's triumph.

“Good luck, Azure,” she told him with a soft smile before immediately looking past him and calling out, “Next!”

Azure knew better than to dawdle. Their business was concluded, and it was time for him to leave. Heading towards the door, he took a brief detour to the Open Quests board. The Bower Boys quest was still there, though he noticed that a few of the others were missing.

*I guess everyone is scared to take this one. I certainly hope I don't run into any of these Bower Boys before someone completes this. They sound like bad news.*

With that in mind, Azure decided to spend the rest of the afternoon in town. He went to the tavern and ordered himself a beer, feeling like he'd earned it. More than likely, he'd waste a good amount of time standing in line at The Adventurer's Guild tomorrow. If the location of his new quest was as spaced out as the fishing quest had been, he'd probably spend the day mostly traveling. Azure could afford to have the slight headache that the beer would inevitably give him.

Opening up his inventory, Azure tried to figure out what he could get away with selling. Harvested plants were taking up a quarter of his inventory slots. They were common, so he didn't really need them. The other items he didn't think he'd need were the sardines, fishing pole, box of basic bait, and jade catfish. Out of all of that, though, he only really wanted to sell the jade catfish. Since the sardines stacked, it made sense to keep them as an easy food source...not that he couldn't always hunt. But that took arrows, and without Manny endlessly supplying him, he would need to buy more when he ran out. Perhaps it was better to save them. The only reason he wanted to keep the fishing pole and bait was just in case he got another fishing quest. Azure knew he'd be kicking himself if he sold them and then ended up needing them again soon after. Maybe he should be looking into buying a bag with more inventory slots instead of selling his stuff.

That could be a project for tomorrow. He would pick up his new quest, budget his time, and then swing by the market before heading out. Once he'd completed a few quests and felt more financially stable, he definitely wanted to take the time to fully explore Squall's End. Time was money, though, and he needed to complete a quest before the week's end so that he could afford his portion of the rent for next week. Blegh. This was just like his world had been, living from paycheck to paycheck.

Azure tried not to think about it as he settled back, enjoying a warm meal and Analyzing the new people that came and went from the tavern. In the two hours that Azure sat there, he only saw ten new faces, but it was enough to level up the skill.

*Congratulations! The skill:* ***Analyze*** *has reached Level 7. This skill allows you to see how dangerous a foe is in relation to your own level. Use this skill frequently to avoid getting yourself killed.*

It felt like it was going to take forever before he'd reach his first perk. Oh well. At least, Azure was in an advantageous place to level the skill quickly. If he kept doing this, he imagined that it would take about a month to get to level fourteen.

Once Azure finished his beer, he went back outside to check out the market. As expected, all of the stalls were closed for the night, so he returned to his room at the inn. Lonnell was absent yet again. Perhaps he had come back last night while Azure was gone, though there was no way to tell. Azure hoped that was the case. To be honest, he was beginning to worry a little. It had now been three days since they'd last seen each other. Hopefully, nothing had happened to Lonnell. Even if it had, there would be no way for Azure to know unless someone reported it in town. And no one from Squall's End knew Lonnell, so he would just end up another John Doe. The thought made Azure uneasy. Made him want to listen more carefully for news and gossip when he was hanging around the tavern.

*I can't let my mind get away from me. Lonnell is perfectly capable of taking care of himself. More than likely, we just haven't been able to cross paths because we've both been busy on these long quests.* They were thoughts that would help him sleep at night.

Azure wondered what his next quest would be. At least this time, he'd have a choice. Ferne had said that the receptionist at the E window could give him up to four quests to choose from. That was exciting.

Thinking back on it now, he'd come a long way since arriving in The Realm. Azure no longer felt like a noob. He had faced fearsome foes with his friends, and now he was mostly on his own. It was a strange thought. There had been so much togetherness in the beginning, but now it felt like he had gone solo. Something told him it wouldn't always be like this, though. Rarely could you play through an entire MMO in solo mode. Eventually, something would give, and he'd be forced to party again. Azure just wondered what that event would be.

For now, he was just happy that he'd hit another milestone. Tonight, he'd go to sleep a nobody. Tomorrow, he'd wake up a true Adventurer.

**The adventure continues in book three. Coming soon...**

# ABOUT THE AUTHOR

Phoenix Grey is the super secret nerd pen name of a USA Today bestselling author. She currently lives in a secluded podunk town outside of San Antonio, Texas where she can hermit away while working on books and playing video games. When she's not busy plotting her world domination, she can be found hosting game nights at the local comic book store or checking out the latest recommended anime.

She loves hearing from and interacting with fans, so feel free to stalk her in the following ways:

1. Phoenix Grey's Mailing List:
http://www.subscribepage.com/TheRealmBetween
Sign up to learn when the next installment of The Realm Between is coming out.

2. The Realm Between's Facebook page:
fb.me/TheRealmBetweenLitRPG

3. Phoenix Grey's Reader Group:
https://www.facebook.com/groups/PhoenixGreyReaderGroup

4. Phoenix Grey's YouTube:
https://www.youtube.com/channel/UCjxdU4nqGlBTLX05tjPq1sw

# Azure's end of book stats:

**Name:** Azure

**Race:** Human

**Level:** 7, 19% of the way to next level

**Health:** 210 / 210

**Mana:** 200 / 200

**Stamina:** 210 / 210

**Vitality:** 14

**Intelligence:** 13

**Strength:** 14

**Agility:** 13

**Dexterity:** 12

**Charisma:** 10

**Luck:** 12

**Skills:** Archery Lvl 3; 50% of the way to next level

Stealth Lvl 3; 57% of the way to the next level

Analyze Lvl 7; 10% of the way to next level

Cooking Lvl 5; 52% of the way to next level

Alchemy Lvl 3; 83% of the way to next level

Foraging Lvl 6; 55% of the way to next level

One-Handed Weapons Lvl 6; 0% of the way to next level

Tracking Lvl 1; 80% of the way to next level

Two-Handed Weapons Level 5; 0% of the way to next level

Fishing Lvl 1; 10% of the way to next level

**Languages:** Common Tongue, Sprite, Goblin-Tongue

## Lonnell's end of book stats:

**Name:** Lonnell Namud

**Race:** Human

**Level:** 7

**Health:** 200

**Mana:** 170

**Stamina:** 210

# End of Book Shit

Hey guys and gals,

Phoenix here again! These past few months have been pretty crazy. I completed my first round of NaNoWriMo(National Novel Writing Month) which is how I was able to finish this book so quickly. I'm hoping that I can keep up the pace in months to come.

For those of you who were wondering why I didn't put the fight with the demon in book one, you probably understand now. The dungeon crawl took up half of this novel, and I really didn't want to feel like I was rushing through it because I wanted to give Uden's death more depth and meaning.

Two Brothers was originally supposed to be a bit longer, but a ton got cut out during the initial edit. Having said that, you can look forward to another Cut Scenes book in the coming days. It's completely free and only available to those subscribed to my mailing list. If you haven't joined yet, you can sign up here:

http://www.subscribepage.com/TheRealmBetween

In other news, I'll be at PAX South in San Antonio, Texas on January 18th, 19th, and 20th of 2019 from 2 – 6PM at the North Star Games booth helping them to demo some of their tabletop games. For more details about that, sign up for my mailing list.

Anyway, I hope you guys have enjoyed reading The Realm Between: Two Brothers.

Much love,

Phoenix Grey

Printed in Great Britain
by Amazon

13639043R00153